'James's whodunit is of very high quality. From the moment a handless corpse in a neat city suit is found in a drifting dinghy off the East Coast, and we meet the ghastly members of a literary community, we're hooked'
Evening Standard

'In ability to set a scene and impress it upon the memory, to catch a character in a phrase, to weave a plot and breathe life into a community Miss P. D. James rivals Margery Allingham at her best. . . . The story telling and writing are both quite exceptional'
Irish Independent

'The best all-round whodunit (plot: people: place) this year. Plus a novel murder-method that gave me a nightmare'
The Sun

Also by P. D. James in Sphere Books

SHROUD FOR A NIGHTINGALE
COVER HER FACE
AN UNSUITABLE JOB FOR A WOMAN
THE BLACK TOWER
DEATH OF AN EXPERT WITNESS

Unnatural Causes

P. D. JAMES

SPHERE BOOKS LIMITED
30/32 Gray's Inn Road, London WC1X 8JL

First published in Great Britain by
Faber and Faber Ltd 1967

Published by Sphere Books Ltd 1973
Reprinted 1976, 1977, 1978, 1979 (three times)

TRADE
MARK

Printed in Canada

Book One

CHAPTER ONE

The corpse without hands lay in the bottom of a small sailing dinghy drifting just within sight of the Suffolk coast. It was the body of a middle-aged man, a dapper little cadaver, its shroud a dark pin-striped suit which fitted the narrow body as elegantly in death as it had in life. The hand-made shoes still gleamed except for some scuffing of the toe caps, the silk tie was knotted under the prominent Adam's apple. He had dressed with careful orthodoxy for the town, this hapless voyager; not for this lonely sea; nor for this death.

It was early afternoon in mid-October and the glazed eyes were turned upwards to a sky of surprising blue across which the light south-west wind was dragging a few torn rags of cloud. The wooden shell, without mast or row-locks, bounced gently on the surge of the North Sea so that the head shifted and rolled as if in restless sleep. It had been an unremarkable face even in life and death had given it nothing but a pitiful vacuity. The fair hair grew sparsely from a high bumpy forehead, the nose was so narrow that the white ridge of bone looked as if it were about to pierce the flesh; the mouth, small and thin-lipped, had dropped open to reveal two prominent front teeth which gave the whole face the supercilious look of a dead hare.

The legs, still clamped in rigor, were wedged one each side of the centre-board case and the forearms had been placed resting on the thwart. Both hands had been taken off at the wrists. There had been little bleeding. On each forearm a trickle of blood had spun a black web between the stiff fair hairs and the thwart was stained as if it had been used as a chopping block. But that was all; the rest of the body and the boards of the dinghy were free of blood.

The right hand had been taken cleanly off and the curved end of the radius glistened white; but the left had been bungled and the jagged splinters of bone, needle sharp, stuck out from the receding flesh. Both jacket sleeves and shirt cuffs had been pulled up for the butchery and a pair of gold initialled cuff links dangled free, glinting as they slowly turned and were caught by the autumn sun.

The dinghy, its paintwork faded and peeling, drifted like a discarded toy on an almost empty sea. On the horizon the divided silhouette of a coaster was making her way down the Yarmouth Lanes; nothing else was in sight. About two o'clock a black dot swooped across the sky towards the land trailing its feathered tail and the air was torn by the scream of engines. Then the roar faded and there was again no sound but the sucking of the water against the boat and the occasional cry of a gull.

Suddenly the dinghy rocked violently, then steadied itself and swung slowly round. As if sensing the strong tug of the on-shore current, it began to move more purposefully. A black-headed gull, which had dropped lightly on to the prow and had perched there, rigid as a figurehead, rose with wild cries to circle above the body. Slowly, inexorably, the water dancing at the prow, the little boat bore its dreadful cargo towards the shore.

CHAPTER TWO

Just before two o'clock on the afternoon of the same day Superintendent Adam Dalgliesh drove his Cooper Bristol gently on to the grass verge outside Blythburgh Church and, a minute later, passed through the north chantry-chapel door into the cold silvery whiteness of one of the loveliest church interiors in Suffolk. He was on his way to Monksmere Head just south of Dunwich to spend a ten-day autumn holiday with a spinster aunt, his only living relative, and this was his last stop on the way. He had started off from his City flat before London was stirring, and instead of taking the direct route to Monksmere through Ipswich, had struck north at Chelmsford to enter Suffolk at Sudbury. He had breakfasted at Long Melford and had then turned west through Lavenham to drive slowly and at will through the green and gold of this most unspoilt and unprettified of counties. His mood would have wholly matched the day if it weren't for one persistent nagging worry. He had been deliberately putting off a personal decision until this holiday. Before he went back to London he must finally decide whether to ask Deborah Riscoe to marry him.

Irrationally, the decision would have been easier if he hadn't known so certainly what her answer would be. This threw upon him the whole responsibility for deciding whether to change the present satisfactory status quo (well, satisfactory for him anyway, and it could be argued surely that Deborah was happier now than she had been a year ago?) for a commitment which both of them, he suspected, would regard as irrevocable no matter what the outcome. There are few couples as unhappy as those who are too proud to admit their unhappiness. Some of the hazards he knew. He knew that she disliked and resented his job. This wasn't surprising nor, in itself, important. The job was his choice and he had never required anyone's approval or encouragement. But it was a daunting prospect that every late duty, every emergency, might have to be preceded by an apologetic telephone call. As he walked to and fro under the marvellous cambered tie-beam roof and smelt the Anglican odour of wax polish, flowers and damp old hymn books, it came to him that he had got what he wanted at almost the precise moment of suspecting that he no longer wanted it. This experience is too common to cause an intelligent man lasting disappointment but it still has power to disconcert. It wasn't the loss of freedom that deterred him; the men who squealed most about that were usually the least free. Much more difficult to face was the loss of privacy. Even the loss of physical privacy was hard to accept. Running his fingers over the carved fifteenth century lectern he tried to picture life in the Queenhithe flat with Deborah always there, no longer the eagerly awaited visitor but part of his life, the legal, certificated next of kin.

It had been a bad time at the Yard to be faced with personal problems, There had recently been a major reorganisation which had resulted in the inevitable disruption of loyalties and of routine, the expected crop of rumours and discontent. And there had been no relief from the pressure of work. Most of the senior officers were already working a fourteen-hour day. His last case, although successful, had been particularly tedious. A child had been murdered and the investigation had turned into a man hunt of the kind he most disliked and was temperamentally least suited for—a matter of dogged, persistent checking of facts carried on in a blaze of publicity and hindered by the fear and hysteria of the neighbourhood. The child's parents had fastened on him like drowning swimmers gulping for reassurance and hope and he could still feel the almost physical load of their sorrow and guilt. He had been required to be at once a comforter and father-confessor, avenger and judge. There was nothing new to him in this. He had felt no personal involvement in their grief, and this detachment had, as always, been his strength, as the anger and intense, outraged commitment of some of his colleagues, faced with the same crime, would have been theirs. But the strain of the case was still with him and it would take more than the winds of a Suffolk autumn to clean his mind of some images. No reasonable woman could have expected him to propose marriage in the middle of this investigation and Deborah had not done so. That he had found time and energy to finish his second book of verse a few days before the arrest was something which neither of them had mentioned. He had been appalled to recognise that even the exercise of a minor talent could be made the excuse for selfishness and inertia. He hadn't liked himself much recently, and it was perhaps sanguine to hope that this holiday could alter that.

Half an hour later he closed the church door quietly behind him and set off on the last few miles of the journey to Monksmere. He had written to his aunt to say that he would probably arrive at half-past two and, with luck, he would be there almost precisely on time. If, as was usual, his aunt came out of the cottage at two-thirty she should see the Cooper Bristol just breasting the headland. He thought of her tall, angular, waiting figure with affection. There was little unusual about her story and most of it he had guessed, picked up as as a boy from snatches of his mother's unguarded talk or had simply known as one of the facts of his childhood. Her fiancé had been killed in 1918 just six months before the Armistice when she was a young girl. Her mother was a delicate, spoilt beauty, the worst possible wife for a scholarly country clergyman as she herself frequently admitted, apparently thinking that this candour both justified and excused in advance the next outbreak of selfishness or extravagance. She disliked the sight of other people's grief since it rendered them temporarily more interesting than herself and she decided to take young Captain Maskell's death very hard. Whatever her sensitive, uncommunicative and rather difficult daughter suffered it must be apparent that her mother suffered more; and three weeks after the telegram was received she died of influenza. It is doubtful whether she intended to go to such lengths but she would have been gratified by the result. Her distraught husband forgot in one night all the irritations and anxieties of his marriage and remembered only his wife's gaiety and beauty. It was, of course, unthinkable that he should marry again, and he never did. Jane Dalgliesh whose own bereavement hardly anyone now had the time to remember, took her mother's place as hostess at the vicarage and remained with her father until his retirement in 1945 and his death ten years later. She was a highly intelligent woman and if she found unsatisfying the annual routine of housekeeping and parochial activities, predictable and inescapable as the liturgical year, she never said so. Her father was so assured of the ultimate importance of his calling that it never occurred to him that anyone's gifts could be wasted in its service. Jane Dalgliesh, respected by the parishioners but never loved, did what had to be done and solaced herself with her study of birds. After her father's death the papers she published, records of meticulous observation, brought her some notice; and in time what the parish had patronisingly described as "Miss Dalgliesh's little hobby" made her one of the most respected of amateur ornithologists. Just over five years ago she had sold her house in Lincolnshire and bought Pentlands, a stone cottage on the edge of Monksmere Head. Here Dalgliesh visited her at least twice a year.

They were no mere duty visits, although he would have felt a responsibility for her if she were not so obviously self-sufficient that, at times, even to feel affection seemed a kind of insult. But the affection was there and both of them knew it. Already he was looking forward to the satisfaction of seeing her, to the assured pleasures of a holiday at Monksmere.

There would be a driftwood fire in the wide hearth scenting the whole cottage, and before it the high-backed armchair once part of his father's study in the vicarage where he was born, the leather smelling of childhood. There would be a sparsely furnished bedroom with a view of sea and sky, a comfortable if narrow bed with sheets smelling faintly of wood-smoke and lavender, plenty of hot water and a bath long enough for a six-foot-two man to stretch himself in comfort. His aunt was herself six foot tall and had a masculine appreciation of essential comforts. More immediately, there would be tea before the fire and hot buttered toast with home made potted meat. Best of all, there would be no corpses and no talk of them. He suspected that Jane Dalgliesh thought it odd that an intelligent man should choose to earn his living catching murderers and she was not a woman to feign polite interest when she felt none. She made no demands on him, not even the demands of affection, and because of this she was the only woman in the world with whom he was completely at peace. He knew exactly what the holiday offered. They would walk together, often in silence, on the damp strip of firm sand between the sea's foam and the pebbled rises of the beach. He would carry her sketching paraphernalia; she would stride a little ahead, hands dug in her jacket pockets, eyes searching out where wheatears, scarcely distinguishable from pebbles, had lighted on the shingle, or following the flight of tern or plover. It would be peaceful, restful, utterly undemanding; but at the end of ten days he would go back to London with a sense of relief.

He was driving now through Dunwich Forest where the Forestry Commission's plantations of dark firs flanked the road. He fancied that he could smell the sea now, the salt tang borne to him on the wind was sharper than the bitter smell of the trees. His heart lifted. He felt like a child coming home. And now the forest ended, the sombre dark green of the firs ruled off by a wire fence from the water-coloured fields and hedges. And now they too passed and he was driving through the gorse and heather of the heathlands on his way to Dunwich. As he reached the village and turned right up the hill which skirted the walled enclosure of the ruined Franciscan friory there was the blare of a car's horn and a Jaguar, driven very fast, shot past. He glimpsed a dark head, and a hand raised in salute before, with a valedictory hoot, the car was out of sight. So Oliver Latham, the dramatic critic, was at his cottage for the weekend. That was hardly likely to inconvenience Dalgliesh for Latham did not come to Suffolk for company. Like his near neighbour, Justin Bryce, he used his cottage as a retreat from London, and perhaps from people, although he was at Monksmere less frequently than Bryce. Dalgliesh had met him once or twice and had recognised in him a restlessness and tension which found an echo in his own character. He was known to like fast cars and fast driving, and Dalgliesh suspected that it was in the drive to and from Monksmere that he found his release. It was difficult to imagine why else he kept on his cottage. He came to it seldom, never brought his women there took no interest in furnishing it, and used it chiefly as a base for wild drives around the district which were so violent and irrational that they seemed a kind of abreaction.

As Rosemary Cottage came into sight on the bend of the road Dalgliesh accelerated. He had little hope of driving past unobserved but at least he could drive at a speed which made it unreasonable to stop. As he shot past he just had time to see out of the corner of his eye a face at an upstairs window. Well it was to be expected. Celia Calthrop regarded herself as the doyenne of the small community at Monksmere and had assigned herself certain duties and privileges. If her neighbours were so ill-advised as not to keep her informed of the comings and goings of themselves and their visitors she was prepared to take some trouble to find out for herself. She had a quick ear for an approaching car and the situation of her cottage, just where the rough track across the headland joined the road from Dunwich, gave her every opportunity of keeping an eye on things.

Miss Calthrop had bought Brodie's Barn, re-named

Rosemary Cottage, twelve years previously. She had got it cheap and by gentle but persistent bullying of local labour, had converted it equally cheaply from a pleasing if shabby stone house to the romanticised ideal of her readers. It frequently featured in women's magazines as "Celia Calthrop's delightful Suffolk residence where, amid the peace of the countryside, she creates those delightful romances which so thrill our readers". Inside, Rosemary Cottage was very comfortable in its pretentious and tasteless way; outside, it had everything its owner considered appropriate to a country cottage, a thatched roof (deplorably expensive to insure and maintain), a herb garden (a sinister looking patch this; Miss Calthrop was not successful with herbs), a small artificial pond (malodorous in summer) and a dovecote (but doves obstinately refused to roost in it). There was also a sleek lawn on which the writers' community—Celia's phrase—was invited in summer to drink tea. At first Jane Dalgliesh had been excluded from the invitations, not because she didn't claim to be a writer but because she was a solitary, elderly spinster and therefore, in Miss Calthrop's scale of values, a social and sexual failure rating only a patronising kindness. Then Miss Calthrop discovered that her neighbour was regarded as a distinguished woman by people well qualified to judge and that the men who, in defiance of propriety, were entertained at Pentlands and who were to be met trudging along the shore in happy companionship with their hostess were frequently themselves distinguished. A further discovery was more surprising. Jane Dalgliesh dined with R. B. Sinclair at Priory House. Not all those who praised Sinclair's three great novels, the last written over thirty years ago, realised that he was still alive. Fewer still were invited to dine with him. Miss Calthrop was not a woman obstinately to persist in error and Miss Dalgliesh became "dear Jane" overnight. For her part she continued to call her neighbour "Miss Calthrop" and was as unaware of the rapprochement as she had been of the original disdain. Dalgliesh was never sure what she really thought of Celia. She seldom spoke about her neighbours and the women were too rarely in each other's company for him to judge.

The rough track which led across Monksmere Head to Pentlands was less than fifty yards from Rosemary Cottage.

It was usually barred by a heavy farm gate but today this stood open, biting deep into the tall hedge of brambles and elders. The car bumped slowly over the potholes and between the stubble of hay which soon gave way to grass and then to bracken. It passed the twin stone cottages belonging to Latham and Justin Bryce but Dalgliesh saw no sign of either man although Latham's Jaguar was parked at his door and there was a thin curl of smoke from Bryce's chimney. Now the track wound uphill and suddenly the whole of the headland lay open before him, stretching purple and golden to the cliffs and shining sea. At the crest of the track Dalgliesh stopped the car to watch and to listen. Autumn had never been his favourite season, but in the moment which followed the stopping of the engine he wouldn't have changed this mellow peace for all the keener sensitivities of spring. The heather was beginning to fade now but the second flowering of the gorse was as thick and golden as the first richness of May. Beyond it lay the sea, streaked with purple, azure and brown, and to the south the mist-hung marshes of the bird reserve added their gentler greens and blues. The air smelt of heather and woodsmoke, the inevitable and evocative smells of autumn. It was hard to believe, thought Dalgliesh, that one was looking at a battlefield where for nearly nine centuries the land had waged its losing fight against the sea; hard to realise that under that deceptive calm of veined water lay the nine drowned churches of old Dunwich. There were few buildings standing on the headland now but not all were old. To the north Dalgliesh could just glimpse the low walls of Seton House, little more than an excrescence on the edge of the cliff, which Maurice Seton, the detective novelist, had built to suit his odd and solitary life. Half a mile to the south the great square walls of Priory House stood like a last bastion against the sea and, on the very edge of the bird reserve, Pentlands Cottage seemed to hang on the brink of nothingness. As his eyes scanned the headland a horse and buggy came into sight on the far north track and bowled merrily over the gorse towards Priory House. Dalgliesh could see a stout little body hunchbacked in the driving seat and the whip, delicate as a wand, erect by her side. It must be R. B. Sinclair's housekeeper bringing home the provisions.

There was a charming domestic touch about the gay little equipage and Dalgliesh watched it with pleasure until it disappeared behind the shield of trees which half hid Priory House. At that moment his aunt appeared at the side of her cottage and gazed up the headland. Dalgliesh glanced at his wrist. It was thirty-three minutes past two. He let in the clutch and the Cooper Bristol bumped slowly down the track towards her.

CHAPTER THREE

Stepping back instinctively into the shadows of his upstairs room. Oliver Latham watched the car as it bounced gently up the headland and laughed aloud. Then he checked himself, silenced by the explosive sound of his laughter in the stillness of the cottage. But this was too much! Scotland Yard's wonder boy, still reeking from his latest blood sport, had come most promptly upon his cue. The car was stopping now on the crown of the headland. It would be pleasant if that damned Cooper Bristol had broken down at last. But no, it looked as if Dalgliesh was pausing simply to admire the view. The poor fool was probably relishing in advance the sweets of a fortnight's cossetting at Pentlands. Well, he was in for a surprise. The question was, would it be prudent for him, Latham, to stay around and watch the fun? Why not? He wasn't due back in town until the first night at the Court Theatre on Thursday week and it would look odd if he dashed back now so soon after his arrival. Besides, he was curious. He had driven to Monksmere on Wednesday expecting to be bored. But now, with luck, it was promising to be quite an exciting holiday.

CHAPTER FOUR

Alice Kerrison drove the buggy behind the fringe of trees which shielded Priory House from the northern part of the headland, bounced down from her seat and led the mare through the wide crumbling archway to a row of sixteenth-century stables. As she busied herself with the unharnessing, grunting a little with the effort, her practical mind complacently reviewed the morning's work and looked forward to the small domestic pleasures to come. First they would drink tea together, strong and over-sweet as Mr. Sinclair liked it, sitting one each side of the great fire in the hall. Even on a warm autumn day Mr. Sinclair liked his fire. And then before the light began to fade and the mists rose, they would take their daily walk together across the headland. And it wouldn't be a walk without a purpose. There was some burying to be done. Well, it was always satisfactory to have an object and for all Mr. Sinclair's clever talk, human remains however incomplete were still human remains and were entitled to respect. Besides, it was high time they were out of the house.

CHAPTER FIVE

It was nearly half-past eight and Dalgliesh and his aunt, their dinner over, sat in companionable silence one each side of the living room fire. The room, which occupied almost the whole of the ground floor of Pentlands, was stone walled with a low roof buttressed by immense oak beams and floor of red quarry tiles. In front of the open fireplace, where a wood fire crackled and spurted, a neat stack of driftwood was drying. The smell of wood smoke drifted through the cottage like incense; and the air vibrated endlessly with the thudding of the sea. Dalgliesh found it hard to keep awake in this rhythmic, somnambulant peace. He had always enjoyed contrast in art or nature and at Pentlands, once night had fallen, the pleasures of contrast were easily self-induced. Inside the cottage there was light and warmth, all the colours and comfort of civilised domesticity; outside under the low clouds there was darkness, solitude, mystery. He pictured the shore, one hundred feet below, where the sea was spreading its fringe of lace over the cold, firm beach; and the Monksmere bird reserve to the south, quiet under the night sky, its reeds hardly stirring in the still water.

Stretching his legs to the fire and wedging his head still more comfortably into the high back of the chair, he looked across at his aunt. She was sitting, as always, bolt upright and yet she looked perfectly comfortable. She was knitting a pair of woollen socks in bright red which Dalgliesh could only hope were not intended for him. He thought it unlikely. His aunt was not given to such domestic tokens of affection. The firelight threw gules on her long face, brown and carved as an Aztec's, the eyes hooded, the nose long and straight above a wide mobile mouth. Her hair was iron grey now, coiled into a huge bun in the nape of her neck. It was a face that he remembered from childhood. He had never seen any difference in her. Upstairs in her room, stuck casually into the edge of a looking glass, was the faded photograph of herself and her dead fiancé taken in 1916. Dalgliesh thought of it now; the boy, in the squashed peak cap and breeches which had once looked slightly ridiculous to him but now epitomised the romance and heartbreak of an age long dead; the girl half an inch taller, swaying towards him with the angular grace of adolescence, her hair dressed wide and ribbon bound, her feet in their pointed shoes just showing beneath the slim flowing skirt. Jane Dalgliesh had never talked to him of her youth and he had never asked. She was the most self-sufficient, the least sentimental woman that he knew. Dalgliesh wondered how Deborah would get on with her, what the two women would make of each other. It was difficult to picture Deborah in any setting other than London. Since her mother's death she hardly ever went home and, for reasons which they both understood only too well, he had never gone back to Martingale with her. He could only see her now against the background of his own City flat, of restaurants, theatre foyers and their favourite pubs. He was used to living his life on different levels. Deborah was not part of his job and as yet she had no place at Pentlands. But if he married her, she would necessarily have some share in both. Somehow, on this brief holiday he knew he had to decide if that was what he really wanted.

Jane Dalgliesh said:

"Would you like some music? I have the new Mahler recording."

Dalgliesh wasn't musical, but he knew that music meant a great deal to his aunt and listening to her records had become part of a Pentlands holiday. Her knowledge and pleasure were infectious; he was beginning to make discoveries. And, in his present mood, he was even ready to try Mahler.

It was then they heard the car.

"Oh, Lord," he said. "Who's this? Not Celia Calthrop, I hope." Miss Calthrop, if not firmly discouraged, was an inveterate dropper in, trying always to impose on the solitariness of Monksmere the cosy conventions of suburban social life. She was particularly apt to call when Dalgliesh was at the cottage. To her a personable and unattached male was natural prey. If she didn't want him herself there was always somebody who did; she disliked seeing anything go to waste. On one of his visits she had actually given a cocktail party in his honour. At the time he had enjoyed it, intrigued by the essential incongruity of the occasion. The little group of Monksmere residents, meeting as if for the first time, had munched canapes and sipped cheap sherry in Celia's pink and white drawing room and made inconsequent polite conversation while, outside, a gale screamed across the headland and the sou'-westers and storm lanterns were stacked in the hall. Here had been contrast indeed. But it was not a habit to encourage.

Jane Dalgliesh said:

"It sounds like Miss Calthrop's Morris. She may be bringing her niece. Elizabeth is home from Cambridge convalescing from glandular fever. I think she arrived yesterday."

"Then she ought to be in bed. It sounds as if there are more than two of them. Isn't that Justin Bryce's bleat?"

It was. When Miss Dalgliesh opened the door they could see through the porch windows the twin lights of the car and a confusion of dark forms which gradually resolved themselves into familiar figures. It looked as if the whole of Monksmere was calling on his aunt. Even Sylvia Kedge, Maurice Seton's crippled secretary, was with them, creeping on her crutches towards the stream of light from the open door. Miss Calthrop walked slowly beside her as if in support. Behind them was Justin Bryce, still bleating inconsequently into the night. The tall figure of Oliver Latham loomed up beside him. Last of all, sulky and reluctant came Elizabeth Marley, shoulders hunched, hands dug into her jacket pockets. She was loitering on the path and peering from side to side into the darkness as if dissociating herself from the party. Bryce called:

"Good evening Miss Dalgliesh. Good evening Adam. Don't blame me for this invasion. It's all Celia's idea. We've come for professional advice my dears. All except Oliver. We met him on the way and he's only come to borrow some coffee. Or so he says."

Latham said calmly:

"I forgot to buy coffee when I was driving from town yesterday. So I decided to call on my one neighbour who could be trusted to provide a decent blend without an accompanying lecture on my inefficient housekeeping. If I'd known you were having a party I might have waited until tomorrow."

But he showed no inclination to go.

They came in, blinking in the light and bringing with them a gust of cold air which billowed the white wood smoke across the room. Celia Calthrop went straight to Dalgliesh's chair and arranged herself as if to receive an evening's homage. Her elegant legs and feet, carefully displayed to advantage, were in marked contrast to her heavy, stoutly-corseted body with its high bosom, and her flabby mottled arms. Dalgliesh supposed that she must be in her late forties but she looked older. As always she was heavily but skillfully made up. The little vulpine mouth was carmine, the deep-set and downward sloping eyes which gave her face a look of spurious spirituality much emphasised in her publicity photographs were blue shadowed, he lashes weighted with mascara. She took off her chiffon headscarf to reveal her hairdresser's latest effort, the hair fine as a baby's through which the glimpses of pink, smooth scalp looked almost indecent.

Dalgliesh had only met her niece twice before and now, shaking hands, he thought that Cambridge had not changed her. She was still the sulky, heavy-featured girl that he remembered. It was not an unintelligent face and might even have been attractive if only it had held a spark of animation.

The room had lost its peace. Dalgliesh reflected that it was extraordinary how much noise seven people could make. There was the usual business of settling Sylvia Kedge into her chair which Miss Calthrop supervised imperiously, although she did nothing active to help. The girl would have been called unusual, perhaps even beautiful, if only one could have forgotten those twisted ugly legs, braced into calipers, the heavy shoulders, the masculine hands distorted by her crutches. Her face was long, brown as a gypsy's and framed by shoulder length black hair brushed straight from a centre parting. It was a face which could have held strength and character but she had imposed on it a look of piteous humility, an air of suffering, meekly and uncomplainingly borne, which sat incongruously on that high brow. The great black eyes were skilled in inviting compassion. She was now adding to the general fluster by asserting that she was perfectly comfortable when she obviously wasn't, suggesting with a deprecating gentleness which had all the force of a command that her crutches should be placed within reach even though this meant propping them insecurely against her knees, and by generally making all present uncomfortably aware of their own undeserved good health. Dalgliesh had watched this play-acting before, but tonight he sensed that her heart wasn't in it, that the routine was almost mechanical. For once the girl looked genuinely ill and in pain. Her eyes were as dull as stones and there were lines running deeply between her nostrils and the corners of her mouth. She looked as if she needed sleep, and when he gave her a glass of sherry he saw that her hand was trembling. Siezed by a spasm of genuine compassion, he wrapped his fingers around hers and steadied the glass until she could drink. Smiling at her he asked gently:

"Well, what's the trouble? What can I do to help?"

But Celia Calthrop had appointed herself spokesman. "It's too bad of us all to come worrying you and Jane on your first evening together. I do realise that. But we're very worried. At least, Sylvia and I are. Deeply concerned."

"While I," said Justin Bryce, "am not so much worried as intrigued, not to say hopeful. Maurice Seton's disappeared. I'm afraid it may only be a publicity stunt for his next thriller and that we shall see him among us again all too soon. But let us not look on the gloomy side."

He did, indeed, look very far from gloomy, squatting on a stool before the fire like a malevolent turtle, twisting his long neck towards the blaze. His had been, in youth, a striking head with its high cheekbones, wide mobile lips and huge luminous grey eyes under the heavy lids. But he was fifty now and becoming a caricature. Though they seemed even larger, his eyes were less bright, and watered perpetually as if he were always fighting against a high wind. The receding hair had faded and coarsened to dull straw. The bones jutted through his skin giving him the appearance of a death's head. Only his hands were unchanged. He held them out now to the fire, soft-skinned, white and delicate as those of a girl. He smiled at Dalgliesh:

"Lost, believed safe. One middle-aged detective writer. Nervous disposition. Slight build. Narrow nose. Buck teeth. Sparse hair. Prominent Adam's apple. Finder, please keep. . . . So we come to you for advice, dear boy. Fresh, as I understand it, from your latest triumph. Do we wait for Maurice to make his reappearance and then pretend we didn't notice that he got lost? Or do we play it his way and ask the police to help us find him? After all, if it is a publicity stunt, it would only be kind to co-operate. Poor Maurice needs all the help in that direction he can get."

"It's not a joking matter, Justin." Miss Calthrop was severe. "And I don't for one moment think that it's a publicity stunt. If I did, I wouldn't come worrying Adam at a time when he particularly needs a peaceful, quiet holiday to recover from the strain of that case. So clever of you, Adam, to catch him before he did it again. The whole case makes me feel sick, physically sick! And now what will happen to him? Kept in prison for a few years at the State's expense, then let out to murder some other child? Are we all mad in this country? I can't think why we don't hang him mercifully and be done with it."

Dalgliesh was glad that his face was in shadow. He recalled again the moment of arrest. Pooley had been such a small man, small, ugly and stinking with fear. His wife had left him a year before and the inexpert patch which puckered the elbow of his cheap suit had obviously been his own work. Dalgliesh had found his eyes held by that patch as if it had the power to assert that Pooley was still a human being. Well, the beast was caged now and the public and press were free to be loud in their praise of the police work in general and of Superintendent Dalgliesh in particular. A psychiatrist could explain, no doubt, why he felt himself contaminated with guilt. The feeling was not new to him and he would deal with it in his own way. After all, he reflected wryly, it had seldom inconvenienced him for long and never once had it made him want to change his job. But he was damned if he was going to discuss Pooley with Celia Calthrop.

Across the room his aunt's eyes met his. She said quietly:

"What exactly do you want my nephew to do, Miss Calthrop? If Mr. Seton has disappeared, isn't that a matter for the local police?"

"But is it? That's our problem!" Miss Calthrop drained her glass as if the Amontillado had been cooking sherry, and automatically held it out to be refilled.

"Maurice may have disappeared for some purpose of his own, perhaps to collect material for his next book. He's been hinting that this is to be something different—a departure from his usual classical detective novel. He's a most conscientious craftsman and doesn't like to deal with anything outside his personal experience. We all know that. Remember how he spent three months with a travelling circus before he wrote *Murder on the High Wire*. Of course, it does imply he's a little deficient in creative imagination. My novels are never restricted to my own experience."

Justin Bryce said:

"In view of what your last heroine went through, Celia darling, I'm relieved to hear it."

Dalgliesh asked when Seton had last been seen. Before Miss Calthrop could answer, Sylvia Kedge spoke. The sherry and the warmth of the fire had put some colour into her cheeks and she had herself well under control. She spoke directly to Dalgliesh and without interruption.

"Mr. Seton went to London last Monday morning to stay at his Club, that's the Cadaver Club in Tavistock Square. He always spends a week or two there in October. He prefers London in the autumn and he likes to do research for his books in the Club Library. He took a small suitcase with him and his portable typewriter. He went by the train from Halesworth. He told me that he was going to make a start on a new book, something different from his usual style, and I got the impression he was rather excited about it although he never discussed it with me. He said that everyone would be surprised by it. He arranged for me to work at the house for mornings only while he was away and said he would telephone me about ten o'clock if he had any messages. That's the usual arrangement when he's working at the Club. He types the manuscript in double spacing and posts it to me in instalments and I make a fair copy. Then he revises the whole book and I type it ready for the publishers. Of course, the instalments don't always connect. When he's in London he likes to work on town scenes—I never know what's going to arrive next. Well, he telephoned on Tuesday morning to say that he hoped to post some manuscript by Wednesday evening and to ask me to do one or two small mending jobs. He sounded perfectly all right, perfectly normal then."

Miss Calthrop could contain herself no longer.

"It was really very naughty of Maurice to use you for jobs like darning his socks and polishing the silver. You're a qualified shorthand typist and it's a dreadful waste of skill. Goodness knows, I've enough stuff on tape waiting for you to type. However, that's another matter. Everyone knows my views."

Everyone did. There would have been more sympathy with them if people hadn't suspected that dear Celia's indignation was chiefly on her own account. If there was any exploiting to be done she expected priority.

The girl took no notice of her interruption. Her dark eyes were still fixed on Dalgliesh. He asked gently:

"When did you next hear from Mr. Seton?"

"I didn't, Mr. Dalgliesh. There was no call on Wednesday when I was working at Seton House but, of course, that didn't worry me. He might not telephone for days. I was there again early this morning to finish some ironing when Mr. Plant rang. He's the caretaker at the Cadaver Club and his wife does the cooking. He said they were very worried because Mr. Seton had gone out before dinner on Tuesday and hadn't returned to the Club. His bed hadn't been slept in and his clothes and typewriter were still there. Mr. Plant didn't like to make too much fuss at first. He thought that Mr. Seton might have stayed out for some purpose connected with his work—but he got worried when a second night went by and still no message. So he thought he'd better telephone the house. I didn't know what to do. I couldn't contact Mr. Seton's half-brother because he recently moved to a new flat and we don't know the address. There aren't any other relations. You see, I wasn't sure whether Mr. Seton would want me to take any action. I suggested to Mr. Plant that we should wait a little longer and we agreed to phone each other the minute there was any news, and then just before lunch time, the post arrived and I got the manuscript."

"We have it here," proclaimed Miss Calthrop. "And the envelope." She produced them from her capacious handbag with a flourish and handed them to Dalgliesh. The envelope was the ordinary commercial, buff-coloured, four-by-nine-inch size and was addressed, in typing, to Maurice Seton, Esq., Seton House, Monksmere, Suffolk. Inside were three quarto sheets of inexpert typescript, double spaced. Miss Kedge said dully:

"He always addressed the manuscript to himself. But

that isn't his work, Mr. Dalgliesh. He didn't write it and he didn't type it."

"How can you be sure?"

It was hardly a necessary question. There are few things more difficult to disguise than typing and the girl had surely copied enough Maurice Seton manuscripts to recognise his style. But before she had a chance to reply, Miss Calthrop said:

"I think it would be best if I just read part of it."

They waited while she took from her handbag a pair of immense jewelled spectacles, settled them on her nose, and arranged herself more comfortably in the chair. Maurice Seton, thought Dalgliesh, was about to have his first public reading. He would have been gratified by the listeners' rapt attention and possibly, too, by Miss Calthrop's histrionics. Celia, faced with the work of a fellow craftsman and sure of the audience, was prepared to give of her best. She read:

"Carruthers pushed aside the bead curtain and entered the night club. For a moment he stood motionless in the doorway, his tall figure elegant as always in the well-cut dinner jacket, his cool ironic eyes surveying with a kind of disdain the close packed tables, the squalid pseudo-Spanish decor, the shabby clientèle. So this was the headquarters of perhaps the most dangerous gang in Europe! Behind this sordid but commonplace night club, outwardly no different from a hundred others in Soho, was a master mind which could control some of the most powerful criminal gangs in the West. It seemed unlikely. But then, this whole fantastic adventure was unlikely. He sat down at the table nearest the door to watch and wait. When the waiter came he ordered fried scampi, green salad and a bottle of chianti. The man, a grubby little Cypriot, took his order without a word. Did they know he was here? Carruthers wondered. And, if they did, how long would it be before they showed themselves.

"There was a small stage at the end of the Club furnished only with a cane screen and a single red chair. Suddenly the lights were dimmed and the pianist began to play a slow sensuous tune. From behind the screen came a girl. She was blonde and beautiful, not young but mature and full bosomed, with a grace and arrogance which Carruthers thought might indicate White Russian blood. She moved forward sensuously to the single chair and with great deliberation began to unzip her evening dress. It fell about her knees to the ground. Underneath she wore nothing but a black brassiere and G string. Sitting now with her back to the audience she twisted her hands to unhook the brassiere. Immediately from the crowded tables there came a hoarse murmuring. 'Rosie! Rosie! Come on Rosie! Give! Give!' "

Miss Calthrop stopped reading. There was complete silence. Most of her listeners seemed stunned. Then Bryce called out:

"Well, go on Celia! Don't stop now it's getting really exciting. Does Rosie fall on the Hon. Martin Carruthers and rape him? He's had it coming to him for years. Or is that too much to hope?"

Miss Calthrop said:

"There's no need to go on. The proof we need is there."

Sylvia Kedge turned again to Dalgliesh.

"Mr. Seton would never call a character Rosie, Mr. Dalgliesh. That was his mother's name. He told me once that he would never use it in any of his books. And he never did."

"Particularly not for a Soho prostitute," broke in Miss Calthrop. "He talked to me about his mother quite often. He adored her. Absolutely adored her. It nearly broke his heart when she died and his father married again."

Miss Calthrop's voice throbbed with all the yearning of frustrated motherhood. Suddenly Oliver Latham said:

"Let me see that."

Celia handed the manuscript to him and they all watched with anxious expectancy while he scanned it. Then he handed it back without a word.

"Well?" asked Miss Calthrop.

"Nothing. I just wanted to have a look at it. I know Seton's handwriting but not his typing. But you say that he didn't type this."

"I'm sure he didn't," said Miss Kedge. "Although I can't exactly say why. It just doesn't look like his work. But it was typed on his machine."

"What about the style?" asked Dalgliesh. The little group considered. At last Bryce said:

"One couldn't really call that typical Seton. After all, the man could write when he chose. It's almost artificial, isn't it? One gets the impression he was trying to write badly."

Elizabeth Marley had been silent until now, sitting alone in the corner like a discontented child who has been dragged unwillingly into the company of boring adults. Suddenly she said impatiently:

"If this is a fake it's obvious we were meant to discover it. Justin's right. The style's completely bogus. And it's too much of a coincidence that the person responsible should have hit on the one name which would arouse suspicion. Why choose Rosie? If you ask me, this is just Maurice Seton trying to be clever and you've all fallen for it. You'll read all about it when his new book comes out. You know how he loves experimenting."

"It's certainly the sort of childish scheme that Seton might think up," said Latham. "I'm not sure I want to be an involuntary participant in any of his damn silly experiments. I suggest we forget the whole thing. He'll turn up in his own time."

"Maurice was always very odd and secretive, of course," agreed Miss Calthrop. "Especially about his work. And there's another thing. I've been able to give him one or two useful little hints in the past. He's definitely used them. But never a word to me subsequently. Naturally I didn't expect a formal acknowledgement. If I can help a fellow writer I'm only too happy. But it's a little disconcerting when a book is published to find one or two of one's own ideas in the plot and never a thank you from Maurice."

"He's probably forgotten by then that he didn't think them out for himself," suggested Latham with a kind of tolerant contempt.

"He never forgot anything, Oliver. Maurice had a very clear mind. He worked methodically too. If I dropped a suggestion he'd pretend to be only half interested and mutter something about trying to work it in sometime or other. But I could see from the look in his eyes that he'd seized on it and was only waiting to get home to file it away on one of those little index cards. Not that I resented it really. It's just that I think he might have acknowledged the help occasionally. I gave him an idea a month or so ago and I bet you anything it will appear in the next book."

No one accepted the offer. Bryce said:

"You're absolutely right about him, Celia. One contributed one's own mite from time to time. God knows why except that one does get the occasional idea for a new method of murder and it seemed a shame to waste it when poor Seton was so obviously near the end of his resources. But, apart from that predatory gleam in his eye— not a sign of appreciation, my dears! Of course, for reasons you all appreciate, he gets no help from me now. Not after what he did to Arabella."

Miss Calthrop said:

"Oh, my idea wasn't for a new method of murder exactly. It was just a situation. I thought it might make rather an effective opening chapter. I kept telling Maurice that you must capture your readers from the very start. I pictured a body drifting out to sea in a dinghy with its hands chopped off at the wrists."

There was a silence, so complete, so sudden that the striking of the carriage clock drew all their eyes towards it as if it were chiming the hour of execution. Dalgliesh was looking at Latham. He had stiffened in his chair and was grasping the stem of his glass with such force that Dalgliesh half expected it to snap. It was impossible to guess what lay behind that pale, rigid, mask. Suddenly Bryce gave his high, nervous laugh and the tension broke. One could almost hear the little gasps of relief.

"What an extraordinarily morbid imagination you have Celia! One would never suspect. You must control these impulses, my dear, or the League of Romantic Novelists will hurl you out of the Club."

Latham spoke, his voice controlled, colourless. He said:

"All this doesn't help with the present problem. Do I take it that we're agreed to take no action about Seton's disappearance? Eliza is probably right and it's just some nonsense Maurice has thought up. If so the sooner we leave Mr. Dalgliesh to enjoy his holiday in peace the better."

He was rising to go as if suddenly wearied of the whole subject when there was a loud authoritative knock on the cottage door. Jane Dalgliesh lifted an interrogative eyebrow at her nephew then got up silently and went through the porch to open it. The party fell silent, listening unashamedly. A caller after dusk was rare in their isolated community. Once night fell they were used to seeing only each other and knew by instinct of long experience whose footstep was approaching their door. But this loud summons had been the knock of a stranger. There was the soft, broken mutter of voices from the porch. Then Miss Dalgliesh reappeared in the doorway, two raincoated men in the shadows behind her. She said:

"This is Detective Inspector Reckless and Sergeant Courtney from the County C.I.D. They are looking for Digby Seton. His sailing dinghy has come ashore at Cod Head."

Justin Bryce said:

"That's odd. It was beached as usual at the bottom of Tanner's Lane at five o'clock yesterday afternoon."

Everyone seemed to realise simultaneously how strange it was that a Detective Inspector and a Sergeant should be calling after dark about a missing dinghy but Latham spoke before the others had formed their questions:

"What's wrong Inspector?"

Jane Dalgliesh replied for him.

"Something very shocking, I'm afraid. Maurice Seton's body was in the boat."

"Maurice's body! Maurice? But that's ridiculous!" Miss Calthrop's sharp didactic voice cut across the room in futile protest.

"It can't be Maurice. He never takes the boat out. Maurice doesn't like sailing."

The Inspector moved forward into the light and spoke for the first time.

"He hadn't been sailing, Madam. Mr. Seton was lying dead in the bottom of the boat. Dead, and with both hands taken off at the wrists."

CHAPTER SIX

Celia Calthrop, as if relishing her own obstinacy, said for the tenth time.

"I keep telling you! I didn't say a word about the plot to anyone except Maurice. Why should I? And it's no good harping on about the date. It was about six months ago—perhaps longer. I can't remember just when. But we were walking along the beach to Walberswick and I suddenly thought that it would make a good start to a detective story if one described a handless corpse drifting out to sea in a boat. So I suggested it to Maurice. I certainly never mentioned it to anyone else until tonight. Maurice may have done so, of course."

Elizabeth Marley burst out irritably:

"Obviously he told someone! We can hardly suppose that he cut his own hands off in the cause of verisimilitude. And it's stretching coincidence too far to suggest that you and the murderer happened to think of the same idea. But I don't see how you can be so certain that you didn't talk about it to anyone else. I believe you mentioned it to me once when we were discussing how slow Maurice was to get his plots under way."

No one looked as if they believed her. Justin Bryce said softly, but not so softly that the others couldn't hear:

"Dear Eliza! So loyal always." Oliver Latham laughed and there was a short, embarrassed silence broken by Sylvia Kedge's hoarse belligerent voice.

"He never mentioned it to me."

"No dear," replied Miss Calthrop sweetly. "But then, there were a great many things which Mr. Seton didn't discuss with you. One doesn't tell everything to one's maid. And that, my dear, was how he thought of you. You should have had more pride than to let him use you as a household drudge. Men prefer a little spirit, you know."

It was gratuitously spiteful and Dalgliesh could sense the general embarrassed surprise. But no one spoke. He was almost ashamed to look at the girl but she had bent her head as if meekly accepting a merited rebuke, and the two black swathes of hair had swung forward to curtain her face. In the sudden silence he could hear the rasping of her breath, and he wished he could feel sorry for her. Certainly Celia Calthrop was intolerable; but there was something about Sylvia Kedge which provoked unkindness. He wondered what lay behind that particular impulse to savagery.

It was nearly an hour since Inspector Reckless and his Sergeant had arrived, an hour in which the Inspector had said little and the rest of the company, except Dalgliesh and his aunt, had said a great deal. Not all of it had been wise. Reckless had settled himself on arrival in a high chair against the wall and sat there still, solid as a bailiff, his sombre eyes watchful in the light of the fire. Despite the warmth of the room he was wearing his raincoat, a grubby gaberdine which looked too fragile to sustain the weight of its armour of metal buttons, buckles and studs. On his lap he nursed with careful hands a pair of immense gauntlet gloves and a trilby hat as if fearful that someone was going to snatch them from him. He looked like an interloper; the minor official there on sufferance, the little man who dares not risk a drink on duty. And that, thought Dalgliesh, was exactly the effect he aimed to produce. Like all successful detectives, he was able to subdue his personality at will so that even his physical presence became as innocuous and commonplace as a piece of furniture. The man was helped by his appearance, of course. He was small—surely only just the regulation height for a policeman—and the sallow, anxious face was as neutral and unremarkable as any of a million faces seen crowding into a football ground on a Saturday afternoon. His voice, too, was flat, classless, giving no clue to the man. His eyes, wide spaced and deep set under jutting brows, had a trick of moving expressionlessly from face to face as people spoke, which the present company might have found disconcerting if they had bothered to notice. By his side, Sergeant Courtney sat with the air of one who has been told to sit upright, keep his eyes and ears open and say nothing, and who is doing just that.

Dalgliesh glanced across the room to where his aunt sat

in her usual chair, she had taken up her knitting and seemed serenely detached from the business in hand. She had been taught to knit by a German governess and held the needles upright in the Continental manner; Celia Calthrop seemed mesmerised by their flashing tips and sat glaring across at them as if both fascinated and affronted by her hostess's unusual expertise. She was less at ease, crossing and uncrossing her feet and jerking back her head from the fire as if she found its heat intolerable. It was certainly getting hot in the sitting room. All the other visitors, except Reckless, seemed to feel it too. Oliver Latham was pacing up and down, his brow wet with sweat, his restless energy seeming to raise the temperature still higher. Suddenly he swung round at Reckless:

"When did he die?" he demanded. "Come on, let's have some facts for a change! When did Seton die?"

"We shan't know that precisely until we get the P.M. report, Sir."

"In other words, you're not telling. Let me phrase it another way then. For what hours are we expected to provide alibis?"

Celia Calthrop gave a little squeak of protest but turned to Reckless as anxiously as the rest for his reply.

"I shall want a statement from all of you covering the time Mr. Seton was last seen, which was I understand, seven-thirty on Tuesday evening, until midnight on Wednesday."

Latham said:

"That's putting it a bit late surely? He must have been shoved out to sea long before midnight. Sunset and evening star and one clear call for me. . . . I'll begin, shall I? I was at the New Theatre Guild first night on Tuesday and afterwards went on to a party given by our dear theatrical knight. I got back to my flat shortly after one and spent what remained of the night with a friend. I can't say who at present but I expect I'll be able to give you the name tomorrow. We got up late, lunched at the Ivy, and parted when I got out my car to drive down here. I arrived at my cottage shortly after seven-thirty yesterday evening and didn't go out again except to take a short walk along the beach before bed. Today I've spent driving around the country and getting in supplies. After dinner I discovered I hadn't bought any coffee and came to the one neighbour who could be relied upon to provide a drinkable blend without a coy accompanying lecture on men and their inefficient housekeeping. To make it easy for you, I would emphasise that I have, apparently, an alibi for the time of death—presuming him to have died on Tuesday—but not for the time he was sent off on his last journey, presuming that to have been yesterday night."

During the first part of this recital Miss Calthrop had assumed a quick variety of expressions—curiosity, disapproval, lubricity and a gentle sadness—as if trying to decide which suited her best. She settled for the gentle sadness, a good woman grieving once more over the frailty of men.

Inspector Reckless said quietly:

"I shall have to ask you for the lady's name Sir."

"Then you'll ask in vain, at least until I've had a chance to talk to her. Charming of you to assume that it was a woman, though. Look Inspector, be reasonable! If I had anything to do with Seton's death I should have fixed my alibi by now. And if I set out to concoct a false one it would hardly involve a woman. Apart from considerations of misplaced chivalry we could hardly fox you for long. No one remembers all the details. You would only have to ask what we talked about, who drew the curtains, on what side of the bed I slept, how many blankets, what we ate for breakfast. It amazes me that anyone tries to concoct an alibi. One would need a better head for detail than I lay claim to."

"Well, you seem to be in the clear, Oliver," proclaimed Celia severely. "It is a matter of murder after all. No reasonable woman could make difficulties."

Latham laughed.

"But she's not reasonable, my dear Celia. She's an actress. Not that I'm expecting trouble. My father gave me one piece of useful advice. Never go to bed with a woman if either of you would be embarrassed to admit the fact next morning. It's a little restricting to one's sex life but now you can see the practical advantages."

Dalglicsh doubted whether Latham found it in fact so very restricting. In his sophisticated circle few people minded a liaison becoming public provided it enhanced their standing, and Oliver Latham, wealthy, handsome, urbane and reputedly hard to get, stood high in the market. Bryce said peevishly:

"Well, you've nothing to worry about then if, as seems likely, Seton died on Tuesday night. Unless, of course, the Inspector is unkind enough to suggest that your sleeping partner would provide you with an alibi in any case."

"Oh, she would provide almost anything if asked nicely," said Latham lightly. "But it would be dangerous surely. It's a question of histrionics. As long as she was playing the gallant little liar, risking her reputation to save her lover from jail, I should be all right. But suppose she decided to change her role? It's probably as well that I shall be requiring her merely to tell the truth."

Celia Calthrop, obviously tired of the general interest in Latham's sex life, broke in impatiently:

"I hardly think I need to describe my movements. I was a very dear friend of poor Maurice, perhaps the only real friend he ever had. However, I haven't any objection to telling you, and I suppose it may help to clear someone else. Every piece of information is important, isn't it? I was at home for most of the time. On Tuesday afternoon however, I drove Sylvia to Norwich and we both had our hair washed and set. *Estelle's* near the Maddermarket. It makes a pleasant little treat for Sylvia and I do think it's important not to let oneself go just because one lives in the country. We had a late tea in Norwich and I took Sylvia home at about eight-thirty; then I drove back to my cottage. I spent yesterday morning working—I dictate on tape—and I drove to Ipswich yesterday afternoon to do some shopping and call on a friend, Lady Briggs of Well Walk. It was just a chance call. Actually she wasn't in, but the maid will remember me. I'm afraid I got a little lost coming home and wasn't back until nearly ten. By then my niece had arrived from Cambridge and she, of course, can vouch for me for the rest of the night. Just before lunch this morning Sylvia telephoned to tell me about the manuscript and Maurice being missing. I wasn't at all sure what to do for the best but when I saw Superintendent Dalgliesh driving past this evening I rang Mr.

Bryce and suggested that we all come to consult him. By then I had a premonition that something was dreadfully wrong; and how right I am proved!"

Justin Bryce spoke next. Dalgliesh was intrigued by the readiness with which the suspects were volunteering information for which no one had yet officially asked. They were reciting their alibis with the glib assurance of converts at a revivalist meeting. Tomorrow, no doubt, they would pay for this indulgence with the usual emotional hangover. But it was hardly his job to warn them. He began to feel a considerably increased respect for Reckless; at least the man knew when to sit still and listen.

Bryce said:

"I was at my Bloomsbury flat in town until yesterday too, but if Seton died late on Tuesday night I'm definitely out of the running my dears. I had to telephone the doctor twice that night. I was really dreadfully ill. One of my asthma attacks; you know how I suffer Celia. My doctor, Lionel Forbes-Denby can confirm it. I phoned him first just before midnight and begged him to visit at once. He wouldn't come, of course. Just told me to take two of my blue capsules and ring again if they hadn't acted in an hour. It was really naughty of him. I told him I thought I was dying. That's why my type of asthma is so dangerous. You can die with it if you think you're going to."

"But not if Forbes-Denby forbids it, surely?" said Latham.

"That's all very well, Oliver, but he can be wrong."

"He was Maurice's doctor, too, wasn't he?" asked Miss Calthrop. "Maurice always swore by him. He had to be terribly careful of his heart and he always said that Forbes-Denby kept him alive."

"Well he should have visited me Tuesday night," said Bryce, aggrieved. "I rang again at three-thirty and he came at six but I was over the worst by then. Still, it's an alibi."

"Not really, Justin," said Latham. "We've no proof that you rang from your flat."

"Of course, I phoned from the flat! I told you. I was practically at death's door. Besides, if I sent a false message and was rushing around London murdering Seton what would I do when Forbes-Denby turned up at the flat? He'd never treat me again!" Latham laughed:

"My dear Justin! If Forbes-Denby says he isn't coming he isn't coming. And well you know it."

Bryce assented sadly; he seemed to take the destruction of his alibi remarkably philosophically. Dalgliesh had heard of Forbes-Denby. He was a fashionable West End practitioner who was also a good doctor. He and his patients shared a common belief in the medical infallibility of Forbes-Denby and it was rumoured that few of them would eat, drink, marry, give birth, leave the country or die without his permission; they gloried in his eccentricities, recounted with gusto his latest rudeness and dined out on the recent Forbes-Denby outrage whether it were hurling their favourite patent medicine through the window or sacking the cook. Dalgliesh was glad that it would be Reckless or his minions who would have the task of asking this unaimiable eccentric to provide medical information about the victim and an alibi for one of the suspects.

Suddenly Justin burst out vith a violence that caused them all to turn and stare at him:

"I didn't kill him, but don't ask me to be sorry about it! Not after what he did to Arabella!"

Celia Calthrop gave Reckless the resigned, slightly apologetic look of a mother whose child is about to make a nuisance of himself but not altogether without excuse. She muttered confidentially:

"Arabella. His Siamese cat. Mr. Bryce thought that Maurice had killed the animal."

"One didn't think, Celia. One knew." He turned to Reckless.

"I ran over his dog about three months ago. It was the purest accident. I like animals. I like them, I tell you! Even Towser who, admit it Celia, was the most disagreeable, ill-bred and unattractive mongrel. It was the most horrible experience! He ran straight under my wheels. Seton was utterly devoted to him. He practically accused me of deliberately running the dog down. And then, four days later, he murdered Arabella. That's the kind of man he was! Do you wonder someone has put a stop to him?"

Miss Calthrop, Miss Dalgliesh and Latham all spoke at once thus effectively defeating their good intentions.

"Justin dear, there really wasn't a particle of proof. . . ."

"Mr. Bryce, no one is going to suppose that Arabella has anything to do with it."

"For God's sake Justin, why drag up. . . ."

Reckless broke in quietly:

"And when did you arrive at Monksmere, Sir?"

"Wednesday afternoon. Just before four. And I didn't have Seton's body in the car with me either. Luckily for me, I had trouble with the gear box all the way from Ipswich and had to leave it in Baines garage just outside Saxmundham. I came on by taxi. Young Baines brought me. So if you want to check the car for blood and fingerprints you'll find it with Baines. And good luck to you."

Latham said:

"Why the hell are we bothering, anyway? What about the next-of-kin? Dear Maurice's half-brother. Shouldn't the police be trying to trace him? After all, he's the heir. He's the one with the explaining to do."

Eliza Marley said quietly:

"Digby was at Seton House last night. I drove him there."

It was only the second time she had spoken since the Inspector's arrival and Dalgliesh sensed that she wasn't anxious to speak now. But no one hoping for a sensation could have wished for a more gratifying response. There was an astounded silence broken by Miss Calthrop's sharp, inquisitorial voice:

"What do you mean, drove him there?"

It was, thought Dalgliesh, a predictable question.

The girl shrugged:

"What I said. I drove Digby Seton home last night. He telephoned from Ipswich station before catching the connection and asked me to meet him off the eight-thirty train at Saxmundham. He knew Maurice wouldn't be at home and I suppose he wanted to save the cost of a taxi. Anyway, I went. I took the Mini."

"You never told me about this when I got home," said Miss Calthrop accusingly. The rest of the party shifted uneasily, apprehensive that they might be in for a family row. Only the dark figure sitting against the wall seemed utterly unconcerned:

"I didn't think you would be particularly interested. Anyway, you were pretty late back, weren't you?"

"But what about tonight? You didn't say anything earlier."

"Why should I? If Digby wanted to beetle off again somewhere it's no business of mine. Anyway, that was before we knew that Maurice Seton was dead."

"So you met Digby at his request off the eight-thirty?" asked Latham, as if anxious to get the record straight.

"That's right. And what's more, Oliver, he was on the train when it pulled in. He wasn't lurking in the waiting room or hanging about outside the station. I bought a platform ticket, saw him get off the train and was with him when he gave up his ticket. A London ticket, incidentally; he was complaining about the cost. The ticket collector will remember him, anyway. There were only about half-a-dozen other passengers."

"And presumably he hadn't a body with him?" asked Latham.

"Not unless he was carrying it in a hold-all measuring about three feet by two."

"And you drove him straight home?"

"Of course. That was the idea. Sax is hardly a haunt of gaiety after eight o'clock and Digby isn't my favourite drinking companion. I was just saving him the cost of a taxi. I told you."

"Well, go on, Eliza," encouraged Bryce. "You drove Digby to Seton House. And then?"

"Nothing. I left him at the front door. The house was quiet and there were no lights. Well, naturally. Everyone knows that Maurice stays in London during mid-October. Digby asked me in for a drink but I said that I was tired and wanted to get home and that Aunt Celia would probably be home and waiting up for me. We said goodnight and Digby let himself in with his own key."

"He had a key, then?" interposed Reckless. "He and his brother were on those terms?"

"I don't know what terms they were on. I only know that Digby has a key."

Reckless turned to Sylvia Kedge.

"You knew about this? That Mr. Digby Seton had open access to the house?"

Sylvia Kedge replied:

"Mr. Maurice Seton gave his brother a key about two

years ago. From time to time he did mention asking for it back but Mr. Digby used it so seldom when his brother wasn't at home that I suppose he thought it didn't matter letting him keep it."

"Why, as a matter of interest, did he want it back?" enquired Bryce. Miss Calthrop obviously considered this the kind of question that Sylvia should not be expected to answer. With an expression and voice clearly indicating "not in front of the servants", she replied:

"Maurice did mention the key to me on one occasion and said that he might ask for it to be returned. There was no question of not trusting Digby. He was merely a little worried in case it got lost or stolen at one of those night clubs Digby is so fond of."

"Well, apparently he didn't get it back," said Latham. "Digby used it to get into the house at about nine o'clock last night. And no one has seen him since. Are you sure the house was empty, Eliza?"

"How could I be? I didn't go in. But I heard no one and there were no lights."

"I was there at half past nine this morning," said Sylvia Kedge. "The front door was locked as usual and the house was empty. None of the beds had been slept in. Mr. Digby hadn't even poured himself a drink."

There was an unspoken comment that something sudden and drastic must indeed have occurred. There were surely few crises which Digby Seton would not suitably fortify himself to meet.

But Celia was speaking.

"That's nothing to go by. Digby always carries a hip flask. It was one of those little idiocyncracies of his that used to irritate Maurice so. But where on earth can he have gone?"

"He didn't say anything to you about going out again?" Latham turned to Eliza Marley. "How did he seem?".

"No, he didn't say anything; I'm not particularly perceptive of Digby's moods but he seemed much as usual."

"It's ridiculous!" proclaimed Miss Calthrop. "Digby surely wouldn't go out again when he'd only just arrived. And where is there for anyone to go? Are you sure he didn't mention his plans?"

Elizabeth Marley said:

"He may have been called out."

Her aunt's voice was sharp.

"Called out! Nobody knew he was there! Called out by whom?"

"I don't know. I only mention it as a possibility. As I was walking back to the car I heard the telephone ring."

"Are you sure?" asked Latham.

"Why do you keep on asking me if I'm sure? You know what it's like up there on the headland; the quietness; the loneliness and mystery of the place; the way sound travels at night. I tell you, I heard the phone ring!"

They fell silent. She was right, of course. They knew what it was like on the headland at night. And the same silence, the same loneliness and mystery waited for them outside. Despite the heat of the room Celia Calthrop shivered. But the heat was really getting intolerable.

Bryce had been crouching on a low stool in front of the fire feeding it compulsively from the wood basket like some demonic stoker. The great tongues of flame leapt and hissed around the drift wood; the stone walls of the sitting room looked as if they were sweating blood. Dalgliesh went over to one of the windows and wrestled with the shutters. As he pushed open the pane the waves of sweet cold air passed over him, lifting the rugs on the floor and bringing in like a clap of thunder the surge of the sea. As he turned again he heard Reckless's flat unemphatic voice:

"I suggest someone takes Miss Kedge home. She looks ill. I shan't want to talk to her tonight."

The girl looked as if she were about to remonstrate but Elizabeth Marley said with brief finality:

"I'll take her. I want to get home myself. I'm supposed to be convalescent and this hasn't exactly been a restful evening, has it? Where's her coat?"

There was a little spurt of activity. Everyone seemed to feel relief in action and there was much fuss over Sylvia Kedge's coat, her crutches and her general comfort. Miss Calthrop handed over her car keys and said graciously that she would walk home escorted, of course, by Oliver and Justin. Sylvia Kedge, surrounded by a bodyguard of helpers, began to hobble her way to the door.

It was then that the telephone rang. Immediately the little party froze into a tableau of apprehension. The raucous sound, at once so ordinary and so ominous, petrified them into silence. Miss Dalgliesh had moved to the telephone and lifted the receiver when Reckless rose swiftly and without apology took it from her hand.

They could make little of the conversation, which on Reckless's part was conducted briefly and in monosyllables He seemed to be speaking to a Police Station. For most of the time he listened in silence interspersed with grunts. He ended:

"Right. Thank you. I shall be seeing him at Seton House first thing in the morning. Goodnight." He replaced the receiver and turned to face the waiting company who were making no effort to hide their anxiety. Dalgliesh half-expected him to disappoint them but instead he said:

"We've found Mr. Digby Seton. He has telephoned Lowestoft Police Station to say that he was admitted to hospital last night after driving his car into a ditch on the Lowestoft road. They are discharging him first thing tomorrow morning."

Miss Calthrop's mouth had opened for the inevitable question when he added:

"His story is that someone telephoned him just after nine o'clock last night to ask him to go at once to Lowestoft Police Station to identify his brother's body. The caller told him that Mr. Maurice Seton's corpse had come ashore in a dinghy with both hands chopped off at the wrists."

Latham said incredulously:

"But that's impossible! I thought you said the body wasn't found until early this evening?

"Nor was it, Sir. No one telephoned from the Lowestoft Police yesterday night. No one knew what had happened to Mr. Maurice Seton until his body came ashore this evening. Except one person, of course."

He looked round at them, the melancholy eyes moving speculatively from face to face. No one spoke or moved. It was as if they were all fixed in a moment of time waiting helplessly for some unavoidable cataclysm. It was a moment for which no words seemed adequate; it cried out for action, for drama. And Sylvia Kedge, as if obligingly doing her best, slid with a moan from Eliza's supporting arms and crumpled to the floor.

CHAPTER SEVEN

Reckless said:

"He died at midnight on Tuesday, give or take an hour. That's my guess based on the stage of rigor and the general look of him. I shall be surprised if the P.M. doesn't confirm it. The hands were taken off sometime after death. There wasn't much bleeding but it looked as if the seat of the dinghy had been used as a chopping block. Assuming that Mr. Bryce was telling the truth and the dinghy was still beached here at five o'clock Wednesday afternoon, he was almost certainly pushed out to sea after the tide turned an hour later. The butchery must have been done after dusk. But he had been dead then for the best part of eighteen hours, maybe longer. I don't know where he died or how he died. But I shall find out."

The three policemen were together in the sitting room. Jane Dalgliesh had made an excuse to leave them alone by offering them coffee; from the kitchen Dalgliesh could hear the faint tinkling sounds of its preparation. It was over ten minutes since the rest of the company had left. It had required little time or effort to revive Sylvia Kedge and once she and Liz Marley were on their way, there had been a general tacit agreement that the excitements of the evening might now be drawn to a close. The visitors looked suddenly bedraggled with weariness. When Reckless, as if gaining energy and animation from their exhaustion, began to question them about a possible weapon, he was met by weary incomprehension. No one seemed able to remember whether he or she owned a chopper, a cleaver or an axe, where these implements were kept or when they had last been used. No one except Jane Dalgliesh. And even Miss Dalgliesh's calm admission that she had lost a chopper from her woodshed some months previously provoked no more than mild interest. The company had had enough of murder for one night. Like over-excited children at the end of the party, they wanted to go home.

It was not until Miss Dalgliesh had also left them that Reckless spoke of the case. This was to be expected but Dalgliesh was irritated to discover how much he resented the obvious implication. Reckless was presumably neither stupid nor crassly insensitive. He would utter no warnings. He wouldn't antagonise Dalgliesh by inviting a discretion and co-operation which both of them knew he had the right to take for granted. But this was his case. He was in charge. It was for him to decide at leisure which pieces of the puzzle he would lay out for Dalgliesh's inspection; how much he would confide and to whom. The situation was a novel one for Dalgliesh and he wasn't sure he was going to like it.

The room was still very close. The fire was dying now into a pyramid of white ash but the heat trapped between the stone walls beat on their faces as if from an oven and the air smelt heavy. The Inspector seemed unaffected by it. He said:

"These people who were here this evening, Mr. Dalgliesh. Tell me about them. Do they all call themselves writers?"

Dalgliesh replied:

"I imagine that Oliver Latham would call himself a dramatic critic. Miss Calthrop likes to be known as a romantic novelist, whatever that may mean. I don't know what Justin Bryce would call himself. He edits a monthly literary and political review which was founded by his grandfather."

Reckless said surprisingly:

"I know. The *Monthly Critical Review*. My father used to take it. That was in the days when sixpence meant something to a working man. And for sixpence the *Monthly Crit.* gave you the message, warm and strong. Nowadays it's about as pink as the *Financial Times;* advice on your investments, reviews of books which nobody wants to read; cosy competitions for the intelligentsia. He can't make a living out of that."

Dalgliesh replied that, so far from making a living, Bryce was known to subsidise the review from his private income.

Reckless said:

"He's apparently one of those men who don't mind people thinking he's a queer. Is he, Mr. Dalgliesh?"

It was not an irrelevant question. Nothing about a suspect's character is irrelevant in a murder investigation, and the case was being treated as one of murder. But, irrationally, Dalgliesh was irritated. He replied:

"I don't know. He may be a little ambivalent."

"Is he married?"

"Not as far as I know. But we surely haven't yet reached the point when every bachelor over forty is automatically suspect?"

Reckless did not reply. Miss Dalgliesh had returned with the tray of coffee and he accepted a cup with grave thanks but with no appearance of really wanting it. When she had again left them he began noisily sipping; his sombre eyes above the rim of the cup fixed on a water colour of avocets in flight by Jane Dalgliesh which hung on the opposite wall. He said:

"They're a spiteful lot, queers. Not violent on the whole. But spiteful. And there was a spiteful crime. That secretary girl, the cripple. Where does she come from, Mr. Dalgliesh?".

Dalgliesh, feeling like a candidate at a viva voce examination, said calmly:

"Sylvia Kedge is an orphan who lives alone in a cottage in Tanner's Lane. She is said to be a highly competent shorthand typist. She worked chiefly for Maurice Seton but she does quite a bit for Miss Calthrop and Bryce. I know very little about her, about any of them."

"You know enough for my needs at present, Mr. Dalgliesh. And Miss Marley?"

"Also an orphan. Her aunt brought her up. At present she's at Cambridge."

"And all these people are friends of your aunt?"

Dalgliesh hesitated. Friendship was not a word his aunt used easily and he thought it doubtful whether she would in fact speak of more than one person at Monksmere as a friend. But one does not willingly deny one's acquaintances when they are about to be suspected of murder. Resisting the temptation to reply that they knew each other intimately but not well, he said cautiously: "You had better ask my aunt. But they all know each other. After all, it's a small and isolated community. They manage to get on together."

Reckless said:

"When they're not killing each other's animals."

Dalgliesh didn't reply. Reckless added:

"They weren't particularly upset were they? Not a word of regret the whole evening. Being writers you'd think one of them might have managed a stylish little epitaph."

"Miss Kedge took it badly," suggested Dalgliesh.

"That wasn't grief. That was shock. Clinical shock. If she isn't better tomorrow someone should get a doctor to her."

He was right, of course, thought Dalgliesh. It had been shock. And that in itself was interesting. Certainly the evening's news had been shocking enough, but would it have been quite so shocking to someone to whom it wasn't news? There had been nothing faked about that final faint and it hardly suggested guilty knowledge.

Suddenly Reckless got up from his chair, looked at his empty cup as if uncertain how it came to be in his hand and replaced it with slow deliberation on the coffee tray. Sergeant Courtney, after a moment's hesitation, did the same with his. It looked as if they were at last preparing to go. But first there was something which Reckless had to be told. Since it was a perfectly straightforward piece of information which might or might not prove to be important, Dalgliesh was irritated at his reluctance to get it out. He told himself that the next few days were going to be difficult enough without letting Reckless inveigle him into a mood of morbid self-analysis. Firmly he said:

"There's something you ought to know about that fake manuscript. I may be wrong—there's not a lot to go on—but I think I recognise the description of the night club. It sounds like the Cortez Club in Soho, L. J. Luker's place. You probably remember the case. It was in 1959. Luker shot his partner, was sentenced to death, but was released when the verdict was quashed by the Court of Criminal Appeal."

Reckless said slowly:

"I remember Luker. Mr. Justice Brothwick's case wasn't it? The Cortez Club would be a useful place to know if you were hoping to pin a murder on someone. And Luker would be as good a man to pin it on as any."

He walked to the door, his Sergeant following him like a shadow. Then he turned for a last word.

"I can see that it's going to be a great advantage having you here, Mr. Dalgliesh."

He made it sound like an insult.

CHAPTER EIGHT

The contrast between the brightness of the sitting room and the cool darkness of the autumn night was absolute. It was like stepping into a pit. As the door of Pentlands closed behind them Celia Calthrop experienced a moment of blind panic. The night pressed around her. She breathed darkness like a physical weight. It was as if the air had thickened with night, had become a heaviness through which she had to fight her way. There was no longer direction nor distance. In this black and numinous void the sullen, melancholy thudding of the sea sounded on all sides, so that she felt menaced and rooted like a lost traveller on some desolate shore. When Latham shone his torch on the path the ground looked unreal and very far away like the surface of the moon. It was impossible that human feet could make contact with this remote and insubstantial soil. She stumbled and would have lost her balance if Latham hadn't gripped her arm with sudden and surprising force.

They started together on the inland path. Celia, who had not expected to walk home, was wearing light, high-heeled shoes which alternately skidded on the smooth sea pebbles which littered the path or sank into soft patches of sand so that she lurched forward in Latham's grip like a graceless and recalcitrant child. But her panic was over. Her eyes were getting accustomed to the night and with every stumble forward the roar of the sea grew fainter and less insistent. But it was a relief when Justin Bryce spoke, his voice unaltered, ordinary:

"Asthma is a peculiar complaint! This has been a traumatic evening—one's first contact with murder—and yet one feels quite well. Yet last Tuesday one had the most appalling attack with no apparent cause. One may get a reaction later of course."

"One certainly may," agreed Latham caustically. "Especially if Forbes-Denby doesn't confirm one's alibi for Tuesday night."

"Oh, but he will, Oliver! And one can't help thinking that his testimony will carry rather more weight than anything your sleeping partner may say."

Celia Calthrop, gaining confidence from their nearness, their normality, said quickly:

"It's such a comfort that Adam Dalgliesh happens to be here. After all, he does know us. Socially I mean. And being a writer himself I feel that he belongs at Monksmere."

Latham gave a shout of laughter.

"If you find Adam Dalgliesh a comfort I envy your capacity for self-deception. Do tell us how you see him, Celia! The gentleman sleuth, dabbling in detection for the fun of it, treating his suspects with studied courtesy? A kind of professional Carruthers, straight out of one of Seton's dreary sagas? My dear Celia, Dalgliesh would sell us all to Reckless if he thought it would enhance his reputation one iota. He's the most dangerous man I know."

He laughed again and she felt his grip tighten on her arm. Now he was really hurting her, hurrying her forward as if she were in custody. Yet she could not bring herself to shake free. Although the lane was wider here, the ground was still uneven. Stumbling and slipping, her feet bruised and her ankles aching, she had no chance of keeping up with them except in Latham's remorseless grip. And she could not bear to be left alone. Bryce's voice fluted in her ear.

"Oliver's right you know, Celia. Dalgliesh is a professional detective and probably one of the most intelligent in the country. I don't see that his two volumes of verse, much as I personally admire them, can alter that."

"Reckless is no fool though." Latham still seemed amused. "Did you notice how he said hardly a word but just encouraged us to babble on in our childish, egotistical way? He probably learned more from us in five minutes than other suspects would tell him in hours of orthodox questioning. When will we learn to keep our mouths shut?"

"As we've nothing to hide I don't see that it matters," said Celia Calthrop. Really Oliver was extraordinarily irritating tonight! One might almost imagine that he was a little drunk. Justin Bryce said:

"Oh, Celia! Everyone has something to hide from the police. That's why one is so ambivalent about them. Wait until Dalgliesh asks why you kept referring to Seton in the past tense, even before we heard that his body had been found. You did, you know. Even I noticed it so it must have struck Dalgliesh. I wonder whether he'll feel it his duty to mention the matter to Reckless."

But Celia was too tough to be intimidated by Bryce. She said irritably. "Don't be stupid Justin! I don't believe you. And, even if I did, it was probably because I was speaking of Maurice as a writer. And one does somehow feel that, as a writer, poor Maurice has been finished for quite a time."

"God yes!" said Latham. "Dead and done for. Finished. Written out. Maurice Seton only wrote one effective passage of prose in his life but that was straight from the heart all right. And from the brain. It produced exactly the effect he intended. Every word selected to wound and the whole —lethal."

"Do you mean his play?" asked Celia. "I thought you despised it. Maurice always said that it was your notice that killed it."

"Celia darling, if my notice could kill a play, half the little pieces now running in London would have folded after the first night." He jerked her forward with fresh impetus and for a minute Justin Bryce lagged behind them. Hurrying to catch them up he called breathlessly:

"Maurice must have been killed on Tuesday night. And his body was pushed out to sea late on Wednesday evening. So how did the murderer get it to Monksmere? You drove from London on Wednesday Oliver. It wasn't in the boot of your Jaguar, was it?

"No dear," said Latham easily. "I'm very particular what I carry in the boot of my Jaguar."

Celia said complacently:

"Well, I'm in the clear. Sylvia can give me an alibi until late on Tuesday and that's obviously the crucial time. I admit that I was out alone on Wednesday night but Reckless will hardly suspect me of mutilating the body. And that reminds me. There's one person who doesn't even claim an alibi for Tuesday or Wednesday, Jane Dalgliesh. And what's more—it was her chopper!"

Latham said:

"Why in God's name should Miss Dalgliesh wish to kill Seton?"

"Why should any of us want to?" retorted Celia. "And I'm not saying she did. I'm merely pointing out that it was apparently her chopper."

Bryce said happily:

"I wanted to at one time. Murder Seton, I mean. After I found Arabella I could willingly have killed him. But I didn't. All the same, I can't feel sorry about it. I wonder if I ought to ask to view the body after the inquest. It might shock me out of this insensitivity which I can't feel is at all healthy."

But Latham was still meditating on the missing chopper. He said fiercely:

"Anyone could have taken it! Anyone! We all walk in and out of each other's houses at will. No one here locks up anything. There's never been the need. And we don't even know yet that it was the weapon."

"My dears," said Bryce. "Consider this and calm yourselves. Until we know the cause of death we can't even be sure that Maurice was murdered."

CHAPTER NINE

They left her at the door of Rosemary Cottage and she watched them disappear into the night. Justin's high voice and Latham's laugh came back to her long after their figures had merged with the darker shadows of hedgerow and tree. There were no lights in the cottage and the sitting room was empty. So Elizabeth was in bed. She must have driven home fast from Tanner's Cottage. Her aunt was uncertain whether to be glad or sorry. She had a sudden need of company but she couldn't face questions or arguments. There would be much to discuss, but not to-night. She was too tired. She switched on the table lamp and, kneeling on the hearthrug, poked ineffectually at the slates and ashes of the dead fire. Then she got unsteadily to her feet, grunting with the effort like an old woman, and let herself down into an armchair. Opposite her an identical chair loomed squat and solid, plump with cushions, empty and poignant. Here Maurice had sat on that October afternoon six years ago. It was the day of the Inquest; a day of cold and sudden squalls. There had been a good fire that evening. She had been expecting him and had taken care that both she and the room were ready. The firelight and the one discreet lamp had shed a nicely calculated glow over the polished mahogany and cast soft shadows on the soft pinks and blues of cushions and carpet. The tray of drinks had been set ready to hand. Nothing had been left to chance. And she had waited for him as eagerly as a young girl before her first date. She had worn a dress of soft blue-grey wool. It had really made her look quite slim, quite young. It still hung in her wardrobe. She had never cared to wear it again. And he had sat opposite her, stiff and black in his formal mourning, an absurd little mannikin with his black tie and armband, his face rigid with grief. But she hadn't understood then that it was grief. How could she? It was impossible that he could be grieving for that shallow, egotistical, monstrous nymphomaniac. Of course, there had been the shock of hearing that Dorothy was dead, had killed herself, the horror of identifying the drowned body, the ordeal of the inquest, of facing the rows of white, accusing faces. He knew what they were saying all right, that he had driven his wife to suicide. No wonder he had looked shocked and ill. But grief? It had never occurred to her that he might grieve. Somehow she had taken it for granted that there must, in his heart, have been a spring of relief. Relief that the long years of torment and self-control were over at last, that he could begin to live again. And she would be there to help him, just as she had helped with her sympathy and advice when Dorothy was alive. He was a writer, an artist. He needed affection and understanding. From tonight he need never be alone ever again.

Had she loved him, she wondered. It was difficult to remember. Perhaps not. Perhaps it had never been love as she imagined love to be. But it had been as close as she would ever get to that longed-for, elusive, oft-imagined cataclysm. She had dealt with its counterfeit in nearly forty novels; but the coin itself had never come within her grasp.

Sitting in front of the dead fire she recalled the second when she had known the truth, and her cheeks burned at the memory. Suddenly he had begun to cry, awkwardly as a child. In that moment all artifice had been forgotten. Only pity remained. She had knelt beside him, cradling his head in her arms, murmuring her comfort and love. And then, it had happened. His whole body stiffened and withdrew. He looked at her, catching his breath, and she saw his face. It was all there. Pity, embarrassment, a trace of fear—and hardest of all to accept—physical repulsion. In one bitter moment of complete clarity she had seen herself with his eyes. He had been grieving for that slim, gay, beautiful creature; and an ugly middle-aged woman had chosen that moment to throw herself into his arms. He had recovered himself, of course. Nothing had been said. Even the dreadful sobbing had been cut off in mid-gasp like that of a child suddenly offered a sweet. She reflected bitterly that there was nothing like personal danger to take the edge off grief. Somehow, gracelessly, she had stumbled back to her own chair, her face burning. He had stayed for as long as politeness dictated and she had handed him his drinks, listened to his sentimental reminiscences about his wife—dear God, had the poor fool forgotten so soon?—and feigned interest in his plans for a long holiday abroad, "to try to forget". It was six months before he had thought it prudent to revisit Rosemary Cottage alone and even longer before he began tentatively to establish the understanding that she would be available whenever he wanted to escort a woman in public. Just before he left for his holiday he had written to tell her that she was named in his Will "in appreciation of your sympathy and understanding on the death of my dear wife". She had understood all right. It was the kind of crude, insensitive gesture which he would consider an adequate, appropriate apology. But her first reaction hadn't been anger or humiliation; she had merely wondered how much it would be. Since then she had wondered increasingly; and now the question had a fascinating immediacy. It might, of course, be a mere hundred or so. It might be thousands. It might even be a fortune. After all, Dorothy was reputed to have been a wealthy woman and Maurice hadn't anyone else to leave it to. He had never had much use for his half-brother and lately they had grown even further apart. Besides, didn't he owe it to her?

A slant of light from the hall fell across the carpet. Silently, Elizabeth Marley came into the room, her feet bare, her red dressing gown glowing in the half light. She stretched herself out stiffly in the chair opposite her aunt, her feet towards the dying fire, her face deep in the shadows. She said:

"I thought I heard you come in. Can I get you anything? Hot milk? Ovaltine?"

The tone was ungracious, embarrassed, but the offer was unexpected and Miss Calthrop was touched.

"No thank you dear. You go back to bed. You'll catch cold. I'll make the drink and bring yours up."

The girl did not move. Miss Calthrop made a fresh attack on the fire. This time a tongue of flame hissed round the coals and she felt the first welcome warmth on hands and face. She asked:

"You got Sylvia home all right? How did she seem?"

"Not too good. But then, she never does."

Her aunt said:

"I wondered afterwards whether we ought to have insisted that she stay here. She really looked very ill, not safe to be alone."

Elizabeth shrugged. "I did tell her that we had a spare bed until the new *au pair* girl comes and that she was welcome to it. She wouldn't consider it. When I pressed her she became overwrought, so I left it. After all, she's thirty, isn't she? She's not a child. I couldn't force her to stay."

"No, of course not." Celia Calthrop thought that her niece would hardly have welcomed Sylvia in the house.

She had noticed that most women were less sympathetic to the girl than were men, and Elizabeth made no secret of her dislike. The voice from the armchair asked:

"What happened after we left?"

"Nothing very much. Jahn Dalgliesh seems to think that he may have been killed with her chopper. Apparently she missed it about four weeks ago."

"Did Inspector Reckless tell you that he was killed that way?"

"No. But surely. . . ."

"Then we still don't know how he died. He could have been killed in a dozen different ways and his hands chopped off after death. I imagine that they were. It wouldn't be an easy thing to do if your victim were alive and conscious. Inspector Reckless must know if it happened that way. There wouldn't be very much bleeding for one thing. And I expect he knows the time of death to an hour or so even without the P.M. report."

Her aunt said:

"Surely he died on Tuesday night? Something must have happened to him on Tuesday. Maurice would never walk out of his Club like that and spend the night away without a word to anyone. He died on Tuesday night when Sylvia and I were at the pictures."

She spoke with stubborn confidence. She wished it to be so, therefore, it must be so. Maurice had died on Tuesday night and her alibi was assured. She added:

"It's unfortunate for Justin and Oliver that they happened to be in town that evening. They've got alibis of a sort, of course. But it's a pity all the same."

The girl said quietly:

"I was in London on Tuesday night too." Before her aunt could speak she went on quickly:

"All right, I know what you're going to say. I was supposed to be on a bed of sickness in Cambridge. Well, they let me up earlier than I told you. I took the first fast train to Liverpool Street on Tuesday morning. I was meeting someone there for lunch. No one you know. Someone from Cambridge. He's gone down now. Anyway he didn't turn up. There was a message of course, very polite, very regretful. It's a pity, though, that we arranged to meet where we were known. I didn't much enjoy seeing the head waiter look sorry for me. Not that I was surprised really. It isn't important. But I wasn't going to have Oliver and Justin gossiping over my affairs. I don't see why I should tell Reckless, either. Let him find out for himself."

Celia thought:

"But you told me!" She felt a surge of happiness so acute that she was glad that they sat in the shadows. This was the first real confidence she had ever received from the girl. And happiness made her wise. Resisting the first impulse to comfort or question she said:

"I'm not sure, dear, that it was sensible of you to spend the whole day in town. You're not really strong yet. Still, it doesn't seem to have done you any harm. What did you do after lunch?"

"Oh, worked for the afternoon in the London Library. Then I went to a news theatre. It was getting lateish then so I thought I'd better stay the night. After all, you weren't expecting me at any particular time. I had a meal at the Coventry Street Lyons and then managed to get a room at the Walter Scott Hotel in Bloomsbury. Most of the evening I spent just walking in London. I suppose I collected my key and went to my room just before eleven."

Miss Calthrop broke in eagerly:

"Then the porter will be able to vouch for you. And perhaps someone will remember you at Lyons. But I think you were right to say nothing about it for the present. It's entirely your own concern. What we'll do is to wait until we know the time of death. We can reconsider the whole matter then."

It was difficult for her to keep the ring of happiness from her voice. This was what she had always wanted. They were talking together, planning together. She was being asked, however obliquely and unwillingly, for reassurance and advice. How odd that it should take Maurice's death to bring them together. She babbled on:

"I'm glad you're not upset about the luncheon date. Young men today have no manners. If he couldn't telephone you by the day before at the latest, he should have made it his business to turn up. But at least you know where you stand."

The girl got up from the chair and walked without speaking to the door. Her aunt called after her:

"I'll get the drinks and we'll have them together in your room. I won't be a moment. You go up and get into bed."

"I don't want anything, thank you."

"But you said you'd like a hot drink. You ought to have something. Let me make you some Ovaltine. Or just hot milk perhaps."

"I said I didn't want anything. And I'm going to bed. I want to be left in peace."

"But Eliza. . . ."

The door closed. She could hear nothing more, not even a soft footfall on the stairs. There was nothing but the hissing of the fire and, outside, the silence, the loneliness of the night.

CHAPTER TEN

Dalgliesh was woken next morning by the ring of the telephone. His aunt must have answered it quickly for the ringing stopped almost immediately and he dozed again into that happy trance between waking and sleeping which follows a good night. It must have been half an hour before the telephone rang again, and this time it seemed louder and more insistent. He opened his eyes wide and saw, framed by the window, a translucent oblong of blue light with only the faintest hairline separating the sea and the sky. It promised to be another wonderful autumn day. It was already another wonderful autumn day. He saw with surprise that his watch showed ten-fifteen. Putting on his dressing gown and slippers, he pattered downstairs in time to hear his aunt answering the telephone.

"I'll tell him, Inspector, as soon as he wakes. Is it urgent? No, except that this is supposed to be his holiday . . . . I'm sure that he'll be glad to come as soon as he's finished breakfast. Goodbye."

Dalgliesh bent over and placed his cheek momentarily against hers. It felt, as always, as soft and tough as a chamois glove.

"Is that Reckless?"

"Yes. He says he is at Seton's house and would be glad if you would join him there this morning."

"He didn't say in what capacity I suppose? Am I supposed to work or merely to admire him working? Or am I, possibly, a suspect?

"It is I who am the suspect, Adam. It was almost certainly my chopper."

"Oh, that's been taken notice of. Even so, you rate lower than most of your neighbours, I imagine. And certainly lower than Digby Seton. We police are simple souls at heart. We like to see a motive before we actually make an arrest. And no motive so gladdens our heart as the prospect of gain. I take it that Digby is his half-brother's heir?"

"It's generally supposed so. Two eggs or one, Adam?"

"Two, please. But I'll see to them. You stay and talk. Didn't I hear two calls? Who telephoned earlier?"

His aunt explained that R. B. Sinclair had rung to invite them both to dinner on Sunday night. She had promised to ring back. Dalgliesh, paying loving attention to his frying eggs, was intrigued. But he said little beyond expressing his willingness to go. This was something new. His aunt, he guessed, was a fairly frequent visitor to Priory House but never when he was at Pentlands. It was after all well understood that R. B. Sinclair neither visited nor received visitors. His aunt was uniquely privileged. But it wasn't hard to guess the reason for this innovation. Sinclair wanted to talk about the murder with the one man who could be expected to give a professional opinion. It was reassuring, if a little disillusioning, to discover that the great man wasn't immune to common curiosity. Violent death held its macabre fascination even for this dedicated non-participant in the human charade. But, of course, Dalgliesh would go to dinner. The temptation was too great to resist. He had lived long enough to know that few experiences can be so disenchanting as meeting the famous. But, with R. B. Sinclair, any writer would be willing to take the risk.

Dalgliesh made an unhurried business of washing-up after his breakfast, put on a tweed jacket over his sweater, and hesitated at the cottage door where a jumbled collection of walking sticks, left by past guests as hostages against a happy return, tempted him to add a final touch to the part of an energetic holiday-maker. He selected a sturdy ash, balanced it in his hand, then replaced it. There was no point in overdoing the act. Calling "Goodbye" to his aunt he set off across the headland. The quickest way would have been by car, turning right at the road junction, driving about half a mile on the Southwold road, then taking the narrow but reasonably smooth track which led across the headland to the house. Perversely, Dalgliesh decided to walk. He was, after all, supposed to be on holiday and the Inspector's summons had made no mention of any urgency. He was sorry for Reckless. Nothing is more irritating and frustrating to a detective than any uncertainty about the extent of his responsibility. In fact, there was none. Reckless was in sole charge of the investigation and both of them knew it. Even if the Chief Constable decided to ask for the help of the Yard it was highly improbable that Dalgliesh would be given the case. He was too personally involved. But Reckless would hardly relish conducting his investigation under the eyes of a C.I.D. Superintendent, particularly one with Dalgliesh's reputation. Well, it was hard luck on Reckless; but harder luck, thought Dalgliesh, on himself. This was the end of his hope of a solitary, uncomplicated holiday, that blessed week of undemanding peace which almost without effort on his part was to soothe his nerves and solve his personal problems. From the first this plan was probably an unsubstantial fabrication built on tiredness and his need to escape. But it was disconcerting to see it fall so early into ruin. He was as little inclined to interfere in the case as Reckless was to seek his help. There would have been tactful telephone calls to and from the Yard, of course. It would be understood by all concerned that Dalgliesh's familiarity with Monksmere and his knowledge of the people concerned would be at the Inspector's service. That was no more than any citizen owed the police. But if Reckless thought that Dalgliesh craved any more positive participation he must be speedily disillusioned.

It was impossible not to rejoice in the beauty of the day and as he walked much of Dalgliesh's irritation fell away. The whole headland was bathed in the yellow warmth of the autumn sun. The breeze was fresh but without chill. The sandy track was firm under his feet, sometimes passing straight between the gorse and heather, sometimes twisting among the thick brambles and stunted hawthorn trees which formed a succession of little caverns where the light was lost and the path dwindled to a thread of sand. For most of the walk Dalgliesh had a view of the sea except when he passed behind the grey walls of Priory House. It stood four square to the sea within a hundred yards of the cliff edge and was bounded on the south by a tall stone wall and on the north by a fringe of fir trees. At night there was something eerie and unwelcoming about the house which reinforced its natural privacy. Dalgliesh thought that Sinclair if he craved seclusion could hardly have found a more perfect site. He wondered how long it would be before Inspector Reckless violated that privacy with his questions. It would hardly take him long to learn that Sinclair had a private flight of steps leading to the beach from his land. Assuming that the body had been taken to the boat and not the boat rowed some considerable distance along the coast to the body, it must have been carried down to the beach by one of three paths. There was no other access. One way, and perhaps the most obvious, was Tanner's Lane which led past Sylvia Kedge's cottage. As the dinghy had been beached at the bottom of Tanner's Lane this would have been the most direct route. The second was the steep and sandy slope which led from Pentlands to the shore. It was difficult enough in daylight. At night it would be hazardous even to the experienced and unburdened. He could not see the murderer risking that route. Even if his aunt did not hear the distant car she would know that someone was passing the cottage. People who lived alone and in so remote a place were quick to sense the unfamiliar noises of the night. His aunt was the most detached, and incurious of women to whom the habits of birds had always appeared of greater interest than those of humans. But even she would hardly watch unconcerned while a dead body was carried past her door. There would, too, be the problem of carrying the corpse the half mile along the shore to where Sheldrake was beached. Unless, of course, the killer left it half buried in the sand while he collected the dinghy and rowed it to the corpse. But that would surely add unnecessarily to the risks and it would be impossible to remove all traces of sand from the body. More to the point, it would require oars and rowlocks. He wondered whether Reckless had checked on these.

The third way of access to the beach was by Sinclair's steps. These were only some fifty yards from the bottom of Tanner's Lane and they led to a small secluded cove where the cliffs, taller here than at any other point, had been crumbled and eroded by the sea into a gentle curve. This was the only part of the beach where the killer—if killer there were— could have worked on the corpse without fear of being watched either from the north or south. Only in the unlikely event of one of the local inhabitants deciding to take a late walk along the shore would there be danger of discovery; and in this place, once dusk had fallen, the countryman did not choose to walk alone on the shore.

Priory House was behind Dalgliesh now and he had come to the thin beech wood which fringed Tanner's Lane. Here the earth was brittle with fallen leaves and through the lattice of the bare boughs there was a haze of blue which could have been sky or sea. The wood ended suddenly and Dalgliesh clambered over a stile and dropped into the lane. Immediately before him was the squat, red-bricked cottage where Sylvia Kedge had lived alone since the death of her mother. It was an ugly building, as uncompromisingly square as a doll's house with its four small windows, each heavily curtained. The gate and the front door had been widened, presumably to take the girl's wheel chair, but the change had done nothing to improve the proportions of the house. No attempt had been made to prettify it. The diminutive front garden was a dark patch cut in two by a gravel path; the paint on doors and windows was a thick, institutional brown. Dalgliesh thought that there must have been a Tanner's Cottage here for generations, each built a little higher up the lane until it too crumbled or was swept away in the great storms. Now this square, red, twentieth-century box stood firm to take its chance against the sea. Obeying an impulse, Dalgliesh pushed open the garden gate and walked up the path. Suddenly his ears caught a sound. Someone else was exploring. Round the corner of the house came the figure of Elizabeth Marley. Unembarrassed, she gave him a cool glance and said: "Oh, it's you! I thought I heard someone snooping around. What do you want?"

"Nothing. I snoop by nature. Whereas you, presumably, were looking for Miss Kedge?"

"Sylvia's not here. I thought she might be in her little dark room at the back but she isn't. I've come with a message from my aunt. Ostensibly she wants to make sure that Sylvia's all right after the shock of last night. Really, she wants her to come and take dictation before Oliver Latham or Justin nab her. There's going to be great competition for La Kedge, and I've no doubt she'll make the most of it. They all like the idea of having a private secretary on call for two bob a thousand words, carbons supplied."

"Is that all Seton paid her? Why didn't she leave?"

"She was devoted to him, or pretended to be. She had her own reasons for staying, I suppose. After all, it wouldn't be easy for her to find a flat in town. It'll be interesting to know what she's been left in the Will. Anyway, she enjoyed posing as the loyal, overworked little help-meet who would be so happy to transfer to auntie if only it didn't mean letting poor Mr. Seton down. My aunt never saw through it, of course. But then, she's not particularly intelligent."

"Whereas you have us all neatly catalogued. But you're not suggesting that someone killed Maurice Seton to get his shorthand typist?"

She turned on him furiously, her heavy face blotched with anger.

"I don't care a damn who killed him or why! I only know that it wasn't Digby Seton. I met him off that train Wednesday night. And if you're wondering where he was on Tuesday night, I can tell you. He told me on the drive home. He was locked up in West Central Police Station from eleven o'clock onwards. They picked him up drunk and he came before the Magistrate on Wednesday morning. So, luckily for him, he was in police custody from eleven o'clock on Tuesday night until nearly midday on Wednesday. Break that alibi if you can, Superintendent."

Dalgliesh pointed out mildly that the breaking of alibis was Reckless's business, not his. The girl shrugged, dug her fists into her jacket pockets, and kicked shut the gate of Tanner's Cottage. She and Dalgliesh walked up the lane together in silence. Suddenly she said:

"I suppose the body was brought down this lane to the sea. It's the easiest way to where Sheldrake was beached. The killer would have had to carry it for the last hundred yards, though. The lane's much too narrow for a car or even a motor cycle. He could have got it by car as far as Coles's meadow and parked the car on the grass verge. There were a couple of plain clothes men there when I came past, looking for tyre marks. They won't get much joy. Someone left the gate open last night and Coles's sheep were all over the lane this morning."

This, as Dalgliesh knew, was not unusual. Ben Coles, who farmed a couple of hundred unproductive acres on the east of the Dunwich road did not keep his gates in the best of repair and his sheep, with the blind perversity of their kind, were as often in Tanner's Lane as in their own meadow. At tripper time the lane became a shambles when the bleating flock in full cry mingled with the herd of horn-happy motorists frantically trying to edge each other out of the only parking space in the lane. But that open gate might have been highly convenient for someone; Coles's sheep in their happy scamperings might have been following an old local tradition. It was well known that, in the smuggling days, the flocks were driven nightly along the sheep paths which crossed the Westleton marshes so that all traces of horses' hoofs were obliterated before the Excise Officers made their morning search.

They walked on together until they came to the stile which gave access to the northern half of Monksmere Head. Dalgliesh was pausing to say goodbye when the girl suddenly blurted:

"I suppose you think I'm an ungrateful bitch. She makes me an allowance, of course. £400 a year in addition to my grant. But I expect you know that. Most people here seem to."

There was no need to ask whom she meant, Dalgliesh could have replied that Celia Calthrop was not the woman to let her generosities go unremarked. But he was surprised by the amount. Miss Calthrop made no secret of the fact that she had no private income—"Poor little me. I'm a working girl. I earn every penny I get"—but it was not therefore assumed that she lacked money. Her sales were large and she worked hard, incredibly hard by the standards of Latham or Bryce who were apt to assume that dear Celia had only to lean back in a comfortable armchair with her tape recorder on and her reprehensible fiction would gush forth in an effortless and highly rewarding stream. It was easy to be unkind about her books. But if one were buying affection, and the price of even a reluctant toleration was a Cambridge education and £400 a year, much might be necessary. A novel every six months; a weekly stint in *Home and Hearth;* appearances whenever her agent could get them on those interminably boring television panels; short stories written under one name or another for the women's weeklies; the gracious appearances at Church bazaars where the publicity was free even if the tea had to be paid for. He felt a spasm of pity for Celia. The vanities and ostentations which were such a source of amused contempt to Latham and Bryce suddenly appeared no more than the pathetic trappings of a life both lonely and insecure. He wondered whether she had really cared for Maurice Seton. And he wondered, too, whether she was mentioned in Seton's Will.

Elizabeth Marley seemed in no hurry to leave him and it was difficult to turn away from that resolutely persistent figure. He was used to being a confidant. That, after all, was part of his job. But he wasn't on duty now and he knew well that those who confided most were apt to regret it soonest. Besides, he had no real wish to discuss Celia Calthrop with her niece. He hoped the girl didn't intend to walk all the way to Seton House with him. Looking at her he could see where at least some of that £400 allowance went. Her fur lined jacket was real leather. The pleated skirt of thin tweed looked as if it had been tailored for her. Her shoes were sturdy but they were also elegant. He remembered something he had once heard Oliver Latham say, he couldn't remember when or why: "Elizabeth Marley has a passion for money. One finds it rather engaging in this age when we're all so busy pretending to have minds above mere cash."

She was leaning back against the stile now, effectively blocking his way.

"She got me to Cambridge, of course. You can't do that without either money or influence if you're only moderately intelligent like me. It's all right for the alpha people. Everyone's glad to get them. For the rest of us it's a matter of the right school, the right crammers, and the right names on your application form. Aunt could manage even that. She has a real talent for making use of people. She's never afraid of being a vulgar nuisance which makes it easier of course."

"Why do you dislike her so much?" enquired Dalgliesh.

"Oh, it's nothing personal. Although we haven't much in common, have we? It's her work. The novels are bad enough. Thank God we haven't the same name. People are pretty tolerant at Cambridge. If, like the waterman's wife, she was a receiver of stolen property under guise of keeping a brothel no one would care a damn. And nor would I. But that column she writes. It's utterly humiliating! Worse even than the books. You know the kind of muck." Her voice rose to a sickly falsetto. "Don't give in to him, dear. Men are only after one thing."

In Dalgliesh's view men, including himself, frequently were but he thought it prudent not to say so. Suddenly he felt middle-aged, bored and irritated. He had neither wanted nor expected company and if his solitude had to be disturbed he could have named more agreeable companions than this peevish and dissatisfied adolescent. He hardly heard the rest of her complaint. She had dropped her voice and the words were blown from him on the freshening breeze. But he caught the final mutterings. "It's so completely amoral in the real sense of the term. Virginity as a carefully preserved bait for eligible males. In this day and age!"

"I haven't much sympathy with that point of view myself," Dalgliesh said. "But then, as a man, your aunt would no doubt consider me prejudiced. But at least it's realistic. And you can hardly blame Miss Calthrop for dishing out the same advice week after week when she gets so many letters from the readers wishing they'd taken it in the first place."

The girl shrugged: "Naturally she has to adopt the orthodox line. The hag rag wouldn't employ her if she dared to be honest. Not that I think she knows how. And she needs that column. She hasn't any money except what she earns and the novels can't go on selling for ever." Dalgliesh caught the note of anxiety in her voice. He said brutally:

"I shouldn't worry. Her sales won't fall. She writes about sex. You may not like the packaging but the basic commodity will always be in demand. I should think your £400 is safe for the next three years."

For a moment he thought she was going to smack his face. Then surprisingly, she gave a shout of laughter and moved away from the stile.

"I deserved that! I've been taking myself too seriously. Sorry for boring you. You're on your way to Seton House, I suppose?" Dalgliesh said that he was and asked if he should give any message to Sylvia Kedge if she were there.

"Not to Sylvia. Why should you pimp for auntie? No, it's to Digby. Just to say that there will be meals for him at the cottage until he gets fixed up if he cares to come. It's only cold meat and salad today so he won't be missing much if he can't make it. But I don't suppose he'll want to depend on Sylvia. They hate each other. And don't get any wrong ideas, Superintendent. I may be willing to drive Digby home and feed with him for a day or two. But that's as far as it goes. I'm not interested in pansies."

"No," said Dalgliesh. "I wouldn't suppose that you were."

For some reason she blushed. She was turning away when, prompted by no more than mild curiosity, Dalgliesh said:

"One thing intrigues me. When Digby Seton telephoned to ask you to meet him at Saxmundham, how did he know you weren't at Cambridge?" She turned back and met his gaze without embarrassment or fear. She didn't even appear to resent the question. Instead, to his surprise, she laughed.

"I wondered how long it would be before someone asked that. I might have known it would be you. The answer's simple. I met Digby in London, quite by chance, on Tuesday morning. At Piccadily Underground to be precise. I stayed in London that night and on my own. So I probably haven't an alibi. . . . Are you going to tell Inspector Reckless? But of course you are."

"No," replied Dalgliesh. "You are."

CHAPTER ELEVEN

Maurice Seton had been fortunate in his architect and his house had that characteristic of all good domestic building: it seemed indigenous to its site. The grey stone walls curved from the heather to buttress the highest point of Monksmere Head, with a view north over Sole Bay and south over the marshes and the bird reserve as far as Sizewell Gap. It was an unpretentious and agreeable building, single-storied and L-shaped, and built only fifty yards from the cliff edge. Presumably, these elegant walls, like those of Sinclair's sturdy bastion, would one day crumble into the North Sea, but there seemed no immediate danger of it. The cliffs here had a strength and height which gave some hope of permanence. The long arm of the L faced south-east and was composed almost entirely of double-glazed windows which opened on to a terrace of paved stones. Here Seton had taken a hand in the planning. Dalgliesh thought it unlikely that the architect had chosen to set up the two ornate urns which marked the ends of the terrace and in which a couple of bushes, their boughs contorted by the cold winds of the Suffolk coast, were failing to thrive, nor the pretentious sign swinging between two low posts on which the words, "Seton House" were carved in Gothic lettering.

It didn't need the car parked at the terrace edge to tell Dalgliesh that Reckless was there. He could see no one, but he knew that his approach was being watched. The tall windows seemed full of eyes. One of them was ajar. Dalgliesh drew it open and stepped into the living room.

It was like walking on to a stage set. Every corner of

the long narrow room was warm with light as if bathed in the glare of arc lamps. It was a modern set. From centre back an open staircase curved to the upper storey. Even the furniture contemporary, functional and expensive-looking added to the air of impermanence and unreality. Almost the whole of the window space was taken up with Seton's desk, an ingeniously designed fitment with a complex of drawers, cupboards and bookcases spreading each side of the central working surface. It had probably been made to the owner's specification, a functional status symbol in light polished oak. On the pale grey walls there were two popular Monet prints unimaginatively framed.

The four people who turned to watch unsmiling as Dalgliesh stepped over the window sill were as immobile and carefully disposed about the room as actors who have taken up their pose ready for the curtains to rise. Digby Seton was lying on a couch placed diagonally across the centre of the room. He was wearing a mauve dressing gown of artifical silk over red pyajmas and might have looked more the part of romantic lead had it not been for the cap of grey stockinette which fitted close to his head and came down level to his eyebrows. The modern method of bandaging is effective but scarcely becoming. Dalgliesh wondered whether Seton had a temperature. He would hardly have been discharged from hospital unfit and Reckless, who was neither inexperienced nor a fool, would have telephoned the doctor to make sure that the man was fit to be questioned. But his eyes were unnaturally bright and a red moon burnt high on each cheekbone so that he looked like a gaudy circus clown, a bizarre focus of interest against the grey couch. Inspector Reckless sat at the desk with Sergeant Courtney by his side. In this morning light Dalgliesh saw the boy clearly for the first time and was struck by his pleasant good looks. He had the type of honest, open face which looks out of advertisements extolling the advantages of a career in banking for the intelligent and ambitious young man. Well, Sergeant Courtney had chosen the police. In his present mood Dalgliesh thought it rather a pity.

The fourth player was hardly on stage. Through the open door which led to the drawing room Dalgliesh caught a glimpse of Sylvia Kedge. She was sitting at the table in her wheelchair. There was a tray of silver in front of her and she was engaged in polishing a fork with as little enthusiasm as a bit player who knows that the attention of the audience is elsewhere. She lifted her eyes momentarily to Dalgliesh and he was shocked by the misery in her drawn face. She looked very ill. Then she bent again to her task.

Digby Seton heaved his legs from the couch, walked deliberately to the dining room door and prodded it gently shut with his stockinged foot. None of the policemen spoke.

Seton said:

"Sorry and all that. Don't want to be rude, but she gives me the willies. Damn it all, I've said I'll pay her the £300 Maurice left her! Thank God you've come, Superintendent! Are you taking over the case?"

It could hardly have been a worse beginning. Dalgliesh said:

"No. It's nothing to do with the Yard. Surely Inspector Reckless has explained to you by now that he's the officer in charge?"

He felt that Reckless deserved that snide innuendo.

Seton protested:

"But I thought they always called in the Yard to tricky cases of murder?"

"What makes you think this is a case of murder?" asked Reckless. He was slowly sorting out papers from the desk and did not turn to Seton as he spoke. His voice was quiet, unemphatic, almost uninterested.

"Well, isn't it? You tell me. You're the experts. But I don't see how Maurice could have cut off his own hands. One perhaps, but hardly two. If that's not murder, then what is it? And damn it all, you've got a Scotland Yard chap on the spot."

"On holiday, remember," said Dalgliesh. "I'm in exactly the same position as you."

"Like hell you are!" Seton twisted himself into a sitting position and groped under the couch for his shoes.

"Brother Maurice hasn't left you £200,000. God, it's crazy! It's unbelievable! Some sod pays off an old score and I get a fortune! Where the hell did Maurice get that kind of money anyway?"

"Apparently partly from his mother and partly from the estate of his late wife," replied Reckless. He had finished with the papers and was now going through a small drawer of index cards with the methodical intentness of a scholar looking for a reference.

Seton gave a snort of laughter.

"Is that what Pettigrew told you? Pettigrew! I ask you, Dalgliesh! Trust Maurice to have a solicitor called Pettigrew. What else could the poor devil be with a name like that? Pettigrew! Doomed from birth to be a respectable provincial solicitor. Can't you picture him? Dry, precise, sixtyish, resplendent watch chain and pin stripes. God I hope he knows how to draw up a valid Will."

"I don't think you need worry on that score," said Dalgliesh. Actually, he knew Charles Pettigrew who was his aunt's solicitor. It was an old firm but the present owner, who had inherited from his grandfather, was a capable and lively thirty year old, reconciled to the tedium of a country practice by the nearness of the sea and a passion for sailing. He said:

"I gather you've found a copy of the Will?"

"It's here." Reckless passed over the single sheet of stiff paper, and Dalgliesh scanned it. The Will was short and soon read. Maurice Seton, after instructing that his body be used for medical research and afterwards cremated, left £2,000 to Celia Calthrop, "in appreciation of her sympathy and understanding on the death of my dear wife", and £300 to Sylvia Kedge, "provided she has been ten years in my service at the time of my death". The remainder of the estate was left to Digby Kenneth Seton, on trust until he married, and then to revert to him absolutely. If he died before his half-brother or died unmarried the estate went absolutely to Celia Calthrop. Seton said:

"Poor old Kedge! She's lost her £300 by two months. No wonder she looks sick! Honestly, I'd no idea about the Will. At least, I knew that I would very likely be Maurice's heir. He more or less said so once. Anyway, he hadn't anyone else to leave it to. We've never been particularly close but we did have the same father and Maurice had a great respect for the old man. But £200,000! Dorothy must have left him a packet. Funny that, when you consider that their marriage was pretty well on the rocks when she died."

"Mrs. Maurice Seton had no other relatives then?" asked Reckless.

"Not that I know of. Lucky for me, isn't it? When she killed herself there was some talk of a sister who ought to be contacted. Or was it a brother? Honestly, I can't remember. Anyway, no one turned up and no one but Maurice was mentioned in the Will. Her father was a property speculator and Dorothy was left pretty well off. And it all came to Maurice. But £200,000!"

"Perhaps your half-brother did well with his books," suggested Reckless. He had finished with the card index but was still seated at the desk, making entries in a note book and seemingly only half-interested in Seton's reactions. But Dalgliesh, himself a professional, knew that the interview was going very much according to plan.

"Oh, I shouldn't think so! Maurice always said that writing wouldn't keep him in socks. He was rather bitter about it. He said that this was the age of 'Soap-powder fiction'. If a writer hadn't a gimmick no one was interested. Bestsellers were created by the advertisers, good writing was a positive disadvantage and the public libraries killed sales. I daresay he was right. If he had £200,000 I don't know why he bothered. Except, of course, that he liked being a writer. It did something for his ego, I suppose. I never understood why he took it seriously, but then, he never understood why I wanted my own Club. And I'll be able to have it now. A whole chain of them if things go my way. You're both invited to the opening night. Bring the whole of West Central with you if you like. No sneaking in on expenses to check on the drinking and see that the floor show isn't too naughty. No women sergeants tarted up to look like provincial tourists on the spree. The best tables. Everything on the house. D'you know, Dalgliesh, I could have made a go of the Golden Pheasant if only I'd had the capital behind me. Well, I've got it now."

"Not unless you also get a wife," Dalgliesh reminded him unkindly. He had noted the names of the trustees in Seton's Will and couldn't see either of those cautious and conservative gentlemen parting with trust funds to finance a second Golden Pheasant. He asked why Maurice Seton had been so anxious for Digby to marry.

"Maurice was always hinting that I ought to settle down. He was a great one for the family name. He hadn't any children himself—none that I know of anyway—and I don't suppose he was keen to marry again after the Dorothy fiasco. Besides, he had a dicky heart. He was afraid, too, that I might set up house with a queer. He didn't want his money shared with a pansy boy friend. Poor old Maurice! I don't think he'd recognise a queen if he met one. He just had the idea that London, and West End Clubs in particular, are full of them."

"Extraordinary!" said Dalgliesh dryly. Seton seemed unaware of the irony. He said anxiously:

"Look, you do believe me about that phone call, don't you? The murderer phoned me as I arrived here Wednesday night and sent me off on a fool's errand to Lowestoft. The idea was to get me away from the house and make sure I hadn't an alibi for the time of death. At least, I suppose that was the idea. It doesn't make sense otherwise. It puts me in a spot all right. I wish to God that Liz had come in with me. I don't see how I can prove that Maurice wasn't in the house when I got here or that I didn't take a late night walk on the beach with him, conveniently armed with the kitchen knife. Have you found the weapon, by the way?"

The Inspector replied briefly that they hadn't. He said:

"It would help me, Mr. Seton, if you could remember more about this phone call."

"Well, I can't." Seton sounded suddenly peevish. He added sullenly: "You keep asking me about it and I keep telling you! I don't remember. Damn it, I've had a bloody great bang on the head since then! If you told me I'd imagined the whole thing I wouldn't be surprised except that it must have happened or I wouldn't have taken out the car. I was dog tired and I wouldn't have set off to Lowestoft just for the fun of it. Someone phoned. I'm sure of that. But I can't remember what the voice sounded like. I'm not even sure if it was a man or a woman."

"And the message?"

"I've told you, Inspector! The voice said it was speaking from Lowestoft Police Station, that Maurice's body had come ashore in my dinghy with the hands chopped off—"

"Chopped or cut?"

"Oh, I don't know! Chopped I think. Anyway, I was to go to Lowestoft at once and identify the body. So I set off. I knew where Maurice keeps the car keys and luckily the Vauxhall had plenty of juice in her. Or unluckily. I damn near killed myself. Oh, I know you're going to say it was my fault. I admit I had a pull or two from my hip flask on the way. Well, do you wonder! And I was bloody tired before I started. I had a lousy night on Tuesday—the West Central's hardly a hotel. And then that long train journey."

And yet you set off for Lowestoft straight away without bothering to check?" asked Reckless.

"I did check! When I got to the road it occurred to me to see if Sheldrake had really gone. So I drove down Tanner's Lane as far as I could and walked to the beach. The boat wasn't there. That was good enough for me. I suppose you think that I ought to have rung back the police station but it never occurred to me that the message might be a hoax until I was on my way and then the easiest thing was to check on the boat. I say. . . ."

"Yes?" enquired Reckless calmly.

"Whoever phoned must have known that I was here. And it couldn't have been Liz Marley because she'd only just left when the phone rang. Now, how could anyone else have known?"

"You could have been seen arriving," suggested Reckless. "And I suppose you put the lights on when you got in. They could be seen for miles."

"I put them on all right. The whole bloody lot. This place gives me the creeps in the dark. Still, it's odd."

It was odd, thought Dalgliesh. But the Inspector's explanation was probably correct. The whole of Monksmere Head could have seen those blazing lights. And when they went out, someone would know that Digby Seton was on his way. But why send him? Was there something still to be done at Seton House? Something to be searched for? Some evidence to be destroyed. Was the body hidden in Seton House? But how was that possible if Digby was telling the truth about the missing boat?

Suddenly Digby said:

"What am I supposed to do about handing the body over for medical research? Maurice never said anything to me about being keen on medical research. Still, if that's what he wanted. . . ."

He looked from Dalgliesh to Reckless enquiringly. The Inspector said:

"I shouldn't worry about that now, Sir. Your brother left the necessary instructions and official forms among his papers. But it will have to wait."

Seton said: "Yes. I suppose so. But I wouldn't like . . . I mean, if that's what he wanted. . . ."

He broke off uncertainly. Much of the excitement had left him and he was looking suddenly very tired. Dalgliesh and Reckless glanced at each other, sharing the thought that there would be little more to be learnt from Maurice's body once Walter Sydenham had finished with it, the eminent and thorough Dr. Sydenham whose textbook on forensic pathology made it plain that he favoured an initial incision from the throat to the groin. Seton's limbs might be useful for raw medical students to practise on, which was probably not what he had in mind. But his cadaver had already made its contribution to medical science.

Reckless was preparing to leave. He explained to Seton that he would be required at the inquest in five days' time, an invitation which was received without enthusiasm, and began putting his papers together with the satisfied efficiency of an insurance agent at the end of a good morning's work. Digby watched him with the puzzled and slightly apprehensive air of a small boy who has found the company of adults a strain but isn't sure that he actually wants them to leave. Strapping up his brief case, Reckless asked his last question with no appearance of really wanting to know the answer:

"Don't you find it rather strange, Mr. Seton, that your half-brother should have made you his heir? It isn't as if you were particularly friendly."

"But I told you!" Seton wailed his protest. "There wasn't anyone else. Besides, we were friendly enough. I mean, I made it my business to keep in with him. He wasn't difficult to get on with if you flattered him about his bloody awful books and took a bit of trouble with him. I like to get on with people if I can. I don't enjoy quarrelling and unpleasantness. I don't think I could have stood his company for long but then I wasn't here very often. I told you I haven't seen him since August Bank Holiday. Besides, he was lonely. I was the only family he had left and he liked to think that there was someone who belonged."

Reckless said:

"So you kept in with him because of his money. And he kept in with you because he was afraid of being completely alone?"

"Well, that's how things are." Seton was unabashed. "That's life. We all want something from each other. Is there anyone who loves you, Inspector, for yourself alone?"

Reckless got up and went out through the open window. Dalgliesh followed him and they stood together on the terrace in silence. The wind was freshening but the sun still shone, warm and golden. On the green-blue sea a couple of white sails moved fitfully like twists of paper blown in the wind. Reckless sat down on the steps which led from the terrace to the narrow strip of turf and the cliff edge. Dalgliesh, feeling unreasonably that he could hardly remain standing since it put Reckless at a disadvantage, dropped down beside him. The stones were unexpectedly cold to his hands and thighs, a reminder that the warmth of the autumn sun had little power. The Inspector said:

"There's no way down to the beach here. You'd have thought Seton would want his own way down. It's a fair walk to Tanner's Lane."

"The cliffs are pretty high here and there's little solid rock. It could be tricky to build a stairway," suggested Dalgliesh.

"Maybe. He must have been a strange sort of chap. Fussy. Methodical. That card index, for instance. He picked up ideas for his stories from newspapers, magazines, and from people. Or just thought of them for himself. But they're all neatly catalogued there, waiting to come in useful."

"And Miss Calthrop's contribution?"

"Not there. That doesn't mean very much though. Sylvia Kedge told me that the house was usually left unlocked when Seton was living here. They all seem to leave their houses unlocked. Anyone could have got in and taken the card. Anyone could have read it for that matter. They just seem to wander in and out of each other's places at will. It's the loneliness I suppose. That's assuming that Seton wrote out a card."

"Or that Miss Calthrop ever gave him the idea," said Dalgliesh. Reckless looked at him.

"That struck you too, did it? What did you think of Digby Seton?"

"The same as I've always thought. It requires an effort of will to understand a man whose passionate ambition is to run his own Club. But then, he probably finds it equally difficult to understand why we should want to be policemen. I don't think our Digby has either the nerve or the brains to plan this particular killing. Basically he's unintelligent."

"He was in the nick most of Tuesday night. I gave West Central a ring and it's true all right. What's more he was drunk. There was nothing feigned about it."

"Very convenient for him."

"It's always convenient to have an alibi, Mr. Dalgliesh. But there are some alibis I don't intend to waste time trying to break. And that's the kind he's got. What's more, unless he was acting just now, he just doesn't know that the weapon wasn't a knife. And he thinks that Seton died on Wednesday night. Maurice couldn't have been in this house alive when Digby and Miss Marley arrived on Wednesday. That's not to say that his body wasn't here. But I can't see Digby acting the butcher and I can't see why he should. Even if he found the body here and panicked he's the sort to hit the bottle then belt off back to town, not to plan an elaborate charade. And he was on the Lowestoft not the London road when he crashed. Besides, I don't see how he could have known about Miss Calthrop's pleasant little opening for a detective story."

"Unless Eliza Marley told him on the way here."

"Why should she tell Digby Seton? It's not a likely topic for conversation on the drive home. But all right. We'll assume that she did know and that she told Digby or that, somehow or other, he knew. He arrives here and finds his brother's body. So he immediately decides to provide a real life mystery by chopping off Maurice's hands and pushing the body out to sea. Why? And what did he use for a weapon? I saw the body, remember, and I'd swear those hands were chopped off, not cut, nor sawed, chopped. So much for the kitchen knife! Seton's chopper is still in the pantry. And your aunt's—if that was the weapon—was stolen three months ago."

"So Digby Seton is out. What about the others?"

"We've only had time for a preliminary check. I'm taking their statements this afternoon. But it looks as if they've all got alibis of a sort for the time of death. All except Miss Dalgliesh. Living alone as she does, that's not surprising."

The flat monotonous voice did not change. The sombre eyes still looked out to sea. But Dalgliesh was not deceived. So this was the reason for the summons to Seton House, for the Inspector's unexpected outburst of confidence. He knew how it must look to Reckless. Here was an elderly unmarried woman living a lonely and isolated life. She had no alibi for the time of death nor for Wednesday night when the body was launched out to sea. She had an almost private access to the beach. She knew where Sheldrake lay. She was nearly six foot tall, a strong, agile country woman, addicted to strenuous walking and accustomed to the night.

Admittedly she had no apparent motive. But what did that matter? Despite what he had said to his aunt that morning Dalgliesh knew perfectly well that motive was not the first concern. The detective who concentrated logically on the "where", "when", and "how", would inevitably have the "why", revealed to him in all its pitiful inadequacy. Dalgliesh's old chief used to say that the four L's—love, lust, loathing and lucre—comprised all motives for murder. Superficially that was true enough. But motive was as varied and complex as human personality. He had no doubt that the Inspector's horribly experienced mind was already busy recalling past cases where the weeds of suspicion, loneliness or irrational dislike had flowered into unexpected violence and death.

Suddenly Dalgliesh was seized with an anger so intense

that for a few seconds it paralysed speech and even thought. It swept through his body like a wave of physical nausea leaving him white and shaken with self disgust. Choked with this anger he was luckily saved from the worst follies of speech, from sarcasm, indignation or the futile protest that his aunt would, of course, make no statement except in the presence of her solicitor. She needed no solicitor. She had him. But, God, what a holiday this was proving to be!

There was a creak of wheels and Sylvia Kedge spun her wheelchair through the french windows and manœuvred it up beside them. She didn't speak but gazed intently down the track towards the road. Their eyes followed hers. A post office van, brightly compact as a toy, was careering over the headland towards the house.

"It's the post," she said.

Dalgliesh saw that her hands were clamped to the chair sides, the knuckles white. As the van drew up before the terrace he watched her body half rise and stiffen as if seized with a sudden rigor. In the silence which followed the stopping of the engine, he could hear her heavy breathing.

The postman slammed the van door and came towards them, calling a cheerful greeting. There was no response from the girl and he glanced puzzled from her rigid face to the still figures of the two men. Then he handed Reckless the post. It was a single, foolscap envelope, buff coloured and with a typewritten address.

"It's the same kind as before, Sir," he said "Like the one I gave her yesterday." He nodded towards Miss Kedge, then, still getting no response, backed awkwardly towards his van muttering "Goodmorning."

Reckless spoke to Dalgliesh:

"Addressed to Maurice Seton, Esq. Posted either late on Wednesday or early on Thursday from Ipswich. Postmarked midday yesterday."

He held the envelope delicately by one corner as if anxious not to impose more finger prints. With his right thumb he edged it open. Inside there was a single sheet of foolscap paper covered with double spaced typescript. Reckless began to read aloud:

"The corpse without hands lay in the bottom of a small

sailing dinghy drifting just within sight of the Suffolk coast. It was the body of a millde-aged man, a dapper little cadaver, its shroud a dark pin-striped suit which fitted the narrow body as elegantly in death as it had been tailored to in life. . ."

Suddenly Sylvia Kedge held out her hand.

"Let me see."

Reckless hesitated, then held the sheet before her eyes.

"He wrote it," she said hoarsely. "He wrote it. And that's his typewriting."

"Maybe," said Reckless. "But he couldn't have posted it. Even if this went into the box late on Wednesday night he couldn't have put it there. He was dead by then."

She cried out:

"He typed it! I know his work, I tell you. He typed it! And he hadn't any hands!"

She burst into peal upon peal of hysterical laughter. It rang over the headland like a wild echo, so startling a flock of gulls that shrieking their alarm they whirled from the cliff edge in a single white cloud.

Reckless looked at the rigid body, the screaming mouth, with speculative unconcern, making no move to comfort or control her. Suddenly Digby Seton appeared in the french windows, his face white under the ridiculous bandage.

"What the hell. . . .?"

Reckless looked at him, expressionless, and said in his flat voice:

"We've just heard from your brother, Mr. Seton. Now isn't that nice?"

CHAPTER TWELVE

It took some time to pacify Miss Kedge. Dalgliesh had no doubt that her hysteria was genuine; this was no play-acting. He was only surprised that she should be so upset. Of all the little community at Monksmere Sylvia Kedge alone seemed to be genuinely shocked and distressed at Seton's death. And, certainly, the shock was real enough.

She had looked and behaved like a woman maintaining a precarious self-control which had snapped at last. But she made visible efforts to pull herself together and was at last well enough to be escorted back to Tanner's Cottage by Courtney who had succumbed entirely to the pathos of her drawn face and pleading eyes and who pushed her wheelchair down the lane like a mother displaying her fragile newborn to the glares of a potentially hostile world. Dalgliesh was relieved to see her go. He had discovered that he did not like her and was the more ashamed of the emotion because he knew that its roots were unreasonable and ignoble. He found her physically repellant. Most of her neighbours used Sylvia Kedge to gratify, at small expense, an easy impulse to pity while ensuring that they got their money's worth. Like so many of the disabled she was at once patronised and exploited. Dalgliesh wondered what she thought of them all. He wished he could feel more sorry for her but it was difficult not to watch, with a kind of contempt, the way in which she made use of her disability. But then what other weapons had she? Despising the young constable for his easy capitulation and himself for lack of feeling, Dalgliesh set off back to Pentlands for lunch. He walked back by the road. It took longer and was less interesting but he had always disliked retracing his footsteps. The route took him past Bryce's cottage. As he reached it an upstairs window was opened and the owner shot his long neck out and called:

"Come in Adam, dear boy. I've been watching out for you. I know you've been spying for that dreary little friend of yours but I don't hold it against you. Just leave your rhino whip outside and help yourself to whatever drink you prefer. I'll be down in a jiffy." Dalgliesh hesitated then pushed open the cottage door. The little sitting room was as untidy as always, a repository of bric-à-brac which could not appropriately be housed in his London flat. Deciding to wait for his drink, Dalgliesh called up the stairs:

"He's not my dreary little friend. He's a highly competent police officer."

"Oh no doubt!" Bryce's voice was muffled. Apparently he was pulling clothes over his head. "Competent enough to nab me if I'm not cunning. I was stopped for speeding on the A13 about six weeks ago and the officer concerned—a beefy brute with one of those metamorphic glares—was most uncivil. I wrote to the Chief Constable about it. It was a fatal thing to do, of course. I see that now. They've got it in for me all right. My name's on a little list somewhere, you may be sure."

He had padded into the room by now and Dalgliesh saw with surprise that he did indeed look concerned. Murmuring reassurance he accepted sherry—Bryce's drinks were always excellent—and settled himself in the latest acquisition, a charming Victorian high-backed chair.

"Well, Adam. Give, as they say. What has Reckless discovered? Such an inappropriate name!"

"I'm not altogether in his confidence. But another instalment of manuscript has arrived. It's rather better written this time. A description of a handless body in a boat and typed apparently by Seton himself."

Dalgliesh saw no reason why Bryce should be denied this bit of information. Sylvia Kedge was hardly likely to keep it to herself.

"Posted when?"

"Before lunch yesterday. From Ipswich."

Bryce wailed his dismay.

"Oh no! Not Ipswich! One was in Ipswich on Thursday. One often is. Shopping you know. One hasn't an alibi."

"You're probably not the only one," Dalgliesh pointed out consolingly. "Miss Calthrop was out in her car. So was Latham. So was I, come to that. Even that woman from Priory House was out in the buggy. I saw her as I drove over the headland."

"That would be Alice Kerrison, Sinclair's housekeeper. I don't suppose she went any further than Southwold. Probably fetching the groceries."

"On Thursday afternoon. Isn't it early closing?"

"Oh Adam dear, what does it matter? I expect she was just out for a drive. She'd hardly drive the buggy as far as Ipswich just to post an incriminating document. She hated Seton, though. She was housekeeper at Seton House before his wife died. Sinclair took her on after Dorothy killed herself and she's been there ever since. It was a most extraordinary thing! Alice stayed with Seton until after the inquest, then, without a word to him, she packed her bags and walked up to Priory House to ask Sinclair if he had a job for her. Apparently Sinclair had reached the point when the urge for self-sufficiency didn't extend to the washing-up and he took her on. As far as I know neither has regretted it."

"Tell me about Dorothy Seton," invited Dalgliesh.

"Oh, she was lovely, Adam! I've got a photograph of her somewhere which I must show you. She was madly neurotic, of course, but really beautiful. Manic depressive is the correct jargon, I believe. Exhaustingly gay one minute and so down the next that one felt positively contaminated with gloom. It was very bad for me, of course. I have enough trouble living with my own neurosis without coping with other people's. She led Seton a terrible life, I believe. One could almost pity him if it weren't for poor Arabella."

"How did she die?" enquired Dalgliesh.

"It was the most appalling thing! Seton strung her up from that meat hook in the beam of my kitchen. I shall never forget the sight of that darling furry body hanging there elongated like a dead rabbit. She was still warm when we cut her down. Look, I'll show you."

Dalgliesh had been half dragged into the kitchen before he grasped that Bryce was talking about his cat. He successfully fought down the first impulse to nervous laughter and followed Bryce. The man was shaking with anger, grasping Dalgliesh's forearm in a surprisingly powerful grip and gesticulating at the hook in impotent fury as if it shared Seton's guilt. There seemed no immediate chance of getting any information about Dorothy Seton's death now that Arabella's end was so vividly recalled. Dalgliesh sympathised with Bryce. His own love of cats was as great if less vocal. If Seton had indeed wantonly destroyed a beautiful animal out of malice and revenge it was difficult to regret him. More to the point, such a man must have made his share of enemies.

Dalgliesh enquired who had found Arabella.

"Sylvia Kedge. She had come up to take some dictation for me and I was delayed arriving from London. I got here about five minutes later. She had phoned Celia to come and cut Arabella down. She couldn't reach the body herself. Naturally both of them were terribly upset. Sylvia was physically sick. We had to push the wheelchair to the kitchen and she threw up all over my washing up. I won't dwell on my own sufferings. But I thought you knew all the details. I asked Miss Dalgliesh to write. I hoped you might have come down to prove Seton did it. The local police were quite hopeless. Now, if it had been a human being, think of the fuss and nonsense! Just like Seton. It's so ridiculous. I'm not one of those sentimentalists who think that human beings are more important than any other form of life. There are too many of us anyway and most of us neither know how to be happy ourselves nor make anyone else happy. And we're ugly. Ugly! You knew Arabella, Adam. Wasn't she the most beautiful creature? Didn't you feel it was a privilege to watch her? She was life-enhancing."

Dalgliesh, wincing at Bryce's choice of words, said the appropriate complimentary things about Arabella who had indeed been a beautiful cat with every appearance of knowing it. His aunt had told him of the incident in one of her fortnightly letters but not surprisingly had made no mention of Bryce's request that he should come down and take over the investigation. Dalgliesh forebore to point out that no actual evidence had been produced against Seton. There had been a great deal of anger, ill-feeling and suspicion but remarkably little rational thought applied to the problem. But he had no stomach for solving it now. He induced Bryce to return to the sitting room and asked again how Dorothy Seton had died.

"Dorothy? She had gone to Le Touquet for an autumn holiday with Alice Kerrison. Things were pretty bad between her and Seton by then. She had become terribly dependent on Alice and I suppose Seton thought it would be a good idea if there were someone to keep an eye on her. When they had been away a week Seton realised that he couldn't face living with her again and wrote to say he wanted a separation. No one knows what exactly was in the letter but Alice Kerrison was with Dorothy when she opened it and said at the inquest that it upset Mrs. Seton terribly and that she said they must go home at once. Seton had written from the Cadaver Club and the house was empty when they got back. Alice said that Dorothy seemed all right, perfectly calm and really much more cheerful than usual. She began preparing supper for the two of them and Dorothy wrote at her desk for a short time. Then she said she would go for a walk along the beach to see the moon on the sea. She walked to the bottom of Tanner's Lane, stripped herself naked, put her clothes in a neat pile with a stone on top and walked out to sea. They recovered the body a week later. It was suicide all right. She left a little note under the stone to say that she realised now that she was no use to herself or to anyone else and had decided to kill herself. It was a very direct note, perfectly clear, perfectly lucid. I remember at the time thinking that most suicides talk about ending it all. Dorothy just wrote that she had decided to kill herself."

"What happened to the letter that Seton wrote her?"

"It was never found. It wasn't with Dorothy's belongings and Alice didn't see her destroy it. But Seton was quite open about it. He was sorry but he had acted for the best. It had become impossible to go on. I didn't realise exactly what living with Dorothy had done to him until I saw his play two years later. It was about marriage to a neurotic but in the play it's the husband who kills himself. Well, naturally. Seton wanted to cast himself in the major role. Not literally, of course. Still, he might just as well have played the part. He couldn't have been much worse than poor Barry. Not that one can blame the actors. Such a very bad play, Adam! And yet written with a kind of terrible honesty and pain."

"Were you there?" enquired Dalgliesh.

"Bang in the middle of the third row of the stalls my dear, and curling with embarrassment. Seton was in a box. He'd got Celia with him and one must say she did him proud. Hardly a stitch above the waist and tinkling away with imitation jewellery like a Christmas tree. Do you think Seton wanted people to think she was his mistress? I've a feeling our Maurice liked to be taken for a naughty boy. My dear, they looked like a couple of minor emigré royalties. Seton even wore a decoration. A Home Guard medal or something of the kind. I was with Paul Markham, such a sensitive boy. He was in tears by the end of the first act. So, admittedly, were a good third of the audience but in their case I suspect it was tears of laughter. We left in the first interval and spent the rest of the evening drinking at Moloneys. I can bear quite an amount of suffering provided it's not my own but I do draw the line at public executions. Celia, gallant girl, stuck it out to the last. They even had a party at the Ivy afterwards. When I think of that evening, oh Arabella, how thou art revenged."

"Latham's notice was Latham at his most vicious wasn't it? Did you get the impression that he had a personal interest in killing the play?"

"Oh, I shouldn't think so." The large eyes bent on Dalgliesh were as innocent as a child's but Adam had a considerable respect for the intelligence behind them.

"Oliver can't tolerate bad writing nor bad acting and when they come together it tends to make him savage. Now if Oliver had been found dead with his hands hacked off one could have understood it. Half those illiterate little secondary-mods who swan around London calling themselves actresses could have done it happily given the wit."

"But Latham knew Dorothy Seton didn't he?"

"Oh Adam! How you do go on about a thing! Not very subtle, my dear. Yes, he knew her. We all did. She was a great dropper-in. Sometimes drunk and sometimes sober and equally tedious either way."

"Were she and Latham lovers?" enquired Dalgliesh bluntly. As he expected Bryce was neither disconcerted nor surprised by the question. Like all inveterate gossips he was fundamentally interested in people. This was one of the first questions he would ask himself about any man or woman in his circle who seemed to find each other's company agreeable.

"Celia always said so, but then she would. I mean the dear girl can't conceive of any other relationship between a heterosexual man and a pretty woman. And where Latham's concerned she's probably right. One could hardly blame Dorothy, stuck in that glass-house with Seton, so dull. She was entitled to find consolation anywhere so long as it wasn't with me."

"But you don't think Latham was particularly fond of her?"

"I don't know. I shouldn't have thought so. Poor Oliver suffers from self-disgust. He pursues a woman, then, when she falls in love with him, he despises her for lack of discrimination. The poor dears simply can't win. It must be so exhausting to dislike oneself so much. Now I'm lucky. I find myself fascinating."

The fascination was beginning to pall on Dalgliesh. He glanced at his watch, said firmly that it was 12.45 and his lunch would be ready and made to go.

"Oh, but you must see that snap of Dorothy. I've got it somewhere. It will given you some idea how lovely she was."

He opened the sliding lid of his writing desk and rummaged among the piles of papers. Dalgliesh thought that it looked a hopeless task. But there must have been some order in the chaos for, in less than a minute, Bryce had found what he wanted. He brought the photograph over to Dalgliesh.

"Sylvia Kedge took it when we were picnicking on the beach one July. She does quite a bit of amateur photography."

There was certainly nothing professional about the photograph. It showed the picnic party grouped around Sheldrake. They were all there, Maurice and Digby Seton; Celia Calthrop with a sulky looking child recognisable as Liz Marley; Oliver Latham and Bryce himself. Dorothy Seton, wearing a bathing costume, was leaning against the hull of the dinghy and laughing at the camera. The snap was clear enough but it told Dalgliesh nothing except that she had an agreeable figure and knew how best to show it off. The face was that of a pretty woman but no more. Bryce looked at the snap over his shoulder. As if struck by this fresh evidence of the perfidy of time and memory he said sadly. "Funny . . . It doesn't really give one any idea of her. . . . I thought it was better than this. . ."

Bryce came to the cottage gate with him. As Dalgliesh was leaving an estate car came lurching up the lane and stopped with a bump at the gate. From it bounded a sturdy, black-haired woman with legs like jambs above her white ankle socks and schoolgirl sandals, who was greeted by Bryce with squeaks of pleasure.

"Mrs. Bain-Porter! You haven't brought them! You have! How perfectly sweet of you."

Mrs. Bain-Porter had the deep, rich, upper-class female voice which is trained to intimidate the helots of empire or to carry across any hockey field in the teeth of a high gale. Her words boomed clearly in Dalgliesh's ears.

"When I got your letter yesterday I thought I'd take a chance. I've brought the three best from the litter. It's so much nicer to choose them in your own home I think. Nicer for them too."

The back of the car was opened now and Mrs. Bain-Porter, helped by Bryce, was carefully lifting out three cat baskets from which there rose at once an agitated squealing, treble descant to Mrs. Bain-Porter's bass and Bryce's joyful chirpings. The concert party disappeared through the cottage door. Dalgliesh trudged home to his lunch in contemplative mood. It was one of those little things which can mean everything or nothing. But if Mrs. Bain-Porter got a letter from Julian Bryce on Thursday it was posted on Wednesday at the latest. Which meant that on Wednesday Bryce had either decided to take a chance on Seton's cat-killing propensities, or had known that there was no longer anything to fear.

CHAPTER THIRTEEN

On Friday afternoon the suspects walked, drove or were driven to the small inn just outside Dunwich which Reckless had taken as his headquarters and there made their statements. They had always thought of the Green Man as their local pub—indeed they took it for granted that George Prike ran the place principally for their benefit—and the Inspector's choice was criticised as showing crass insensitivity and a general disregard for the comfort of others. Celia Calthrop was particularly bitter although she used the Green Man less than most and was scathing in her denunciation of George's folly in allowing himself to be inveigled into such an invidious position. She was not at all sure she would be happy to continue to buy her sherry from George if she were going to be reminded of Inspector Reckless every time she had a drink and a visit to the Saloon Bar would become intolerably traumatic. Latham and Bryce shared her view of the Inspector. Their first impression of him hadn't been favourable and thinking it over later they decided that they disliked him. Perhaps, as Bryce suggested, a too-close acquaintance with Seton's Inspector Briggs had spoilt them for the real thing. Briggs, who was occasionally called Briggsy by the Honourable Martin in an excess of spurious camaraderie, had a humility which they hadn't detected in Inspector Reckless. Despite his eminence at the Yard Briggsy was always happy to play second fiddle to Carruthers, and so far from resenting the Honourable Martin's interference with his cases, made a practice of calling him in when his special expertise was required. Since Carruthers was an expert on wine, women, heraldry, the landed gentry, esoteric poisons and the finer points of the minor Elizabethan poets, his opinion was frequently invaluable. As Bryce pointed out, Inspector Briggs did not turn people out of their favourite pub nor gaze at them fixedly from dark, morose eyes as if hearing only half they were saying and disbelieving that. Nor did he give the impression of regarding writers as no different from lesser men except in their capacity to invent more ingenious alibis. Inspector Briggs's suspects, if required to make statements—which was seldom—made them in the comfort of their own homes attended by obsequious policemen and with Carruthers present to ensure, in the nicest possible way, that Inspector Briggs kept his place.

They were careful not to arrive at the inn together; the artless confidences of Thursday night had been followed by a certain wariness. By Friday afternoon there had been time to think and Seton's death was seen less as a bizarre excursion of fiction into life than as a highly embarrassing fact. Certain unpalatable truths were recognised. Seton, admittedly, had last been seen alive in London, but his mutilated body had been floated out to sea from Monksmere Beach. It hardly needed any complicated calculations with charts, wind force or tide drift and race, to convince anyone of that. He might well have run into trouble in

London in his naive search for copy, but the forged manuscript, the severed hands, the telephone call to Seton House, had a more local flavour. Celia Calthrop was the most voracious supporter of the London-gang-of-crooks theory, but even she could advance no convincing explanation of how the criminals knew where Sheldrake was beached or why they had chosen to bring the corpse back to Suffolk. "To throw suspicion on us, of course", was generally thought to beg more questions than it answered.

After the statements were made there was a certain amount of telephoning. Cautiously, as if half-believing that the lines were being tapped, the little community exchanged those scraps of information, rumour, or guesswork which pieced together probably told as much as there was to know. They were reluctant at present to meet each other, afraid of what they might be told, or worse, inadvertently tell. But they were avid for information.

Telephone calls to Pentlands were invariably answered by Jane Dalgliesh, courteous, uncooperative and uncommunicative. No one liked to betray himself by asking to speak to Adam except Celia Calthrop and she met with such little success that she found it more convenient to believe that he had nothing to tell. But they spoke to each other, gradually abandoning caution in their need to confide and their hunger for news. The snippets of information, most of which changed subtly in the telling and some of which were founded on hope rather than fact, built up an incomplete and amphigoric picture. No one had changed his or her story and the various alibis for Tuesday night which had been put forward with such eager confidence had stood up to such investigation as there had been time for. It was understood that Latham's house guest had made no trouble in supporting his story, but as Reckless was completely uncommunicative and Latham was maintaining a gentlemanly reticence, the general curiosity about her name seemed likely to remain unsatisfied. The news that Eliza Marley had admitted to spending Tuesday night in London created a certain amount of pleasurable speculation, stimulated by Celia's frequent and unconvincing explanations of her niece's need to visit the London Library. As Bryce said to Latham, one could understand it if the poor girl had been at a Redbrick but there had been quite a number of books in Cambridge when he was up. Both Bryce's and Latham's cars had been examined by the police but the owners had made so little protest over the proceedings that it was commonly agreed that they had nothing to fear. It was reported that Dr. Forbes-Denby had been gratifyingly offensive to Inspector Reckless on the telephone while Bryce was at the Green Man and had insisted on regarding Bryce's telephone call as a matter of sacred confidence between himself and his patient. Eventually, however, on Bryce's almost hysterical insistence he had agreed that it had been made. Celia's story that she had given Seton the idea for a floating corpse was supported by an old Walberswick fisherman who called at the Green Man to say that he remembered Mr. Seton enquiring some months previously where a body in a dinghy would come ashore if it were pushed out from Monksmere Beach. As no one had doubted Celia's statement this wasn't regarded as more than mildly interesting. In face of their united wish to find support for the London-gang-of-crooks theory it was depressing that no one except Bryce had seen any strangers at Monksmere on the Wednesday night. He had been outside bringing in wood from his shed shortly after seven when a motor cyclist had come roaring down the lane from the road and had reversed just outside his cottage. Justin abominated motor cycles and the noise had been quite unendurable. He had shouted his protest and the lad had retaliated by roaring up and down in front of the cottage for several minutes, making what Bryce described as obscene gestures. Eventually with a parting blast of his horn he had roared away. It wasn't known what Reckless made of this although he did ask Bryce for a full description of the cyclist, and would probably have noted it down if Bryce had been able to provide it. But the man had worn a black leather suit with helmet and goggles and Bryce could say no more than that he was obviously young and his manners were abominable. But Celia was sure he was a member of the gang. What else would he be doing at Monksmere?

By midday on Saturday the rumours had grown and multiplied. Digby had been left one hundred thousand, two hundred thousand, half a million; the post-mortem was held up because Dr. Sydenham couldn't discover the cause of death; the cause of death was drowning, strangulation, poison, suffocation, haemorrhage; Forbes-Denby had told Reckless that Seton was good for another twenty years; Seton's heart was liable to give out at any moment; Adam Dalgliesh and the Inspector were hardly on speaking terms; Reckless would have arrested Jane Dalgliesh if only he could have discovered a motive; Sylvia Kedge was being very difficult and wouldn't accept the legacy of £300 which Digby had offered to pay her; Reckless had called at Priory House late on Friday night and he and his men had been seen with torches on the cliff-path; the inquest was to be held on Wednesday at two-thirty. Only on the last was there unanimity. The inquest was certainly arranged for the following Wednesday. Digby Seton and Sylvia Kedge had been summoned to attend. Those who had a choice in the matter were uncertain whether their presence would arouse curiosity, help allay suspicion or be prudent as showing a proper respect for the dead.

On Saturday morning it was made known that Inspector Reckless had left Monksmere for London by car late on Friday and wasn't expected back until Sunday morning. Presumably he had gone to check on the London alibis and investigate the Cadaver Club. There was no surprise that he was expected back so shortly. It was plain that he knew only too well where his business lay. But even this temporary absence was a relief. It was as if a cloud lifted from Monksmere Head. That gloomy, silent, accusing presence had taken his preoccupations elsewhere and the air felt freer for his going. He left behind a restlessness which found relief in action. Everyone seemed anxious to get away from Monksmere. Even Jane Dalgliesh and her nephew who were the least affected by Reckless, were seen to set off early along the beach in the direction of Sizewell laden with painting paraphernalia, binoculars and knapsacks. It was obvious that they wouldn't be back until after dark. Latham drove off soon afterwards; the Jaguar was doing sixty-five when it passed Rosemary Cottage and Celia observed tartly that Oliver was off again on one of his attempts to break his neck. She and Eliza were to take Sylvia Kedge on a picnic to Aldeburgh but Eliza changed her mind just before they were due to start and set off on a solitary walk to Walberswick. No one knew what Digby Seton had planned, but a telephone call to Seton House by Miss Calthrop who hoped to persuade him to join the picnic, met with no reply. Bryce told everyone that he was driving to a country-house sale just outside Saxmundham where he hoped to bid for some seventeenth-century porcelain. By half-past nine he too was far away and Monksmere was left to the half dozen autumn trippers who came in ones and twos throughout the day to park their cars in Tanner's Lane and to the occasional couple of walkers from Dunwich or Walberswick trudging along the sand dunes to the bird sanctuary.

Reckless must have driven back to Monksmere late on Saturday. When dawn broke his car was already outside the Green Man, and soon after nine o'clock Sergeant Courtney had rung most of the suspects to request their presence at the inn. The invitation was perfectly polite but no one was under the illusion that there was any choice in the matter. They took their time about arriving and, once again, their was a tacit understanding that they wouldn't arrive together. Sylvia Kedge was collected as usual in a police car by Sergeant Courtney. There was a feeling that Sylvia was, on the whole, quite enjoying herself.

Maurice Seton's portable typewriter was ready for them at the Inn, placed squat and shining on the edge of a small oak table in the saloon bar. The attentions of the finger-print men and the typewriter experts seemed to have given it an added lustre. It looked at once ordinary and menacing, innocent and dangerous. It was, perhaps, the most intimate object that Seton had owned. Looking at the gleaming keyboard it was impossible not to think with repugnance of those bleeding stumps, to wonder what had happened to the severed hands. They knew at once why it was there. They were required to type two passages of prose; the description of Carruther's visit to the nightclub and of the handless corpse, drifting out to sea.

Sergeant Courtney, who was in charge of the exercise, was beginning to fancy himself as a student of human nature and the different reactions of his suspects provided gratifying material. Sylvia Kedge took some time to settle herself but once started the strong fingers, bony as a man's, danced above the keys to produce, in an incredibly short time, two accurate copies elegantly set out and perfectly typed. It is always satisfying to see a job performed perfectly and Sergeant Courtney received Miss Kedge's effort in respectful silence. Miss Dalgliesh, who arrived at the Inn twenty minutes later, was unexpectedly competent. She had been used to typing her father's sermons and the Church magazine and had taught herself with the aid of a manual. She used all five fingers correctly although her speed was only moderate and, unlike Miss Kedge, she kept her eyes firmly on the keys. Miss Calthrop, staring at the machine as if she hadn't seen one before, protested shortly that she couldn't type—all her work was dictated on tape—and didn't see why she should waste her time trying. Eventually she was persuaded to make a start and after thirty minutes' effort, produced an appallingly typed two pages which she flourished at the Sergeant with the air of a vindicated martyr. Observing the length of Miss Calthrop's nails, Courtney was only surprised that she had managed to depress the keys. Bryce, when he could bring himself to touch the typewriter, was surprisingly quick and accurate although he found it necessary to keep up a scathing commentary on the style of the prose. Latham was almost as expert as Miss Kedge and rattled away in sullen silence. Miss Marley said briefly that she couldn't type but had no objection to trying. She refused Courtney's help, spent about five minutes examining the keyboard and the carriage and settled down to the laborious task of copying the passage, word by word. The result was quite creditable and Sergeant Courtney privately marked Miss Marley as an intelligent worker, in contrast to her aunt's assessment of "Could do better if she tried". Digby Seton was hopeless, but even Courtney couldn't believe that the man was faking. In the end, to everyone's relief he was allowed to give up. Predictably, none of the copies, including Digby's abortive effort, bore any resemblance to the originals. Sergeant Courtney, who believed that the second, and probably the first also, had been typed by Maurice Seton, would have been surprised if they had. But the final verdict would not be his. The copies would now be sent to an expert and examined for more subtle similarities. He didn't tell his suspects this;

but then, he didn't need to. They hadn't read their Maurice Seton for nothing.

Before they left the inn their finger prints were taken. When her turn came, Miss Calthrop was outraged. She began for the first time to regret the desire to economise which had made her earlier decide not to seek the help of her solicitor. But she mentioned his name freely, together with that of her Member of Parliament, and the Chief Constable. Sergeant Courtney, however, was so reassuring, so understanding of her feelings, so anxious for her help, so different in every way from that uncouth Inspector, that, she was at last persuaded to cooperate. "Silly old bitch," thought the Sergeant as he directed the pudgy fingers. "If the rest of them make half this fuss I'll be lucky to be through before the old man gets back."

But the rest of them made no fuss at all. Digby Seton was tediously facetious about the whole proceedings, attempting to hide his nervousness by an exaggerated interest in the technique. Eliza Marley was sulkily acquiescent, and Jane Dalgliesh's thoughts appeared to be elsewhere. Bryce disliked it most. There was something portentous and irrevocable about parting with a symbol so uniquely peculiar to himself. He understood why primitive tribes were so careful that no scraps of their hair should fall into an enemy's hand. As he pressed his fingers on the pad with a moue of distaste he felt that virtue had gone out of him.

Oliver Latham jabbed his fingers into the pad as if it were Reckless's eye. When he looked up, he saw that the Inspector had come quietly in and was watching him. Sergeant Courtney got to his feet. Reckless said:

"Good evening, Sir. That's just a formality."

"Oh, I know all about that, thank you. The Sergeant has trotted out all the routine reassurance. I was wondering where you'd got to after your trip to town. I hope you enjoyed yourself questioning—as you would no doubt term her—'my lady friend'. And the porter at the flat? Duncombe was cooperative, I hope?"

"Everyone was very helpful, thank you, Sir."

"Oh, I'm sure they were! I've no doubt they enjoyed themselves immensely. Things are a bit quiet in town at present. I must be providing the best bit of gossip in weeks. And as we're all being so cooperative, what about a little cooperation from your end? I suppose there's no objection to my knowing how Seton died?"

"None at all, Sir—in due course. But we haven't got the P.M. report yet."

"Your chap's being a bit slow, isn't he?"

"On the contrary, Sir. Dr. Sydenham is very quick. But there are still a number of tests to be done. This isn't a straightforward case."

"I should rank that remark, Inspector, as the understatement of the year."

Taking his handkerchief from his pocket Latham carefully wiped his already clean fingers. Watching him the Inspector said quietly:

"If you're so impatient, Mr. Latham, why not ask some of your friends? You know as well as I do that someone at Monksmere could tell you precisely how Maurice Seton died."

CHAPTER FOURTEEN

Since his half-brother's death Digby Seton had taken to dropping in at Rosemary Cottage for meals, and his neighbours didn't fail to remark with wry amusement on just how often the Vauxhall was seen parked on the grass verge outside the cottage. They conceded that Celia was unlikely to discourage the company of a very rich young man but Digby's motives were less obvious. No one assumed that the charms of Eliza attracted him or that he saw in her sullen gracelessness a means of getting his hands on Maurice's capital. On the whole, people thought that he probably preferred Celia's food, uninteresting though it was, to the tedium of driving twice a day into Southwold or the effort of cooking for himself and that he was glad to get out of the way of Sylvia Kedge. Since the murder the girl had haunted Seton House with the persistence of a funeral mute waiting for her pay. The obsessional care which she had given to Maurice's work now seemed to be devoted to his house and she tidied, polished, cleaned, counted linen and dragged herself about on her crutches, duster in hand as if she expected the late owner to appear at any minute and run his fingers over the window ledges. As Digby told Eliza Marley, it made him nervous. He had never liked Seton House which, despite its bright modernity, he found curiously sinister and depressing. Now, when those smouldering black eyes were liable to turn on him from every corner and cupboard, he felt he was living in one of the gloomier Greek dramas with the Eumenides lurking outside ready to make their entrance.

The remark had interested Eliza since it suggested that Digby might be more perceptive and sensitive than was commonly assumed. Without being in the least attracted to him physically she was beginning to find him interesting, even a little intriguing. It was surprising what the possession of £200,000 could do for a man. Already she could detect the subtle patina of success, the assurance and complacency which the possession of power or money invariably gives. The glandular fever had left her depressed and fatigued. In this mood, without the energy to work and fretted by boredom, almost any company was better than none. Despising the easy capitulation to self interest which had changed her aunt's opinion of him overnight from Maurice's problem brother to a perfectly charming young man, she nevertheless was beginning to admit that there might be more in Digby Seton than met the eye. But not much more.

He hadn't accepted Miss Calthrop's invitation to dinner on Sunday night but he turned up at Rosemary Cottage shortly aften nine and having arrived was apparently in no hurry to leave. It was now nearly eleven but he was still there, swivelling himself to and fro on the piano stool and spasmodically playing snatches of his own or other people's tunes. Eliza, curled into her fireside chair, watched and listened and was in no hurry for him to go. He didn't play badly. There was no real talent there, of course, but when he was taking trouble, which was seldom, he was agreeably competent. She remembered that there had once been talk by Maurice of making a pianist out of Digby. Poor Maurice! That was when he was still desperately trying to persuade himself that his only living relative had some qualities to justify the relationship. Even when Digby was still at school his modest successes, the time he had won the boxing championship, for example, had been trumpeted by Maurice as major achievements. It was unthinkable that Maurice Seton's half-brother should be entirely without some talent. And nor was he. He had, single-handed, designed and built Sheldrake and had sailed her with competence even if his enthusiasm had only lasted a couple of seasons. But this hearty gamesmanship, in some way so untypical of Digby, was hardly likely to impress an intellectual snob like Maurice. In the end, of course, he had given up pretending just as Celia had given up hope that her niece was pretty, that she was going to have an orthodox success as a woman. Eliza glanced across at the large coloured photograph of herself that bore witness to Celia's humiliating and ludicrous ambitions. It had been taken when she was eleven, three years after the death of her parents. The thick dark hair was preposterously curled and ribboned, the white organdie dress with its pink sash looked vulgarly inappropriate to such a heavy featured and graceless child. No, it hadn't taken her aunt long to shed that particular delusion. But then, of course, it had been succeeded by another; dear Eliza, if she couldn't be pretty, had to be clever. Now the theme was: "My niece has a brilliant brain. She's at Cambridge, you know." Poor Aunt Celia! It was petty to grudge her this vicarious intellectual pleasure. After all she was paying hard cash for it. But Eliza felt some sympathy with Digby Seton. To an extent both of them had suffered from the pressure of another's personality, both had been accepted for qualities which they had no hope of ever possessing, both had been marked down as a bad buy.

On impulse she suddenly asked him:

"Which of us do you think killed your brother?"

He was syncopating a number from one of the recent London shows, inaccurately and rather too loudly for comfort. He had almost to shout above the noise of his own row:

"You tell me. You're the one who's supposed to be clever."

"Not as clever as Aunt makes out. But clever enough to wonder why it was I you phoned to meet you at Saxmundham. We've never been particularly friendly."

"Perhaps I thought it was time we were. Anyway, assuming I wanted a free lift to Monksmere, who else could I phone?"

"There is that. And, assuming you wanted an alibi for the time of the train journey."

"I had an alibi. The ticket collector recognised me; and I had an interesting chat with an old gentleman in the carriage about the naughtiness of the modern generation. I expect he would remember me. I can prove I was on that train, darling, without your help."

"But can you prove where you got on?"

"Liverpool Street. It was pretty crowded so I don't suppose anyone noticed me; but let Reckless try to prove that I didn't. Why are you so suspicious all of a sudden?"

"I'm not really. I don't see how you could have done it."

"Thank you for nothing. Nor do the police at West Central Station."

The girl shivered and said with sudden force: "Those hands—it was a horrible thing to do. Horrible! Don't you feel that? Particularly to a writer. Horrible and significant. I don't think you hated him that much."

He dropped his hands from the keys and swung round to face her.

"I didn't hate him at all. Damn it, Eliza! Do I look like a murderer?"

"How should I know? You're the one with the motive. £200,000 worth."

"Not until I get a wife. What about applying for the job?"

"No thank you. I like men to have an I.Q. at least approximate to mine. We wouldn't suit. What you want for the Club, surely, is a glamorous blonde with a forty-inch bust, a heart of low carat gold, and a mind like a calculating machine."

"Oh no!" he said seriously. "I know what I want for the Club. And now I've got the money I can pay for it. I want class."

The door into the study opened and Miss Calthrop poked her head through and gave them a vaguely puzzled look. She spoke to Eliza:

"I seem to have lost one of my new tapes. You haven't seen it, I suppose?"

Her niece's only response was a disinterested shrug but Digby sprang to his feet and peered hopefully around the room as if expecting the reel to materialize on top of the piano or pop out from under the cushions. Watching his ineffectual antics Eliza thought:

"Quite the little gentleman, aren't we? He's never bothered with Auntie before. What the hell is he playing at, anyway?"

The search was, of course, unsuccessful and Digby turned his charming deprecatory smile on Miss Calthrop.

"So sorry. It doesn't seem to be here."

Celia, who had been waiting with ill-concealed impatience, thanked him and went back to her work. As soon as the door closed behind her Digby said:

"She's taking it rather well, isn't she?"

"Taking what?"

"Maurice's Will. After all, if it weren't for me she'd be a very wealthy woman."

Did the fool really imagine that they didn't know it, that the arithmetic had somehow escaped them? She glanced across at him and caught his look of secret satisfaction, complacent, amused. It came to her suddenly that he must know something about Maurice's death, that the secret smile meant more than a momentary satisfaction at their disappointment and his own good luck. It was on the tip of her tongue to utter a warning. If he really had discovered something he would be in danger. He was typical of the fool who stumbles on part of the truth and hasn't the sense to keep his mouth shut. But she checked herself, irritated by that glimpse of secret satisfaction. Probably she was only being fanciful. Probably he had guessed nothing. And if he had? Well, Digby Seton would have to look after himself, would have to take his chance like the rest of them.

CHAPTER FIFTEEN

In the dining room at Priory House, dinner was nearly over. Dalgliesh had enjoyed his meal. He wasn't sure exactly what he had expected. It could have been a six course dinner served on Sévres china or a nut cutlet eaten off wooden plates and followed by communal washing-up. Neither would have surprised him. They had, in fact, been given an agreeable chicken casserole cooked with herbs and followed by a salad and cheeses. The Bordeaux rouge had been cheap and a little rough but there had been plenty of it and Dalgliesh, no wine snob, had never subscribed to the view that the only proper alternative to good wine is no wine at all. He sat now, content, almost happy, in a gentle daze of well-being and let his eyes wander over the immense room, where the four of them sat, dwarfed as puppets, round the simple oak table.

It was easy to see that the house had once been part of a monastry. This room must have been the refectory. It was a huge version of the sitting room at Pentlands but here the oak hammer beams smoked with age, arched against the roof like great trees and merged into a black void nearly twenty feet above the faint sphere of the six tall candles which lit the dining table. The fireplace was the stone hearth of Pentlands but magnified into a small cavern in which the great logs burned steady as coal. The six vaulted windows to seawards were shuttered now but Dalgliesh could still hear the murmer of the sea and, from time to time, a soft moan which suggested the wind was rising.

Alice Kerrison sat opposite Sinclair, a plump, quiet, self-possessed woman, sure of her place and chiefly concerned, as far as Dalgliesh could see, to ensure that Sinclair over-ate. When they were first introduced he had the immediate sensation that he had met her before, that he had even known her well. Then almost instantly he realized why. Here, personified, was the Mrs. Noah of his childhood's Noah's ark. Here was the same straight hair, black and smooth as paint, drawn back from a centre parting into a tight little bun at the nape of the neck. Here was the same dumpy and compact figure with its tiny waist and the well-recalled face, round, ruddy cheeked and beaded with two bright eyes. Even her clothes were familiar. She wore a plain black dress, long sleeved and bordered at neck and cuffs with narrow bands of lace. The whole was as evocative of the doldrums of childhood Sundays at his father's vicarage as the sound of Church bells or the morning smell of clean woollen underwear.

He glanced across at her as she poured the coffee and wondered what her relationship with Sinclair was. It was hard to guess. She didn't treat him as if he were a genius; he didn't treat her as a servant. Obviously she enjoyed looking after him but there was something matter-of-fact, almost irreverent in her calm acceptance of him. At times, bringing the food to the table together as was their obvious habit, conferring a little anxiously over the wine, they seemed as close and secret as conspirators. He wondered what had prompted her to pack her bags that morning, six years ago, and leave Maurice Seton for Sinclair. It struck him that Alice Kerrison probably knew more about Seton and his relationship with his wife than anyone else in the world. He wondered what else she knew.

He let his eyes slew round to where Sinclair sat with his back to the fire. The writer looked smaller than his photographs suggested but the broad shoulders, the long, almost simian arms, still gave an impression of great strength. His face was thickening with age so that the features were smudged and amorphous as an underexposed print. The heavy folds of skin hung about his face. The tired eyes were sunk so deep under the springing brows that they were almost invisible, but there was no mistaking the proud carriage of his head nor that great dome of white hair which shone now like a burning bush in the light of the fire, reinforcing the impression of some archaic Jehovah. How old was he, Dalgliesh wondered. The last of his three great novels had been published over thirty years ago and he had been middle-aged then. Three books were a slight foundation for such a solid reputation. Celia Calthrop, peeved by her failure to persuade Sinclair to participate in a Monksmere Literary Festival, accept the dedication of one of her novels, or even invite her to tea, was fond of saying that he was overrated, that it was quantity as well as quality that constituted greatness. Sometimes Dalgliesh thought that she had a point. But, always, one returned to the novels with a sense of wonder. They stood like great rocks on the foreshore where so many literary reputations had crumbled like sandcastles in the changing tide of fashion. Priory House would one day disappear beneath the sea but Sinclair's reputation would stand.

Dalgliesh was not so naive as to suppose that a great writer is necessarily a good talker nor presumptuous enough to expect Sinclair to entertain him. But his host had not been silent during the meal. He had spoken knowledgeably and appreciatively of Dalgliesh's two volumes of verse but not, his guest felt, out of any desire to please. He had the directness and self absorption of a child. As soon as the topic ceased to interest him he changed the subject. Most of the talk was of books although he had no further interest it seemed in his own, and his favourite light reading was, it appeared, detective fiction. He was completely unconcerned with world affairs. "Men will either have to learn to love each other, my dear Dalgliesh, in the entirely practical and unsentimental use of the word or they will destroy themselves. I have no further influence either way." And yet, Dalgliesh felt that Sinclair was neither disillusioned nor cynical. He had detached himself from the world but neither out of disgust nor despair; it was merely that, in extreme old age, he had simply ceased to care.

He was talking now to Jane Dalgliesh, discussing apparently whether the avocet was likely to nest that year. Both of them were giving the subject the serious attention which other topics had failed to excite. Dalgliesh looked across the table at his aunt. She was wearing a cherry red blouse in fine wool, high necked and with the sleeves buttoned almost as high as the elbows. It was an appropriate dress for dining out on the cold eastern seaboard and she had worn it with little variation as long as he remembered. But now inexplicably, it was in fashion and to her individual, dégagé elegance was added the hint of a contemporary smartness which Dalgliesh found alien to her.

Her left hand was resting against her cheek. The long brown fingers were heavy with the family rings which she wore only in the evenings. In the candle light the rubies and diamonds struck fire. They were talking now of a skull which Sinclair had recently picked up on his stretch of the beach. It was usual for the drowned graveyards to yield up their bones and, after a storm, walkers on the shore could expect to find an occasional femur or scapula bleached by the sea and friable with age. But it was less usual to find a whole skull. Sinclair was discussing its probable age and with some expertise. But so far there had been no mention of that other, more recent body. Perhaps, thought Dalgliesh, he had been wrong about the motive for this dinner party. Perhaps Sinclair wasn't interested in Seton's murder after all. But it was difficult to believe that he had merely had a whim to meet Jane Dalgliesh's nephew. Suddenly his host turned to him and said in his slow, rumbling voice:

"I suppose a great many people ask you why you choose to be a detective?"

Dalgliesh answered evenly:

"Not many whom I care to answer . . . I like the job; it's one I can do reasonably well; it allows me to indulge a curiosity about people and, for most of the time, anyway, I'm not bored by it."

"Ah yes! Boredom. The intolerable state for any writer. But isn't there something else? Doesn't being a policeman protect your privacy? You have a professional excuse for remaining uninvolved. Policemen are separate from other men. We treat them, as we do parsons, with superficial fellowship but essential distrust. We are uneasy in their company. I think you are a man who values his privacy."

"Then we are alike," suggested Dalgliesh. "I have my job, you have Priory House." Sinclair said:

"It didn't protect me this afternoon. We had a visit from your colleague, Inspector Stanley Gerald Reckless. Tell Mr. Dalgliesh about it, Alice."

Dalgliesh was wearying of disclaiming any responsibility for Reckless but was curious to know how Sinclair had discovered the Inspector's full names. Probably by the simple expedient of asking.

Alice Kerrison said:

"Reckless. It isn't a Suffolk name. He looked ill to me. An ulcer most likely. Worry and overwork maybe. . . ."

She could be right about the ulcer, thought Dalgliesh, remembering the pallor, the pain-filled eyes, the deep clefts between nose and mouth. He heard the calm voice continue.

"He came to ask if we had killed Mr. Seton."

"But with more tact, surely?" suggested Dalgliesh.

Sinclair said:

"He was as tactful as he knew how to be. But that's what he came for, nevertheless. I explained to him that I didn't even know Seton although I had tried to read one of his books. But he never came here. Just because I can no longer write myself I'm under no obligation to spend my time with those who never could. Fortunately Alice and I can give each other an alibi for Tuesday and Wednesday nights which we understand are the significant times. I told the Inspector that neither of us had left the house. I am not sure that he altogether believed me. Incidentally, Jane, he asked whether we had borrowed your chopper. I deduced from that question that you had unwittingly supplied the weapon. We showed the Inspector our two choppers, both in excellent order I am glad to say, and he could see for himself that no one had used them to chop off poor Maurice Seton's hands."

Alice Kerrison said suddenly:

"He was a wicked man and he's better dead. But's there's no excuse for murder."

"In what way was he wicked?" asked Dalgliesh.

The question was a formality. He was going to be told whether he wanted it or not. He could feel Sinclair's amused and interested eyes searching his face. So this was one reason for the dinner party. It wasn't just that Sinclair hoped to gain information. He had some to give. Alice Kerrison was sitting bolt upright, her face blotched with emotion, her hands clasped under the table. She gave Dalgliesh the truculent, half-pleading look of an embarrassed child and muttered:

"That letter he wrote to her. It was a wicked letter, Mr. Dalgliesh. He drove her to death as surely as if he'd forced her into the sea and held her head under the water."

"So you read the letter?"

"Not all of it. She handed it to me almost unthinking and then took it back again when she'd pulled herself together. It wasn't a letter any woman would want another woman to read. There were things in it I couldn't ever tell a soul. Things I'd rather forget. He meant her to die. That was murder." Dalgliesh asked:

"Can you be sure he wrote it?"

"It was in his handwriting, Mr. Dalgliesh. All five pages of it. He only typed her name at the top, nothing more. I couldn't mistake Mr. Seton's hand." Of course not, thought Dalgliesh. And Seton's wife would have been even less likely to mistake it. So Seton had deliberately driven his wife to suicide. If this were true it was an act of wanton cruelty greater in degree but of the same nature as the killing of Bryce's cat. But somehow this picture of a calculating sadist was subtly out of focus. Dalgliesh had only met Seton twice but the man had never struck him as a monster. Was it really possible that this pedantic, nervous and self-opinionated little man with his pathetically overvalued talent could have nourished so much hatred? Or was this scepticism merely the arrogance of a detective who was beginning to fancy himself as a diagnostician of evil? After all even if one gave little Crippen the benefit of the doubt, there were still plenty of nervous, ineffectual men on record who had proved far from ineffectual when it came to getting rid of their wives. How could he, after two brief meetings, know the essential Seton as well as Alice Kerrison must have known him? And there was the evidence of the letter, a letter which Seton, whose carefully filed correspondence at Seton House was all typewritten, had taken the trouble to write with his own hand.

He was about to ask what Dorothy Seton had done with it when the telephone rang. It was an incongruously strident noise in the silence of that immense, candle-lit room. Dalgliesh, startled, realised that he had unreasonably taken it for granted that there was no electricity at Priory House. He peered around for the instrument. The bell seemed to be ringing from a bookcase in the dark recess at the far end of the room. Neither Sinclair nor Alice Kerrison made any move to answer it. Sinclair said:

"That will be a wrong number. No one ever rings us. We only have the telephone in case of emergency but the number isn't in the book." He glanced across at the instrument complacently as if gratified to know that it was actually in working order. Dalgliesh got up. "Excuse me." he said. "But it may be for me." He groped for the instrument and laid hold of its smooth coldness among the impedimenta which littered the top of the bookcase. The irritating noise ceased. In the quiet he could almost believe that everyone present could hear Inspector Reckless speaking.

"Mr. Dalgliesh? I'm speaking from Pentlands. Something has happened which I think you should know about. Would it be convenient for you to come now?

Then, as Dalgliesh hesitated, he added:

"I've got the P.M. report. I think it will interest you."

He made it sound like a bribe, thought Dalgliesh. But he would, of course, have to go. The formal, unemphatic tone of the request didn't deceive either of them. If they had been working on a case together Superintendent Dalgliesh would have summoned Inspector Reckless, not the other way round. But they weren't working on a case together. And if Reckless wanted to interview a suspect—or even the nephew of a suspect—he could choose his own time and place. All the same, it would be interesting to know what he was doing at Pentlands. Miss Dalgliesh hadn't locked the cottage when they left for Priory House. Few people at Monksmere bothered to lock up and the possible murder of a neighbour hadn't induced his aunt to change her habits. But it was unlike Reckless to make himself so at home.

He made his excuses to his host who accepted them with little sign of regret. Dalgliesh suspected that Sinclair, unused to company other than his aunt, was glad enough to see their party reduced to the familiar three. For some reason of his own he had wanted Dalgliesh to hear Alice Kerrison's story. Now it had been told and he could speed his guest with satisfaction and some relief. He merely reminded Dalgliesh to pick up his torch on the way out and instructed him not to return for his aunt as he and Alice would escort her home. Jane Dalgliesh seemed happy enough with this arrangement. Dalgliesh suspected that she was being tactful. Reckless had only asked to see him and his aunt had no wish to be an unwelcome third even in her own house.

He saw himself out, stepping into darkness so impermeable that at first his eyes could distinguish nothing but the white blur of the path at his feet. Then the clouds moved from the face of the moon and the night became visible, a thing of forms and shadows heavy with mystery and pungent with the sea. Dalgliesh thought how in London one could rarely experience the night, riven as it was by the glare of lights and the restlessness of men. Here it was an almost palpable presence so that there moved along his veins the stirring of an atavistic fear of darkness and the unknown. Even the Suffolk countryman, no alien to the night, could hardly walk these cliff paths without a sense of mystery. It was easy to understand how the local legends had grown that sometimes, on an autumn night, one could hear the muffled beats of horses' hoofs as smugglers brought their kegs and bales from Sizewell Gap to hide them in the marshes or carry them inland across the desolate Westleton heathlands. Easy, too, on such a night to hear from the sea faint bells of long drowned churches, St. Leonard's, St. John's, St. Peter's and All Saints clanging their dirges for the souls of dead men. And now there might be new legends to keep the countryman indoors on the autumn nights. The October legends. One of a naked woman, pale under the moon, walking through the waves to her death: one of a dead and handless man drifting out on the tide.

Dalgliesh perversely decided to walk home along the edge of the cliff. It would add fifteen minutes to his journey but it wouldn't hurt Reckless, comfortably ensconced at Pentlands, to wait another quarter of an hour. He found the path with his torch and followed the little pool of light which moved before him like a wraith. He looked back at the house. It was formless now, a black mass against the night sky with no sign of habitation except the thin shafts of light between the dining room shutters and one high round window which blazed out like a cyclops eye. While he watched, the light went out. Someone, probably Alice Kerrison, had gone upstairs.

He was nearing the edge of the cliff now. The waves thudded more clearly in his ears and somewhere, piercingly shrill, a sea bird called. He thought that the wind might be rising although it was still little more than a strong breeze. But here, on this exposed headland, it was as if sea, land and sky shared a perpetual and gentle turbulence. The path was becoming more overgrown. For the next twenty yards it was little more than a tortuous clearing through the brambles and gorse whose thorned branches caught at his legs. He was beginning to think that it would have been wiser to take the inland path. The gratification of making Reckless wait struck him now as irrational and childish and certainly not worth the ruining of a pair of perfectly good trousers. If Seton's body had been carried from Priory House through this prickly jungle there should be some evidence of its passing. Reckless would certainly have gone over the ground with care; he wondered what, if anything, he had found. And it wasn't only the path. There would be forty or so rackety wooden steps down to the beach to be negotiated. Sinclair was a strong man despite his age and Alice Kerrison was a healthy countrywoman; but Seton small as he was, would have been literally a dead weight. It would have been an exhausing, almost impossible journey.

Suddenly he saw a white shape to the left of the path. It was one of the few remaining tombstones on this part of the cliff. Most of them had long since crumbled with age or been swept under the sea to yield in time their quota of bones to the human debris washed up by the tides. But this one stood and, on impulse, Dalgliesh went over to examine it. It was taller than he had expected and the lettering was cut clear and deep. Crouching low, he shone his torch on the inscription:

In Memory of
Henry Willm. Scrivener
Shot from his horse by a party of
smugglers while travelling in these
parts, 24th Sept. 1786.

The cruel balls have pierced me to the heart
No time have I to pray ere I depart.
Traveller pause, thou knowest not the Day
When thou must meet thy Maker on the Way

Poor Henry Scrivener! What ill chance, Dalgliesh wondered, had brought him travelling on the lonely road to Dunwich. He must have been a man of some substance. It was a fine stone. He wondered how many years it would be before Scrivener, his stone and its pious exhortation were in turn swept away and forgotten. He was scrambling to his feet when the torch jerked in his hand and shone full on the grave itself. He saw with surprise that someone had opened it. The turf had been replaced, the brambles twisted together again to form a dense and prickly panoply, but the grave had undoubtedly been disturbed. He knelt again and gently shifted the soil with his gloved hands. It was light and friable. Hands other than his had been there before. Within a few seconds he unearthed a femur, then a broken scapula and, finally, a skull. Henry Scrivener had been given companions in death. Dalgleish guessed at once what had happened. This was Sinclair or Alice Kerrison's way of disposing of the bones they found on the beach. All of them were very old, all bleached by the sea. Someone, and he thought it was probably Alice, had wanted to give them a reburial in consecrated ground.

He was musing over this fresh insight into the ways of that odd couple at Priory House and turning the skull over in his hands when he caught the soft thud of approaching footsteps. There was a rustle of parted branches and suddenly a dark figure was standing over him, blotting out the night sky. He heard Oliver Latham's light, ironic voice:

"Still detecting, Superintendent? You look, if I may say so, like an under-rehearsed First Grave Digger. What a glutton for work you are! But surely you can let poor Henry Scrivener rest in peace? It's a little late, I should have thought, to start investigating that particular murder. Besides, aren't you trespassing?"

"Rather less than you are at the moment," said Dalgliesh evenly.

Latham laughed:

"So you've been dining with R. B. Sinclair. I hope you appreciated the honour. And what did our great apostle of universal love have to say about Seton's peculiarly unpleasant end?"

"Not much."
Dalgliesh scooped a hole in the soft earth and began covering up the skull. He smoothed soil over the pale forehead and trickled it into the eye sockets and the gaps between the teeth. Without looking up he said:
"I didn't know you were fond of nocturnal walks."
"It's a habit I've only recently taken up. It's most rewarding. One sees such interesting sights."
He watched Dalgliesh as the reburial was completed and the turfs replaced. Then, without speaking, he turned to go. Dalgliesh called quietly after him:
"Did Dorothy Seton send you a letter shortly before she died?"
The dark figure stood stock still, then slowly turned. Latham asked softly:
"Is that any concern of yours?" And, as Dalgleish hesitated he added.
"Then why ask?"
Without another word he turned again and disappeared into the darkness.

CHAPTER SIXTEEN

The light was on over the cottage porch but the sitting room was almost in darkness. Inspector Reckless was sitting alone in front of the dying fire rather like a guest who, unsure of his welcome, is making a propitiatory gesture of economising on the lights. He rose as Dalgliesh entered and switched on a small table lamp. The two men faced each other in its soft but inadequate glow.
"Alone Mr. Dalgliesh? You had some trouble perhaps in getting away?"
The Inspector's voice was expressionless. It was impossible to detect either criticism or enquiry in the flat statement.
"I got away all right. I decided to walk back along the cliff. How did you know where to find me?"
"When I found the cottage empty I supposed you and Miss Dalgliesh would be dining somewhere in the dis-

trict. I tried the most likely house first. There are developments which I wanted to discuss with you tonight and I didn't want to talk on the phone."

"Well, talk away. But what about something to drink?"

Dalgleish found it almost impossible to keep the note of cheerful encouragement from his voice. He felt uncomfortably like a housemaster jollying along a promising but nervous examination candidate. And yet Reckless was entirely at ease. The sombre eyes gazed at him with no trace of embarrassment or servility. "For God's sake, what's wrong with me?" thought Dalgliesh. "Why can't I feel at ease with the man?"

"I won't have anything now, thank you Mr. Dalgliesh. I thought you'd be interested in the pathologist's report, I got it early this evening. Dr. Sydenham must have been up all last night with him. Would you like to take a guess at the cause of death?"

"No," thought Dalgliesh, "I wouldn't. This is your case and I wish to God you'd get on with solving it. I'm not in the mood for guessing games." He said:

"Asphyxia?"

"It was natural causes, Mr. Dalgliesh. He died of a heart attack."

"What?"

"There's no doubt of it. He had a mild angina complicated by a defect of the left antrim. That adds up to a pretty poor heart and it gave out on him. No asphyxia, no poisoning, no marks of violence apart from the severed hands. He didn't bleed to death, and he didn't drown. He died three hours after his last meal. And he died of a heart attack."

"And the meal was? As if I need to ask!"

"Fried scampi with sauce tartare. Green salad with French dressing. Brown bread and butter, danish blue cheese and biscuits, washed down with Chianti."

"I shall be surprised if he ate that at Monksmere," said Dalgliesh. "It's a typical London restaurant meal. What about the hands, by the way?"

"Chopped off some hours after death. Dr. Sydenham thinks they may have been taken off on Wednesday night, and that would be logical enough, Mr. Dalgliesh. The seat of the dinghy was used as a chopping block.

There wouldn't be much bleeding but if the man did get blood on him there was plenty of sea to wash it away. It's a nasty business, a spiteful business, and I shall find the man who did it, but that's not to say it was murder. He died naturally."

'A really bad shock would have killed him, I suppose?"

"But how bad? You know how it is with these heart cases. One of my boys has seen this Dr. Forbes-Denby and he says that Seton could have gone on for years with care. Well, he was careful. No undue strain, no air travel, a moderate diet, plenty of comfort. People with worse hearts than his go on to make old bones. I had an aunt with that trouble. She survived two bombing-outs. You could never count on killing a man by shocking him to death. Heart cases survive the most extraordinary shocks."

"And succumb to a mild attack of indigestion. I know. That last meal was hardly the most appropriate eating for a heart case, but we can't seriously suppose that someone took him out to dinner with the intention of provoking a fatal attack of indigestion."

"Nobody took him out to dinner, Mr. Dalgliesh. He dined where you thought he might have done. At the Cortez Club in Soho, Luker's place. He went there straight from the Cadaver Club and arrived alone."

"And left alone?"

"No. There's a hostess there, a blonde called Lily Coombs. A kind of right-hand woman to Luker. Keeps an eye on the girls and the booze and jollies along the nervous customers. You know her, I daresay, if she was with Luker in fifty-nine when he shot Martin. Her story is that Seton called her to his table and said that a friend had given him her name. He was looking for information about the drug racket and had been told that she could help." Dalgliesh said.

"Lil isn't exactly a Sunday school teacher but, as far as I know, she's never been mixed up in the dope business. Nor has Luker—yet. Seton didn't tell her the name of his friend, I suppose?"

"She says that she asked but he wouldn't tell. Anyway, she saw the chance of making a few quid and they left the Club together at nine-thirty. Seton told her that they couldn't go back to his Club to talk because women weren't admitted. That's true; they aren't. So they drove around Hyde Park and the West End in a taxi for about forty minutes, he paid her five quid for her information —I don't know what sort of a yarn she pitched him—and he got out at Paddington Underground Station leaving her to take the cab back to the Cortez. She arrived back at ten-thirty and remained there in view of about thirty customers until one in the morning."

"But why leave in the first place? Couldn't she have spun him the yarn at his table?"

"She said he seemed anxious to get out of the place. The waiter confirmed that he looked nervy and on edge. And Luker doesn't like her to spend too much time with one customer."

"If I know Luker he'd take an even poorer view of her leaving the Club for forty minutes to take a trip round Hyde Park. But it all sounds very respectable. Lil must have changed since the old days. Did you think it a likely story?"

Reckless said:

"I'm a provincial police officer, Mr. Dalgliesh. I don't take the view that every Soho tart is necessarily a liar. I thought she was telling the truth, although not necessarily the whole truth. And then you see, we've traced the cab driver. He confirmed that he picked them up outside the Club at nine-thirty and dropped Seton outside the District Line entrance at Paddington about forty minutes later. He said they seemed to be talking together very seriously for the whole of the journey and that the gentleman made notes in a pocket book from time to time. If he did I should like to know what happened to it. There was no pocket book on him when I saw the body."

Dalgliesh said:

"You've worked quickly. So the time he was last seen alive is pushed forward to about ten-ten. And he died less than two hours later."

"Of natural causes, Mr. Dalgliesh."

"I think he was intended to die."

"Maybe. But I'm not arguing with facts. Seton died at midnight last Tuesday and he died because he had a weak heart and it stopped beating. That's what Dr.

Sydenham tells me and I'm not going to waste public money trying to prove that he's wrong. Now you're telling me that someone induced that heart attack. I'm not saying it's impossible. I am saying that there's no evidence yet to support it. I'm keeping an open mind on this case. There's a lot we don't know yet."

That remark struck Dalgliesh as a considerable understatement. Most of the facts Reckless didn't yet know were surely almost as crucial as the cause of death. He could have catalogued the unanswered questions. Why had Seton asked to be dropped at Paddington? Who, if anyone, was he on the way to meet? Where had he died? Where was his body from midnight on Tuesday onwards? Who moved it to Monksmere and why? If the death had indeed been premeditated how did the murderer contrive so successfully to make it look like natural death? And this led on to a question which Dalgliesh found the most intriguing of all. Having done so, why didn't he leave the body in London, dumped perhaps at the side of the road to be later identified as that of a middle-aged, unimportant detective novelist, who had been walking in London on his own mysterious business and had been overcome by a heart attack. Why bring the body back to Monksmere and stage an elaborate charade which couldn't fail to arouse suspicion of foul play and which would inevitably bring the whole Suffolk C.I.D. buzzing around his ears?

As if he could read Dalgliesh's thoughts Reckless said:

"We've no evidence that Seton's death and the mutilation of his body are directly related. He died of natural causes. Sooner or later we shall find out where. Then we shall get a lead on the person responsible for all the subsequent nonsense; the mutilation; the false telephone call to Digby Seton—if it were made; the two manuscripts sent to Miss Kedge—if they were sent. There's a joker in this pack and I don't like his sense of humour; but I don't think he's a killer."

"So you think that it's all an elaborate hoax? With what purpose?"

"Malice, Mr. Dalgliesh. Malice against the dead, or the living. The hope of throwing suspicion on other people. The need to make trouble. For Miss Calthrop, maybe. She doesn't deny that the handless corpse in a dinghy was her idea. For Digby Seton. He stands to gain most by his half-brother's death. For Miss Dalgliesh, even. After all, it was her chopper."

Dalgliesh said:

"That's pure conjecture. The chopper's missing, that's all we know. There's no evidence whatsoever that it was the weapon."

"There's evidence now. You see, it's been returned. Switch on the lights, Mr. Dalgliesh, and you'll see."

The chopper had, indeed, been returned. At the far end of the room stood a small eighteenth-century sofa table, a delicate and charming thing which Dalgliesh remembered from his childhood as part of the furniture of his grandmother's sitting room. The chopper had been driven into the centre, the blade splitting the polished wood almost in two, the shaft curving upward. In the bright centre light which now flooded the room Dalgliesh could see clearly the brown stains of blood on the blade. It would be sent for analysis, of course. Nothing would be left to chance. But he had no doubt that it was Maurice Seton's blood.

Reckless said:

"I came to let you know the P.M. report. I thought you might be interested. The door was half open when I arrived so I came in, calling for you. I saw the chopper almost at once. In the circumstances I thought I'd take the liberty of staying around until you arrived."

If he were gratified by the success of his little charade, he made no sign. Dalgliesh hadn't credited him with a dramatic instinct. It had been quite cleverly stage managed; the soft conversation in the gloaming, the sudden blaze of light, the shock of seeing something beautiful and irreplaceable wantonly and maliciously destroyed. He would have liked to have asked whether Reckless would have broken his news with such spectacular éclat if Miss Dalgliesh had been present. Well, why not? Reckless knew perfectly well that Jane Dalgliesh could have driven that chopper into the table before she and Dalgliesh left for Priory House. A woman who could cleave off a dead man's hands to provide herself with a little private entertainment was hardly likely to jib at the sacrifice of a sofa table in the same cause. There had been method in the Inspector's excursion into drama. He had been hoping to watch his suspect's eyes for the absence of that first unmistakable flicker of surprise and shock. Well, he hadn't got much out of Dalgliesh's reaction. Suddenly, cold with anger, he made up his mind. As soon as he could control his voice he said:

"I shall be going to London tomorrow. I would be grateful if you would keep an eye on this place. I don't expect to be any longer than one night."

Reckless said:

"I shall be keeping an eye on everyone at Monksmere, Mr. Dalgliesh. I shall have some questions for them. What time did you and your aunt leave the cottage?"

"At about six-forty-five."

"And you left together?"

"Yes. If you're asking whether my aunt popped back on her own to fetch a clean hankie the answer is no. And, just to get the record straight, the chopper was not where it is now when we left."

Unprovoked, Reckless said calmly:

"And I arrive here just before nine. He had nearly two hours. Did you tell anyone about the dinner engagement, Mr. Dalgliesh?"

"No. I didn't, and I'm sure my aunt wouldn't have talked about it. But that's not really significant. We can always tell at Monksmere whether people are at home by the absence of lights."

"And you always leave your doors conveniently unlocked. It's all made very easy. And if things run true to form on this case, either all of them will be able to produce alibis, or none of them will." He walked over to the sofa table, and pulling an immense white handkerchief from his pocket he wrapped it round the shaft of the chopper and jerked the blade out of the table. He carried it to the door, then turned to face Dalgliesh:

"He died at midnight, Mr. Dalgliesh. Midnight. When Digby Seton had been in police custody for over an hour; when Oliver Latham was enjoying himself at the theatrical party in full view of two Knights, three Dames of the British Empire and half the culture hangers-on in London; when Miss Marley was safely tucked up in her hotel bed as far as I or anyone else knows; and when Justin Bryce was battling with his first attack of asthma. At least two of them have fool-proof alibis and the other two don't seem particularly worried. . . . I forgot to tell you, by the way. There was a telephone call for you while I was waiting. A Mr. Max Gurney. He wants you to ring back as soon as possible. He said that you knew the number."

Dalgliesh was surprised. Max Gurney was the last of his friends to ring him when he was on holiday. More to the point, Gurney was a senior partner in the firm which published Maurice Seton. He wondered whether Reckless knew this. Apparently not, since he made no comment. The Inspector had been working at tremendous pace and there were few people connected with Seton who hadn't been interviewed. But either he hadn't yet got round to seeing Seton's publisher, or he had decided that there was nothing to be gained.

Reckless finally turned to go:

"Goodnight, Mr. Dalgliesh. . . . Please tell your aunt that I'm sorry about the table. . . . If you're right about this being murder we know one thing about our killer, don't we? He reads too many detective stories."

He was gone. As soon as the departing roar of his car had died away, Dalgliesh telephoned Max Gurney. Max must have been waiting for he answered immediately.

"Adam? Good of you to telephone so promptly. The Yard were very naughty about letting me know where you were but I guessed it might be Suffolk. When are you coming back to town? Could I see you as soon as you do?"

Dalgliesh said that he would be in London next day. He could hear Max's voice lighten with relief.

"Then could we lunch together? Oh, lovely. At one o'clock say? Have you any preference about the place?"

"Max, weren't you once a member of the Cadaver Club?"

"I still am; would you like to lunch there? The Plants really do one very well. Shall we say one o'clock then at the Cadaver? Are you sure that's all right?"

Dalgliesh said that nothing would suit him better.

CHAPTER SEVENTEEN

In the ground floor sitting room of the dolls' house in Tanner's Lane Sylvia Kedge heard the first sighs of the rising wind and was afraid. She had always hated a stormy night, hated the contrast between the violence around her and the deep calm of the cottage wedged damply into the shelter of the cliff. Even in a high wind the surrounding air was heavy and still as if the place bred a miasma of its own which no external force could disturb. Few storms shook the windows or set the doors and timbers of Tanner's Cottage creaking. Even in a high wind the branches of the elder bushes which clustered against the back windows only moved sluggishly as if they lacked strength to tap against the panes. Her mother, squatting in animal comfort in the fireside chair, used to say:

"I don't care what anyone says. We're very snug in here. I shouldn't like to be at Pentlands or Seton House on a night like this." It was her mother's favourite phrase. "I don't care what anyone says." Spoken always with the truculence of the widow with a grievance, permanently at odds with the world. Her mother had had an obsessional need of snugness, of smallness, of security. To her all nature was a subtle insult and in the peace of Tanner's Cottage she could shut from her thoughts more than the violence of the wind. But Sylvia would have welcomed the onslaught of cold, sea-heavy gusts against her doors and windows. It would at least have reassured her that the external world existed and that she was part of it. It would have been infinitely less harrowing than this unnatural calm, this sense of isolation so complete that even nature seemed to pass her by as unworthy of notice.

But tonight her fear was sharper, more elemental than the unease of loneliness and isolation. She was afraid of being murdered. It had begun as a flirtation with fear, a nicely judged indulgence of that half pleasurable frisson which a sense of danger can bring. But suddenly and terrifyingly, her imagination was out of control. Imagined fear had become fear itself. She was alone in the cottage, and helpless. And she was horribly afraid. She pictured the lane outside, the path soft and moist with sand, the hedges rising black and high on either side. If the killer came for her tonight she would have no chance of hearing his approach. Inspector Reckless had asked her often enough and her answer had always been the same. It would be possible for a man treading warily to pass by Tanner's Cottage at night unseen and unheard. But a man burdened with a corpse? That had been more difficult to judge but she still thought it possible. When she slept she slept soundly with windows closed and curtains drawn. But tonight he wouldn't be carrying a body. He would be coming for her, and alone. Coming perhaps with a hatchet, or a knife, or twisting a length of rope in his hands. She tried to picture his face. It would be a face she knew; it had not needed the Inspector's insistent questions to convince her that someone living at Monksmere had killed Maurice Seton. But tonight the familiar features would be changed into a mask white and rigid with intent, the face of the predator stalking light footed towards his prey. Perhaps he was even now at the gate, pausing with his hand on the wood, wondering whether to risk the soft creak as it swung open. Because he would know that the gate creaked. Everyone at Monksmere must know. But why should he worry? If she screamed there would be no one near to hear. And he would know that she couldn't run away.

Desperately she looked round the sitting room at the dark and heavy furniture which her mother had brought with her when she married. Either the great ornate bookcase or the corner cupboard would have made an effective barrier to the door if only she could have moved them. But she was helpless. Heaving herself from the narrow bed she grasped her crutches and swung herself into the kitchen. In the glass of the kitchen cabinet she saw her face reflected, a pale moon with eyes like black pools, the hair heavy and dank like the hair of a drowned woman. A witch's face. She thought. "Three hundred years ago they would have burned me alive. Now they aren't even afraid of me." And she wondered whether it was worse to be feared or pitied. Jerking open the cabinet drawer she seized a fistful of spoons and forks. These she balanced in a row on the edge of the narrow window ledge. In the silence she could hear her own breath rasping against the pane. After a moment's thought she added a couple of glasses. If he tried to climb in through the kitchen window at least she would have some warning in the tinkle of falling silver and the smashing of glass. Now she looked round the kitchen for a weapon. The carving knife? Too cumbersome and not really sharp enough. The kitchen scissors perhaps? She opened the blades and tried to pull them apart but the rivet was too strong even for her tough hands. Then she remembered the broken knife which she used to peel vegetables. The tapering blade was only six inches long but it was keen and rigid, the handle short and easy to grasp. She whetted the blade against the stone edge of the kitchen sink and tested it with her finger. It was better than nothing. Armed with this weapon she felt better. She checked again that the bolts on the front door were secure and placed a row of small glass ornaments from the corner cupboard on the window ledge of the sitting room. Then, without taking the braces from her legs she propped herself upright on the bed, a heavy glass paper weight on the pillow beside her, the knife in her hand. And there she sat, waiting for fear to pass, her body shaken with her heart beats, her ears straining to hear through the far away sighing of the wind, the creak of the garden gate, the tinkle of falling glass.

Book Two

CHAPTER ONE

Dalgliesh set out next morning after an early and solitary breakfast, pausing only to telephone Reckless to ask for Digby Seton's London address and the name of the hotel at which Elizabeth Marley had stayed. He didn't explain why he wanted them and Reckless didn't ask but gave the information without comment except to wish Mr. Dalgliesh a pleasant and successful trip. Dalgliesh replied that he doubted whether it would be either but that he was grateful for the Inspector's cooperation. Neither troubled to disguise the irony in his voice. Their mutual dislike seemed to be crackling along the wire.

It was a little unkind to call on Justin Bryce so early but Dalgliesh wanted to borrow the photograph of the beach party. It was several years old but was a good enough likeness of the Setons, Oliver Latham and Bryce himself to help an identification.

Bryce came paddling down in response to his knock. The earliness of the hour seemed to have bereft him of sense as well as speech and it was some time before he grasped what Dalgliesh wanted and produced the snap. Only then, apparently, was he struck with doubt about the wisdom of handing it over. As Dalgliesh was leaving he came scurrying down the path after him, bleating anxiously: "You won't tell Oliver that I let you have it, will you Adam? He'll be absolutely furious if he learns that one is collaborating with the police. Oliver is the teeniest bit distrustful of you, I'm afraid. One must implore secrecy."

Dalgliesh made reassuring noises and encouraged him back to bed, but he was too familiar with Justin's vagaries to take him at face value. Once Bryce had breakfasted and gained strength for the day's mischief he would almost certainly be telephoning Celia Calthrop for a little cosy mutual speculation about what Adam Dalgliesh could be up to now. By noon all Monksmere including

Oliver Latham would know that he had driven to London, taking the photograph with him.

It was a comparatively easy journey. He took the quickest route and, by half past eleven, he was approaching the city. He hadn't expected to be driving into London again so soon. It was like a premature ending to a holiday already spoilt. In a half propitiatory hope that this might not really be so, he resisted the temptation to call at his flat high above the Thames near Queenhithe and drove straight on to the West End. Just before noon he had garaged the Cooper Bristol in Lexington Street and was walking towards Bloomsbury and the Cadaver Club.

The Cadaver Club is a typically English establishment in that its function, though difficult to define with any precision, is perfectly understood by all concerned. It was founded by a barrister in 1892 as a meeting place for men with an interest in murder and, on his death, he bequeathed to the Club his pleasant house in Tavistock Square. The Club is exclusively masculine; women are neither admitted as members nor entertained. Among the members there is a solid core of detective novelists, elected on the prestige of their publishers rather than the size of their sales, one or two retired police officers, a dozen practising barristers, three retired judges, most of the better known amateur criminologists and crime reporters and a residue of members whose qualification consists in the ability to pay their dues on time and discuss intelligently the probable guilt of William Wallace or the finer points of the defence of Madeline Smith. The exclusion of women means that some of the best crime writers are unrepresented but this worries no one; the Committee take the view that their presence would hardly compensate for the expense of putting in a second set of lavatories. The plumbing at the Cadaver has, in fact, remained virtually unaltered since the Club moved to Tavistock Square in 1900 but it is a canard that the baths were originally purchased by George Joseph Smith. The Club is old-fashioned in more than its plumbing; even its exclusiveness is justified by the assumption that murder is hardly a fit subject for discussion in front of women. And murder at the Cadaver seems itself a civilised archaism, insulated from reality by time or the panoply of the law, having nothing in common with the sordid and pathetic crimes which took up most of Dalgliesh's working life. Murder here evokes the image of a Victorian maidservant, correct in cap and streamers, watching through a bedroom door as Adelaide Bartlett prepares her husband's medicine, of a slim hand stretched through an Edinburgh basement railing proffering a cup of cocoa and, perhaps, arsenic; of Dr. Lamson handing round Dundee cake at his wealthy brother-in-law's last tea party; or of Lizzie Borden, creeping, axe in hand, through the quiet house in Fall River in the heat of a Massachusetts summer.

Every club has its peculiar asset. The Cadaver Club has the Plants. The members are apt to say "What shall we do if we lose the Plants?" much as they might ask "What shall we do if they drop the Bomb?" Both questions have their relevance but only the morbid dwell on them. Mr. Plant has sired—one would almost believe for the benefit of the Club—five buxom and competent daughters. The three eldest, Rose, Marigold and Violet, are married and come in to lend a hand. The two youngest, Heather and Primrose, are employed in the dining room as waitresses. Plant himself is steward and general factotum and his wife is generally acknowledged one of the best cooks in London. It is the Plants who give the Club its atmosphere of a private town house where the family's comfort is in the hands of loyal, competent and discreet family servants. Those members who once enjoyed these benefits have the comfortable illusion that they are back in their youth, and the others begin to realise what they are missed. Even the eccentricities of the Plants are odd enough to make them interesting without detracting from their efficiency and there are few Club servants of whom this can be said.

Dalgliesh, although he was not a member of the Club, had occasionally dined there and was known to Plant. Luckily, too, by that curious alchemy which operates in these matters, he was approved of. Plant made no difficulties about showing him round or answering his questions; nor was it necessary for Dalgliesh to emphasise his present amateur status. Very little was said but both men understood each other perfectly. Plant led the way to the small front bedroom on the first floor which Seton had always used and waited just inside the door while Dalgliesh examined the room. Dalgliesh was used to working under scrutiny or he might have been disconcerted by the man's stolid watchfulness. Plant was an arresting figure. He was six feet three inches tall, and broad shouldered, his face pale and pliable as putty with a thin scar sliced diagonally across his left cheekbone. This mark, the result of an undignified tumble from a bicycle on to iron railings in his youth looked so remarkably like a duelling scar that Plant had been unable to resist adding to its effect by wearing a pince-nez and cropping his hair en brosse, like a sinister Commander in an anti-Nazi film. His working uniform was appropriate, a dark blue serge with a miniature skull on each lapel; this vulgar conceit, introduced in 1896 by the Club's founder, had now, like Plant himself, been sanctified by time and custom. Indeed, members were always a little puzzled when their visitors commented on Plant's unusual appearance.

There was little to be seen in the bedroom. Thin terylene curtains were drawn against the grey light of the October afternoon. The drawers and wardrobe were empty. The small desk of light oak in front of the window held nothing but a clean blotter and a supply of club writing paper. The single bed, freshly made up, awaited its next occupant. Plant said:

"The officers from the Suffolk C.I.D. took away his typewriter and clothes, Sir. They looked for papers, too, but he hadn't any to speak of. There was a packet of buff envelopes and about fifty sheets of foolscap and a sheet or two of unused carbon paper but that's all. He was a very tidy gentleman, Sir."

"He stayed here regularly every October didn't he?"

"The last two weeks in the month, Sir. Every year. And he always had this room. We've only got the one bedroom on this floor and he couldn't climb stairs because of his bad heart. Of course, he could have used the lift but he said he hadn't any confidence in lifts. So it had to be this room."

"Did he work in here?"

"Yes Sir. Most mornings from ten until half past twelve. That's when he lunched. And again from two-thirty until half past four. That's if he was typing. It it was a matter of reading or making notes he worked in the library. But there's no typing allowed in the library on account of disturbing other members.

"Did you hear him typing in here on Tuesday?"

"The wife and I heard someone typing, Sir, and naturally we thought it was Mr. Seton. There was a notice on the door saying not to disturb but we wouldn't have come in anyway. Not when a member's working. The Inspector seemed to think it might have been someone else in here."

"Did he now? What do you think?"

"Well, it could have been. The wife heard the typewriter going at about eleven o'clock in the morning and I heard it again at about four. But we wouldn't either of us know whether it was Mr. Seton. It sounded pretty quick and expert like but what's that to go on? That Inspector asked whether anyone else could have got in. We didn't see any strangers about but we were both busy at lunch time and downstairs most of the afternoon. People walk in and out very freely, Sir, as you know. Mind you, a lady would have been noticed. One of the members would have mentioned it if there'd been a lady about the Club. But otherwise—well I couldn't pretend to the Inspector that the place is what he'd call well-supervised. He didn't seem to think much of our security arrangements. But, as I told him Sir, this is a Club not a police station."

"You waited two nights before you reported his disappearance?"

"More's the pity, Sir. And even then, I didn't call the police. I phoned his home and gave a message to his secretary, Miss Kedge. She said to do nothing for the moment and she would try to find Mr. Seton's half-brother. I've never met the gentleman myself but I think Mr. Maurice Seton did mention him to me once. But he's never been to the Club that I remember. That Inspector asked me particularly."

"I expect he asked about Mr. Oliver Latham and Mr. Justin Bryce too."

"He did, Sir. They're both members and so I told him.

But I haven't seen either gentleman recently and I don't think they'd come and go without a word to me or the wife. You'll want to see this first floor bathroom and lavatory. Here we are. Mr. Seton used this little suite. That Inspector looked in the cistern."

"Did he indeed? I hope he found what he was looking for."

"He found the ballcock, Sir and I hope to God he hasn't put it out of action. Very temperamental this lavatory is. You'll want to see the library, I expect. That's where Mr. Seton used to sit when he wasn't typing. It's on the next floor as I think you know."

A visit to the library was obviously scheduled. Inspector Reckless had been thorough and Plant was not the man to let his protégé get away with less. As they crushed together into the tiny claustrophobic lift, Dalgliesh asked his last few questions. Plant replied that neither he nor any member of his staff had posted anything for Mr. Seton. No one had tidied his room or destroyed any papers. As far as Plant knew there had been none to destroy. Except for the typewriter and Seton's clothes, the room was still as he had left it on the evening he disappeared.

The library, which faced south over the square, was probably the most attractive room in the house. It had originally been the drawing room and, except for the provision of shelves along the whole of the west wall, looked much as it was when the Club took over the house. The curtains were copies of the originals, the wallpaper was a faded pre-Raphaelite design, the desks set between the four high windows were Victorian. The books made up a small but reasonably comprehensive library of crime. There were the notable British Trials and Famous Trials series, text books on medical jurisprudence, toxicology and forensic pathology, memoirs of judges, advocates, pathologists and police officers, a variety of books by amateur criminologists dealing with some of the more notable or controversial murders, text books on criminal law and police procedure, and even a few treatises on the sociological and psychological aspects of violent crime which showed few signs of having been opened. On the fiction shelves a small section held the Club's few first editions of Poe, Le Fanu and Conan Doyle; for the rest, most British and American crime writers were represented and it was apparent that those who were members presented copies of their books. Dalgliesh was interested to see that Maurice Seton had had his specially bound and embellished with his monogram in gold. He also noted that, although the Club excluded women from membership, the ban did not extend to their books, so that the library was fairly representative of crime writing during the last one hundred and fifty years.

At the opposite end of the room stood a couple of show cases containing what was, in effect, a small museum of murder. As the exhibits had been given or bequeathed by members over the years and accepted in the same spirit of uncritical benevolence they varied as greatly in interest as, Dalgliesh suspected, in authenticity. There had been no attempt at chronological classification and little at accurate labelling and the objects had been placed in the show cases with more apparent care for the general artistic effect than for logical arrangement. There was a flintlock duelling pistol, silver mounted and with gold-lined flashpans which was labelled as the weapon used by the Rev. James Hackman, executed at Tyburn in 1779 for the murder of Margaret Reay, mistress of the Earl of Sandwich. Dalgliesh thought it unlikely. He judged that the pistol was made some fifteen years later. But he could believe that the glittering and beautiful thing had an evil history. There was no need to doubt the authenticity of the next exhibit, a letter, brown and brittle with age from Mary Blandy to her lover thanking him for the gift of "powder to clean the Scotch pebbles"—the arsenic which was to kill her father and bring her to the scaffold. In the same case a Bible with the signature "Constance Kent" on the flyleaf, a tattered rag of pyjama jacket said to have formed part of the wrapping around Mrs. Crippen's body, a small cotton glove labelled as belonging to Madeline Smith and a phial of white powder, "arsenic found in the possession of Major Herbert Armstrong". If the stuff were genuine there was enough there to cause havoc in the dining room and the show cases were unlocked. But when Dalgliesh voiced his concern Plant smiled:

"That's not arsenic, Sir. Sir Charles Winkworth said just the same as yourself about nine months ago. 'Plant', he said, ' if that stuff's arsenic we must get rid of it or lock it up.' So we took a sample and sent it off to be analysed on the quiet. It's bicarbonate of soda, Sir, that's what it is. I'm not saying it didn't come from Major Armstrong and I'm not denying it wasn't bicarb that killed his wife. But that stuff's harmless. We left it there and said nothing. After all, it's been arsenic for the last thirty years and it might as well go on being arsenic. As Sir Charles said, start looking at the exhibits too closely and we'll have no museum left. And now, Sir, if you'll excuse me I think I ought to be in the dining room. That is, unless there's anything else I can show you."

Dalgliesh thanked him and let him go. But he lingered himself for a few more minutes in the library. He had a tantalising and irrational feeling that somewhere, and very recently, he had seen a clue to Seton's death, a fugitive hint which his sub-conscious mind had registered but which obstinately refused to come forward and be recogsed. This experience was not new to him. Like every good detective, he had known it before. Occasionally it had led him to one of those seemingly intuitive successes on which his reputation partly rested. More often the transitory impression, remembered and analysed, had been found irrelevant. But the subconscious could not be forced. The clue, if clue it were, for the moment eluded him. And now the clock above the fireplace was striking one. His host would be waiting for him.

There was a thin fire in the dining room, its flame hardly visible in the shaft of autumn sunlight which fell obliquely across tables and carpet. It was a plain, comfortable room, reserved for the serious purpose of eating, the solid tables well spaced, flowerless, the linen glistening white. There was a series of original "Phiz" drawings for the illustrations to Martin Chuzzlewit on the walls for no good reason except that a prominent member had recently given them. They were, Dalgliesh thought, an agreeable substitute for the series of scenes from old

Tyburn which had previously adorned the room but which he suspected the Committee, tenacious of the past, had taken down with some regret.

Only one main dish is served at luncheon or dinner at the Cadaver Club, Mrs. Plant holding the view that, with a limited staff, perfection is incompatible with variety. There is always a salad and cold meats as alternative and those who fancy neither this nor the main dish are welcome to try if they can do better elsewhere. Today, as the menu on the library notice board had proclaimed, they were to have melon, steak and kidney pudding, and lemon soufflé. Already the first puddings, napkin swathed, were being borne in.

Max Gurney was waiting for him at a corner table, conferring with Plant about the wine. He raised a plump hand in episcopal salute which gave the impression both of greeting his guest and of bestowing a blessing on the lunches generally. Dalgliesh felt immediately glad to see him. This was the emotion which Max Gurney invariably provoked. He was a man whose company was seldom unwelcome. Urbane, civilised and generous he had an enjoyment of life and of people which was infectious and sustaining. He was a big man who yet gave an impression of lightness, bouncing along on small, high-arched feet, hands fluttering, eyes black and bright behind the immense horn-rimmed spectacles. He beamed at Dalgliesh.

"Adam! This is delightful. Plant and I have agreed that the Johannisberger Auslese 1959 would be very pleasant, unless you have a fancy for something lighter. Good. I do dislike discussing wine longer than I need. It makes me feel I'm behaving too like the Hon. Martin Carruthers."

This was a new light on Seton's detective. Dalgliesh said that he hadn't realised that Seton understood wine.

"Nor did he, poor Maurice. He didn't even care for it greatly. He had an idea that it was bad for his heart. No, he got all the details from books. Which meant, of course, that Carruther's taste was deplorably orthodox. You are looking very well, Adam. I was afraid that I might find you slightly deranged under the strain of having to watch someone else's investigation."

Dalgliesh replied gravely that he had suffered more in pride than in health but that the strain was considerable. Luncheon with Max would, as always, be a solace.

Nothing more was said about Seton's death for twenty minutes. Both were engaged with the business of eating. But when the pudding had been served and the wine poured Max said:

"Now, Adam, this business of Maurice Seton. I may say I heard of his death with a sense of shock and"—he selected a succulent piece of beef, and speared it to a button mushroom and half a kidney—"outrage. And so, of course, have the rest of the firm. We do not expect to lose our authors in such a spectacular way."

"Good for sales, though?" suggested Dalgliesh mischievously.

"Oh no! Not really dear boy. That is a common misconception. Even if Seton's death were a publicity stunt, which, admit it, would suggest somewhat excessive zeal on poor Maurice's part, I doubt whether it would sell a single extra copy. A few dozen old ladies will add his last book to their library lists but that isn't quite the same thing. Have you read his latest, by the way? *One for the Pot,* an arsenic killing set in a pottery works. He spent three weeks last April learning to throw pots before he wrote it, so conscientious always. But no, I suppose you wouldn't read detective fiction."

"I'm not being superior," said Dalgliesh. "You can put it down to envy. I resent the way in which fictional detectives can arrest their man and get a full confession gratis on evidence which wouldn't justify me in applying for a warrant. I wish real life murderers panicked that easily. There's also the little matter that no fictional detective seems to have heard of the Judges's Rules.

"Oh, the Honourable Martin is a perfect gentleman. You could learn a lot from him, I'm sure. Always ready with the apt quotation and a devil with the women. All perfectly respectable of course but you can see that the female suspects are panting to leap into bed with the Hon. if only Seton would let them. Poor Maurice! There was a certain amount of wish fulfilment there I think."

"What about his style?" asked Dalgliesh who was beginning to thing that his reading had been unnecessarily restricted.

"Turgid but grammatical. And, in these days, when every illiterate debutante thinks she is a novelist, who am I to quarrel with that? Written I imagine with Fowler on his left hand and Roget on his right. Stale, flat and, alas, rapidly becoming unprofitable. I didn't want to take him on when he left Maxwell Dawson five years ago but I was outvoted. He was almost written out then. But we've always had one or two crime novelists on the list and we bought him. Both parties regretted it, I think, but we hadn't yet come to the parting of the ways."

"What was he like as a person?" asked Dalgliesh.

"Oh, difficult. Very difficult, poor fellow! I thought you knew him? A precise, self-opinionated, nervous little man perpetually fretting about his sales, his publicity or his book jackets. He overvalued his own talent and undervalued everyone else's, which didn't exactly make for popularity."

"A typical writer, in fact?" suggested Dalgliesh mischievously.

"Now Adam, that's naughty. Coming from a writer, it's treason. You know perfectly well that our people are as hard-working, agreeable and talented a bunch as you'll find outside any mental hospital. No, he wasn't typical. He was more unhappy and insecure than most. I felt sorry for him occasionally but that charitable impulse seldom survived ten minutes in his company."

Dalgliesh asked whether Seton had mentioned that he was changing his genre.

"Yes, he did. When I last saw him about ten weeks ago. I had to listen to the usual diatribe about the decline of standards and the exploitation of sex and sadism but then he told me that he was planning to write a thriller himself. In theory, of course, I should have welcomed the change, but, in fact, I couldn't quite see him pulling it off. He hadn't the jargon or the expertise. It's a highly professional game and Seton was lost when he went outside his own experience."

"Surely that was a grave handicap for a detective writer?"

"Oh, he didn't actually do murder as far as I know.

At least, not in the service of his writing. But he kept to familiar characters and settings. You know the kind of thing. Cosy English village or small town scene. Local characters moving on the chess board strictly according to rank and station. The comforting illusion that violence is exceptional, that all policemen are honest, that the English class system hasn't changed in the last twenty years and that murderers aren't gentlemen. He was absolutely meticulous about detail though. He never described a murder by shooting, for example, because he couldn't understand firearms. But he was very sound on toxicology and his forensic medical knowledge was considerable. He took a great deal of trouble with rigor mortis and details like that. It peeved him when the reviewers didn't notice it and the readers didn't care."

Dalgliesh said:

"So you saw him about ten weeks ago. How was that?"

"He wrote and asked to see me. He came to London purposely and we met in my office just after 6.15 when most of the staff had left. Afterwards we came here to dine. That's what I wanted to talk to you about Adam. He was going to alter his Will. This letter explains why." He took a folded sheet of writing paper from his wallet and handed it to Dalgliesh. The paper was headed "Seton House, Monksmere Head, Suffolk." The letter, dated 30th July, was typed and the typing, although accurate, was inexpert, with something about the spacing and the word division at the end of lines which marked it as the work or an amateur. Dalgliesh realised immediately that he had recently seen one other typescript by the same hand. He read:

Dear Gurney,

I have been thinking over our conversation of last Friday—and here I must digress to thank you again for a most enjoyable dinner—and I have come to the conclusion that my first instinct was right. There is absolutely no sense in doing things by half. If the Maurice Seton literary prize is to fulfill the great purpose which I plan for it the capital outlay must be adequate, not only to ensure that the monetary value of the award is commensurate with its importance, but also to finance the prize in perpetuity. I have no dependents with a legitmate claim on my estate. There are those people who may think they have a claim but that is a very different matter. My only living relative will be left a sum which hard work and prudence will enable him to augment should he choose to exercise these virtues. I am no longer prepared to do more. When this and other small bequests have been made there should be a capital sum of approximately £120,000 available to endow the prize. I tell you this so that you may have some idea of what I intend. As you know my health is not good and although there is no reason why I should not live for many years yet, I am anxious to get this affair under way. You know my views. The prize is to be awarded biennially for a major work of fiction. I am not interested particularly in encouraging the young. We have suffered enough in recent years from the self-pitying emotionalism of the adolescent writer. Nor do I favour realism. A novel should be a work of imaginative craftsmanship not the dreary shibboleths of a social-worker's case book. Nor do I restrict the prize to detective fiction; what I understand by detective fiction is no longer being written.

Perhaps you will think over these few ideas and let me know what you suggest. We shall need trustees of course and I shall consult lawyers in regard to the terms of my new Will. At present, however, I am saying nothing about this plan to anyone and I rely on you to be equally discreet. There will inevitably be publicity when the details are known but I should much deplore any premature disclosures. I shall, as usual, be staying at the Cadaver Club for the last two weeks in October and I suggest that you get in touch with me there.

Yours sincerely,
MAURICE SETON.

Dalgliesh was conscious of Gurney's little black eyes on him as he read. When he had finished he handed back the letter, saying:

"He was expecting rather a lot of you, wasn't he? What was the firm getting out of it?"

"Oh, nothing, my dear Adam. Just a lot of hard work and worry and all of course for the greater glory of Maurice Seton. He didn't even restrict the prize to our list. Not that it would have been reasonable, I admit. He wanted to attract all the really big names. One of his chief worries was whether they would bother to apply. I told him to make the prize large enough and they'd apply all right. But £120,000! I never realized he was worth that."

"His wife had money. . . . Did he talk to anyone else about his plan do you know, Max?

"Well, he said not. He was rather like a schoolboy about it. Tremendous swearings to secrecy and I had to promise I wouldn't even telephone him about it. But you see my problem. Do I, or do I not, hand this over to the police?"

"Of course. To Inspector Reckless of the Suffolk C.I.D., to be precise. I'll give you his address. And you'd better phone him to say it's on the way."

"I thought you'd say that. It's obvious, I suppose. But one has these irrational inhibitions. I know nothing of his present heir. But I imagine that this letter gives someone a whacking great motive."

"The best. But we've no evidence that his heir knew. And, if it's any comfort to you, the man with the strongest financial motive also has the strongest alibi. He was in police custody when Maurice Seton died."

"That was clever of him . . . I suppose I couldn't just hand this letter over to you, Adam?"

"I'm sorry, Max. I'd rather not."

Gurney sighed, replaced the letter in his wallet, and gave his attention to the meal. They did not talk again of Seton until lunch was over and Max was enveloping himself in the immense black cloak which he invariably wore between October and May, and which gave him the appearance of an amateur conjuror who had seen better days.

"I shall be late for our Board meeting if I don't hurry. We have become very formal, Adam, very efficient. Nothing is decided except by resolution of the whole Board. It's the effect of our new buildings. In the old days we sat closeted in our dusty cells and made our own decisions. It led to a certain ambiguity about the firm's policy but I'm not sure that was such a bad thing . . . Can I drop you anywhere? Who are you off to investigate next?"

"I'll walk, thank you Max. I'm going to Soho to have a chat with a murderer." Max paused, surprised.

"Not Seton's murderer? I thought you and the Suffolk C.I.D. were baffled. D'you mean I've been wrestling with my conscience for nothing?"

"No, this murderer didn't kill Seton although I don't suppose he would have had any moral objections. Certainly someone is hoping to persuade the police that he's implicated. It's L. J. Luker. Remember him?"

"Didn't he shoot his business partner in the middle of Piccadilly and get away with it? It was in 1959, wasn't it?"

"That's the man. The Court of Criminal Appeal quashed the verdict on grounds of misdirection. Mr. Justice Brothwick, through some extraordinary aberration, suggested to the jury that a man who made no reply when charged probably had something to hide. He must have realised the consequences as soon as the words were out of his mouth. But they were said. And Luker went free, just as he said he would."

"And how does he tie up with Maurice Seton? I can't imagine two men with less in common."

"That," said Dalgliesh, "is what I'm hoping to find out."

CHAPTER TWO

Dalgliesh walked through Soho to the Cortez Club. With his mind still freshened by the clean emptiness of Suffolk he found these canyoned streets, even in their afternoon doldrums, more than usually depressing. It was difficult to believe that he had once enjoyed walking through this shoddy gulch. Now even a month's absence made the return less tolerable. It was largely a matter of mood, no doubt, for the district is all things to all men, catering comprehensively for those needs which money can buy. You see it as you wish. An agreeable place to dine; a cosmopolitan village tucked away behind Piccadilly with its own mysterious village life, one of the best shopping centres for food in London, the nastiest and most sordid nursery of crime in Europe. Even the travel journalists, obsessed by its ambiguities, can't make up their minds. Passing the strip clubs, the grubby basement stairs, the silhouettes of bored girls against the upstairs window blinds, Dalgliesh thought that a daily walk through these ugly streets could drive any man into a monastery, less from sexual disgust than from an intolerable ennui with the sameness, the joylessness of lust.

The Cortez Club was no better and no worse than its neighbours. There were the usual photographs outside and the inevitable group of middle-aged, depressed-looking men eyeing them with a furtive lack of interest. The place wasn't yet open but the door yielded to his push. There was no one in the small reception kiosk. He went down the narrow stairs with their scruffy red carpet and drew aside the curtain of beads which divided the restaurant from the passage.

It was much as he remembered it. The Cortez Club, like its owner, had an innate capacity for survival. It looked a little smarter although the afternoon light showed up the tawdriness of the pseudo-Spanish decorations and the grubbiness of the walls. The floor was cluttered with tables, many only large enough for one and all too closely packed for comfort. But then, the customers did not come to the Cortez Club for family dinner parties, nor were they primarily interested in the food.

At the far end of the restaurant there was a small stage furnished only with a single chair and a large cane screen. To the left of the stage was an upright piano, its top littered with manuscript paper. A thin young man in slacks and sweater was curved against the instrument picking out a tune with his left hand and jotting it down with his right. Despite the sprawling attitude, the air of casual boredom, he was completely absorbed. He glanced up briefly as Dalgliesh came in but returned immediately to his monotonous stabbing at the keys.

The only other person present was a West African who was pushing a broom in leisurely fashion around the floor. He said in a soft, low voice:

"We're not open yet, Sir. Service doesn't begin until six-thirty."

"I don't want to be served, thank you. Is Mr. Luker in?"

"I'll have to enquire Sir."

"Please do so. And I'd like to see Miss Coombs too."

"I'll have to enquire, Sir. I'm not sure that she's here."

"Oh, I think you'll find that she's here. Tell her please that Adam Dalgliesh would like to speak to her."

The man disappeared. The pianist continued his improvisation without looking up, and Dalgliesh settled himself at the table just inside the door to pass the ten minutes which he judged Luker would feel it appropriate to keep him waiting. He spent the time thinking of the man upstairs.

Luker had said he would kill his partner and he had killed. He had said he wouldn't hang for it and he didn't hang. Since he could hardly have counted on Mr. Justice Brothwick's cooperation, the prediction had shown either uncommon prescience or remarkable confidence in his own luck. Some of the stories which had grown around him since his trial were no doubt apocryphal but he was not the man to repudiate them. He was known and accepted by the professional criminal classes without being one of them. They gave him the reverent half-superstitious respect of men who know exactly how much it is reasonable to risk, for one who in one irretrievable stride has stepped outside all the limits. There was an ambience of awe about any man who had come so close to that last dreadful walk. Dalgliesh was sometimes irritated to find that even the police weren't immune to it. They found it hard to believe that Luker, who had killed so casually to satisfy a private grudge, could content himself with running a string of second-class night clubs. Some more spectacular wickedness was expected of him than the manipulation of Licensing Laws or Income Tax returns and the selling of mildly erotic entertainment to his dreary expense account customers. But if he had other enterprises, nothing as yet was known of them. Perhaps there was nothing to know. Perhaps all he craved was this prosperous, semi-respectability, the spurious reputation, the freedom of this no-mans-land between two worlds.

It was exactly ten minutes before the coloured man returned to say that Luker would see him. Dalgliesh made his own way up the two flights to the large front room from which Luker chose to direct not only the Cortez but all his Clubs. It was warm and airless, over furnished and under ventilated. There was a desk in the middle of the room, a couple of filing cabinets against one wall, an immense safe to the left of the gas fire and a sofa and three easy chairs grouped around a television set. In the corner was a small washstand basin. The room was obviously designed to serve both as an office and a sitting room and succeeded in being neither. There were three people present; Luker himself, Sid Martelli, his general factotum at the Cortez, and Lily Coombs. Sid, in his shirt sleeves, was heating himself a small saucepan of milk on a gas ring at the side of the fire. He was wearing his usual expression of resigned misery. Miss Coombs, already in her evening black, was squatting on a pouffe in front of the gas fire varnishing her nails. She raised a hand in salute and gave Dalgliesh a wide, unworried smile. Dalgliesh thought that the manuscript description of her, whoever had written it, fitted her well enough. He couldn't personally detect the Russian aristocratic blood but this hardly surprised him since he knew perfectly well that Lil had been bred no further east than the Whitechapel Road. She was a large, healthy-looking blonde with strong teeth and the thick, rather pale skin which stands up well to ageing. She might be in her early forties. It was difficult to tell. She looked exactly as she had when Dalgliesh had first seen her five years earlier. Probably she would look much the same for another five years.

Luker had put on weight since their last meeting. The expensive suit was strained across his shoulders, his neck bulged over the immaculate collar. He had a strong, unpleasant face, the skin so clear and shining that it might have been polished. His eyes were extraordinary. The irises were set exactly in the centre of the whites like small grey pebbles and were so lifeless that they gave the whole face a look of deformity. His hair, strong and black, came down low to a widow's peak imposing an incongruous touch of femininity to his face. It was cut short all over and shone like dog's hair, glossy and coarse. He looked like he was. But when he spoke his voice betrayed his origins. It was all there; the small town vicarage, the carefully fostered gentility, the minor public school. He had been able to change much. But he had not been able to alter his voice.

"Ah, Superintendent Dalgliesh. This is very pleasant.

I'm afraid we're booked out this evening but Michael may be able to find you a table. You're interested in the floor show no doubt."

"Neither dinner nor the show, thank you. Your food seemed to disagree with the last of my acquaintances who dined here. And I like my women to look like women, not nursing hippopotami. The photographs outside were enough. Where on earth do you pick them up?"

"We don't. The dear girls recognise that they have, shall we say, natural advantages, and come to us. And you mustn't be censorious, Superintendent. We all have our private sexual fantasies. Just because yours aren't catered for here it doesn't mean that you don't enjoy them. Isn't there a little saying about motes and beams? Remember, I'm a parson's son as well as you. It seems to have taken us rather differently, though." He paused as if for a moment interested in their separate reactions, then went on lightly:

"The Superintendent and I have a common misfortune, Sid. We both had a parson for a dad. It's an unhappy start for a boy. If they're sincere you despise them as a fool: if they're not you write them off as a hypocrite. Either way, they can't win."

Sid, who had been sired by a Cypriot bartender on a mentally subnormal skivvy, nodded in passionate agreement.

Dalgliesh said:

"I wanted a word with you and Miss Coombs about Maurice Seton. It isn't my case so you don't have to talk if you don't want to. But you know that, of course."

"That's right. I don't have to say a damn word. But then I might be in a helpful accommodating mood. You can never tell. Try me."

"You know Digby Seton, don't you?"

Dalgliesh could have sworn that the question was unexpected. Luker's dead eyes flickered. He said:

"Digby worked here for a few months last year when I lost my pianist. That was after his Club failed. I lent him a bit to try and see him over but it was no go. Digby hasn't quite got what it takes. But he's not a bad pianist."

"When was he here last?"

Luker spread his hands and turned to his companions:

"He did a week for us in May, didn't he, when Ricki Carlis took his overdose? We haven't seen him since."

Lil said:

"He's been in once or twice L.J. Not when you were here though." Luker's staff always called him by his initials. Dalgliesh wasn't sure whether the idea was to emphasise the general cosiness of their relationship with him or to make Luker feel like an American tycoon. Lil went on helpfully, "Wasn't he in with a party in the summer, Sid?"

Sid assumed an expression of lugubrious thought:

"Not summer, Lil. More like late spring. Didn't he come in with Mavis Manning and her crowd after her show folded up in May?"

"That was Ricki, Sid. You're thinking of Ricki. Digby Seton was never with Mavis."

They were as well-drilled, thought Dalgliesh, as a song and dance act. Luker smiled smoothly:

"Why pick on Digby? This isn't murder and, if it was, Digby's safe enough. Look at the facts. Digby had a rich brother. Nice for both of them. The brother had a dicky heart which might give out on him any minute. Hard luck on him but, again nice for Digby. And one day it does give out. That's natural causes, Superintendent, if the expression means anything at all. Admittedly someone drove the body down to Suffolk and pushed it out to sea. And did some rather messy and unpleasant things to it first, I hear. It looks to me as if poor Mr. Seton was rather unpopular with some of his literary neighbours. I'm surprised, Superintendent, that your aunt cares to live among these people, let alone leaving her chopper handy for the dead."

"You seem well informed," said Dalgliesh. He was remarkably quickly informed too. Dalgliesh wondered who had been keeping him so clearly in the picture.

Luker shrugged.

"There's nothing illegal in that. My friends tell me things. They know I'm interested in them."

"Particularly when they inherit £200,000?"

"Listen, Superintendent. If I want money I can make it, and make it legally. Any fool can make a fortune outside the law. It takes a clever man, these days, to make it legally. Digby Seton can pay me back the fifteen hundred I lent him when he was trying to save the Golden Pheasant if he likes. I'm not pressing him."

Sid turned his lemur-like eyes on his boss. The devotion in them was almost indecent.

Dalgliesh said:

"Maurice Seton dined here the night he died. Digby Seton is connected with this place. And Digby stands to inherit £200,000. You can't blame people if they come asking questions, particularly as Miss Coombs was the last person to see Maurice alive."

Luker turned to Lil:

"You'd better keep your mouth shut, Lil. Or, better still, get yourself a lawyer. I'll phone Bernie."

"What the hell do I want Bernie for? I've told it all to him once when that C.I.D. chap was here. I'm telling the truth. Michael and the boys saw him call me over to his table and we sat there until nine-thirty when we left together. I was back here by ten-thirty. You saw me Sid, and so did the whole bloody Club."

"That's right, Superintendent. Lil was back by half past ten."

"Lil should never have left the Club," said Luker smoothly. "But that's my concern, not yours."

Miss Coombs appeared magnificently unconcerned at the thought of Luker's displeasure. Like all his employees she knew exactly how far she could go. The rules were few and simple and were well understood. Leaving the Club for an hour on a slack evening was venial. Murder, under certain well-understood circumstances, was probably venial too. But if someone at Monksmere hoped to pin this killing on Luker he was in for a disappointment. Luker was not the man to murder for someone else's benefit nor did he trouble to cover up his tracks. When Luker killed he had no objection to leaving his prints on the crime.

Dalgliesh asked Lil what had happened. There was no more mention of lawyers and no difficulty in getting her story. Dalgliesh did not miss Lil's quick glance at her boss before she begun her story. For some reason best known to himself Luker was willing to let her talk.

"Well, he came in about eight o'clock and took the table

nearest the door. I noticed him at once. He was a funny little man, small, very neat, nervous-looking. I thought he was probably a Civil Servant out for a spree. We get all types here. The regulars usually come with a party but we get the odd solitary chap. Mostly they're looking for a girl. Well, we don't cater for that kind of thing and it's my business to tell them so." Miss Coombs assumed an expression of pious severity which deceived no one and wasn't intended to. Dalgliesh enquired what had happened next.

"Michael took his order. He asked for fried scampi, green salad, bread and butter and a bottle of Ruffino. He seemed to know exactly what he wanted. No mucking about. When Michael served him he asked if he could speak to me. Well I went across and he asked me what I would drink. I had a gin and lime and drank it while he started picking at the scampi. Either he hadn't an appetite or he just wanted something to push around the plate while we were talking. He got a quite a bit of the meal down eventually but he didn't look as if he was enjoying it. He drank the wine, though. Fairly put it away. Nearly the whole bottle."

Dalgliesh enquired what they had talked about.

"Dope," said Miss Coombs frankly. "That's what he was interested in. Dope. Not for himself, mind you. Well, it was plain enough he wasn't a junkie and he wouldn't have come to me if he was. Those boys know well enough where they can get the stuff. We don't see them in the Cortez. This chap told me he was a writer, a very well known one, quite famous, and he was writing a book about dope peddling. He didn't tell me his name and I never asked. Anyway, someone had told him that I might give him some useful information if he made it worth my while. Apparently this friend had said that if you want to know anything about Soho go to the Cortez and ask for Lil. Very nice, I must say. I've never seen myself as an authority on the dope racket. Still, it looked as if someone was trying to do me a good turn. There was money in it and the chap wasn't the sort to know whether he was getting genuine information. All he wanted was a bit of local colour for his book and I reckoned I could provide that. You can buy anything you want in London if you've got the cash and know where to go. You know that ducky, as well as I do. I daresay I could have given him the name of a pub or two where they say the stuff is passed. But what good would that be to him? He wanted a bit of glamour and excitement and there's no glamour about the dope racket, nor the junkies either, poor devils. So I said that I might be able to give him a bit of information and what was it worth? He said ten quid and I said O.K. And don't you go talking about false pretences. He was getting value."

Dalgliesh said that he was sure Miss Coombs always gave value and Miss Coombs, after a brief struggle, decided prudently to let the remark pass. Dalgliesh asked:

"Did you believe this story of being a writer?"

"No dear. Not at first, anyway. I'd heard it too often before. You'd be surprised the number of chaps who want to meet a girl 'just to get authentic background for my new novel'. If it's not that then they're doing sociological research. I'll bet they are! He looked that type. You know, insignificant, nervous and eager at the same time. But when he suggested we should take a taxi and I could dictate the stuff to him and he type it straight away, I began to wonder. I said I couldn't leave the Club for more than an hour at most and I'd rather we went to my place. When you don't know who you're playing keep to the home ground, I always say. So I suggested we took a taxi to my flat. He said all right and we left just before nine-thirty. That right, Sid?"

"That's right Lil. Nine-thirty it was." Sid lifted sad eyes from his glass of milk. He had been contemplating, without enthusiasm, the puckered skin which had slowly formed on its surface. The smell of hot milk, sickly and fecund, seemed to permeate the claustrophobic office. Luker said:

"For God's sake drink the stuff or chuck it away, Sid. You make me nervous."

"Drink it up, darling," encouraged Miss Coombs. "Think of your ulcer. You don't want to go the way of poor Solly Goldstein."

"Solly died of a coronary and milk never helped that. The opposite I should think. Anyway, the stuff's practically radioactive. Full of strontium 90. It's dangerous, Sid."

Sid trotted to the washbasin and poured the milk away. Resisting the urge to throw open the window Dalgliesh asked:

"How did Mr. Seton appear while you were sitting together?"

"Nervy, dear. Excited but on edge at the same time. Michael wanted to move him to another table, it's a bit draughty near the door, but he wouldn't budge. He kept looking at the door while we were talking."

"As if he was expecting someone?"

"No dear. More as if he wanted to make sure it was still there. I half expected him to do a bunk. He was an odd fish and no mistake."

Dalgliesh asked what had happened when they left the Club.

"The same as I told that C.I.D. chap from Suffolk. We got a taxi at the corner of Greek Street and I was going to give the cabbie my address when Mr. Seton suddenly said that he'd rather just drive around for a bit and would I mind. If you ask me he'd suddenly got cold feet. Scared of what might happen to him, poor little twerp. Anyway, that suited me and we cruised around the West End a bit and then went into Hyde Park. I strung him a bit of a yarn about the dope racket and he made notes in a little book. If you ask me he was a bit drunk. Suddenly he got hold of me and tried to kiss me. Well, I was a bit fed up with him by then and didn't fancy being pawed about by that little twit. I got the impression that he only made a pass at me because he thought he ought to. So I said I ought to be back at the Club. He asked to be put down outside Paddington Underground and said he'd take a tube. No hard feelings. He gave me two fivers and an extra pound for the taxi fare."

"Did he say where he was going?"

"No. We came up Sussex Gardens—it's one way only down Praed Street now, as you know—and put him down outside the District Line. But he could have crossed the road to the Bakerloo I suppose. I didn't watch to see. I said goodbye to him at about quarter past ten outside

Paddington Underground and that's the last I saw of him. And that's the truth."

Even if it weren't, thought Dalgliesh, it was difficult to see how the story could be disproved. There was too much corroborative evidence and Lil was the last woman in London to be panicked into changing a good story. It had been a waste of time coming to the Cortez. Luker had been unnaturally, almost suspiciously cooperative but Dalgliesh had learnt nothing which Reckless couldn't have told him in half the time.

Suddenly he felt again some of the uncertainties and the inadequacies which had tormented the young Detective Constable Dalgliesh nearly twenty years ago. When he took out Bryce's photograph of the beach party and handed it round it was with no hope of success. He felt like a doorstep salesman proferring his unwanted rubbish. They looked at it politely enough. Perhaps, like kindly householders, they were rather sorry for him. Doggedly, persevering, he asked whether any of the people shown had been seen at the Cortez Club. Lil screwed up her eyes in an agony of effort while holding the snap at arm's length, thus effectively blurring her vision. Lil, Dalgliesh remembered, was like most women. She lied most effectively when she could convince herself that, essentially, she was telling the truth.

"No, dear, I can't say I recognise them. Except Maurice Seton and Digby, of course. That's not to say they haven't been here. Better ask them."

Luker and Sid, less inhibited, merely glanced at the photograph and averred that they hadn't seen the subjects in their lives.

Dalgliesh looked at the three of them. Sid had the pained, rather anxious look of an underfed little boy, hopelessly at sea in the world of wicked adults. Dalgliesh thought that Luker might be secretly laughing if the man had ever been known to laugh. Lil was looking at him with the encouraging, motherly, almost pitying look which, he thought bitterly, was usually reserved for her customers. There was nothing more to be learned from them. He thanked them for their help—he suspected that the note of cool irony wasn't lost on Luker—and let himself out.

CHAPTER THREE

When Dalgliesh had left Luker jerked his head at Sid. The little man left without a word or a backward glance. Luker waited until his footsteps had been heard going downstairs. Lil, alone with the boss, showed no particular anxiety but settled herself more comfortably in the shabby armchair on the left of the gas fire and watched him with eyes as bland and incurious as the eyes of a cat. Luker went to a wall safe. She watched his broad back as he stood there, motionless, turning the combination lock. When he turned round she saw that he held a small parcel, the size of a shoe box, covered with brown paper and loosly tied with thin white string. He laid it on his desk.

"Have you seen this before?" he asked.

Lil disdained to show curiosity.

"It came for you by this morning's post, didn't it? Sid took it in. What's wrong with it?"

"Nothing's wrong with it. On the contrary it is an admirable parcel. I've undone it once, as you can see, but it was a very neat little job when it arrived. You see the address? L. J. Luker, Esq., The Cortez Club. W.1. Neat capital letters, characterless, printed in Biro. Not very easy to identify that hand. I like the esquire. My family is not armigerous as it happens, so the writer is being a little pretentious but as he shares that failing with my Income Tax inspector and half the tradesmen in Soho, we can hardly consider it a clue. Then there's the paper. Perfectly ordinary brown paper; you can buy it in sheets from any stationer, And the string. Do you see anything remarkable about the string, Lil?"

Lil, watchful, admitted that there was nothing remarkable about the string. Luker went on:

"What is rather strange, though, is the amount of postage he—or she—paid. At least a shilling on the generous side by my estimate. So we take it that the parcel was stamped outside a post office and then pushed over the counter at a busy time. No waiting for it to be weighed. There would be less chance of the customer being noticed that way."

"Where was it posted?"

"In Ipswich on Saturday. Does that mean anything to you?"

"Only that it was posted a hell of a long way from here. Isn't Ipswich near that place where they found Maurice Seton?"

"The nearest large town to Monksmere. The nearest place where one could be certain of being unrecognised. You could hardly post this in Walberswick or Southwold and expect that no one would remember."

"For God's sake, L.J.! What's in it?"

"Open it and see for yourself."

Lil advanced cautiously but with an assumption of unconcern. There were more layers of the brown wrapping paper than she had expected. The box itself was revealed as an ordinary white shoe box but with the labels torn away. It looked very old, the kind of box that could be found tucked away in a drawer or cupboard in almost any house. Lil's hands hovered over the lid.

"If there's some bloody animal in here that jumps out at me I'll kill you L.J., God help me if I don't. I hate damn silly jokes. What's the stink, anyway?"

"Formaline. Go on, open it."

He was watching her closely, the cold grey eyes interested, almost amused. He had her worried now. For a second her eyes met his. Then she stepped back from the desk and, reaching forward, flipped of the lid with one jerk of her wrist.

The sweetly acrid smell rose like an anaesthetic. The severed hands were lying on their bed of damp cotton wool curved as if in a parody of prayer, palms touching briefly, finger tips pressed together. The puffy skin, what was left of it, was chalk white, and so crumpled that it looked as if the phalanges were loosely clothed with a pair of old gloves which would peel off at a touch. Already the flesh was shrinking from the butchered wrists and the nail of the right index finger had shifted from its bed.

The woman stared at the hands, fascinated and repelled. Then she seized the lid of the box and rammed it home. The cardboard buckled under her force.

"It wasn't murder, L.J. I swear it! Digby hadn't anything to do with it. He hasn't the nerve."

"That's what I would have said. You've told me the truth Lil?"

"Of course. Every word L.J. Look, he couldn't have done it. He was in the nick all Tuesday night."

"I know all about that. But if he didn't send these, who did? He stood to make £200,000, remember.

Lil said suddenly:

"He said that his brother would die. He told me that once."

She gazed at the box, fascinated and horrified.

Luker said:

"Of course he was going to die. Some time. He had a dicky heart, didn't he? That's not to say Digby put him away. It was natural causes."

Lil may have detected some tinge of uncertainty in his voice. She glanced at him and said quickly:

"He's always been keen to come in with you L.J. You know that. And he's got £200,000."

"Not yet. And he may never get his hands on it. I don't want a fool in with me, capital or no capital."

"If he put Maurice away and made it look like natural death, he's not all that of a fool, L.J."

"Maybe not. Let's wait and see if he gets away with it."

"And what about . . . those?" asked Lil jerking her head towards the innocuous looking box.

"Back in the safe. Tomorrow I'll get Sid to parcel them up and send them off to Digby. That should tell us something. It would be a rather nice touch to enclose my visiting card. It's time Digby Seton and I had a little talk."

CHAPTER FOUR

Dalgliesh closed the door of the Cortez Club behind him and gulped in the Soho air as if it were as sweet as the sea wind on Monksmere Head. Luker had always had this effect of seeming to contaminate the atmosphere. He was glad to be out of that stuffy little office and free from the stare of those dead eyes. It must have rained briefly while he was in the Club for the cars were hissing over a wet road and the pavement was tacky under his feet. Soho was wakening now and the narrow street was swirling its gaudy flotsam from kerb to kerb. A stiff breeze was blowing, drying the road as he watched. He wondered if it were blowing on Monksmere Head. Perhaps even now his aunt would be closing the shutters against the night.

Walking slowly towards Shaftesbury Avenue he pondered his next move. So far this dash to London, prompted by angry impulse, had told him little that he couldn't have learnt in greater comfort by staying in Suffolk. Even Max Gurney could have told his news over the telephone although Max was, of course, notoriously cautious. Dalgliesh didn't altogether regret his journey; but it had been a long day and he wasn't disposed to make it longer. It was the more irritating, therefore, to find himself harassed by the conviction that there was still something to be done.

It was difficult to decide what. None of the possibilities was attractive. He could visit the fashionable and expensive flats where Latham lived and attempt to get something out of the hall porter but, in his present unofficial capacity, he was unlikely to succeed. Besides, Reckless or his men would have been there before him and if Latham's alibi could be broken they would have broken it. He could try his luck at the eminently respectable Bloomsbury Hotel where Eliza Marley claimed to have spent last Tuesday night. There too his reception would hardly be cordial and, there too, Reckless would have been before his. He was getting a little tired of following in the Inspector's footsteps like a tame dog.

He could take a look at Justin Bryce's flat in the City; but there seemed little point in it. Since Bryce was still in Suffolk there could be no chance of seeing inside and he didn't imagine that there was much to be learned from an examination of the building itself. He already knew it well since it was one of the pleasanter architectural conceits in the City. Bryce lived over the offices of the *Monthly Critical Review* in a small eighteenth century courtyard off Fleet Street, so carefully preserved that it looked wholly artificial. Its only outlet to the street was through Pie Crust Passage, almost too narrow for a single man. Dalgliesh didn't know where Bryce garaged his car but it certainly wasn't in Pie Crust Court. He had a sudden fantastic vision of the little man staggering down Pie Crust Passage with Seton's body slung over his shoulder and stowing it in the back of his car under the interested gaze of the local traffic wardens and half the City police. He wished he could believe it.

There was, of course, another way to spend the evening. He could telephone Deborah Riscoe at her office—she would be almost due to leave—and ask her to join him at his flat. She would come, of course. Those days, sweet to the memory despite their occasional torments, when he could never be sure that she would come, were over now. Whatever else she might have planned for the evening, she would come. Then all the boredom, the irritation and the uncertainties would find at least a physical relief. And, tomorrow, the problem would still remain, casting its shadow between him and the first light.

Suddenly he made up his mind. He turned briskly towards Greek Street, hailed the first taxi that he saw, and asked to be put down outside Paddington Underground Station.

He decided to walk from Paddington Underground to Digby Seton's address. If Maurice Seton had come this way he might have taken a bus or even another taxi (had Reckless checked on that, Dalgliesh wondered) but the chances were that he had walked. Dalgliesh timed himself. It took exactly sixteen minutes of fast walking before he arrived at the archway of brickwork and crumbling stucco which led into Carrington Mews. Maurice Seton might have taken longer.

The cobbled entrance was uninviting, ill-lit and smelt strongly of urine. Dalgliesh, unobserved, since the place was obviously deserted, passed under the archway into a wide yard lit only by a solitary and unshaded bulb over one of a double row of garages. The premises had apparently once been the headquarters of a driving school and a few tattered notices still clung to the garage doors. But they were dedicated now to a nobler purpose, the improvement of London's chronic housing shortage. More accurately, they were being converted into dark, undersized and over priced cottages soon, no doubt, to be advertised as "bijou town residences" to tenants or owners prepared to tolerate any expense or inconvenience for the status of a London address and the taste for contomporary chi-chi. The existing double garages were being halved to provide a downstairs room while retaining space for one small car, and the lofts enlarged to form a couple of cells for bedroom and bath.

Digby Seton's cottage was the only one completed and the decor was depressingly orthodox. It had an orange door with a brass knocker in the shape of a mermaid, window boxes at the two minute square windows, and a lamp in a wrought iron holder above the lintel. The lamp wasn't alight but this was hardly surprising since, as far as Dalgliesh could see, it wasn't connected to the power. It struck him as being coy without being attractive and vulgar without being functional; in this it was symbolic of the whole house. The orange window boxes were sagging with their weight of caked earth. They had been planted with chrysanthemums and, when fresh, their gaiety had no doubt justified another two guineas on the rent. But the flowers, once golden, were now faded and brittle, the dead leaves stank of decay.

He prowled around the cobbled yard shining his pocket torch into the dark eyes of the windows. The two adjoining garages with the rooms above were now being modernised. The interiors had been completely stripped and the double garage doors taken off so that he could step inside the shell and note with interest that there was to be a connecting door betwen the sitting room and the garage. Everywhere there was a smell of new timber, paint and brickdust. The district had a long way to go, of course, before it became socially acceptable let alone fashionable, but it was on the way up. Digby had merely been the first to sniff the returning tide.

And that, of course, led to the intriguing question of why exactly he had come here. It wasn't an unlikely house for him to choose. In many ways this squalid little status symbol was entirely appropriate to Digby. But wasn't it altogether too much of a coincidence that he had chosen a house so convenient for murder? It was within twenty minutes walk of where Maurice Seton had been put down; it was in a dark inconspicuous yard which, once the workmen had left, would be uninhabited except for Digby; it had a garage with a direct door into the house itself. And there was another fact, perhaps the most significant of all. Digby Seton had only recently moved and he hadn't given his new address to anyone at Monksmere. When she had wanted to contact him after Maurice's death Sylvia Kedge hadn't known where to find him. And this meant that Maurice, if indeed he had been sent to Carrington Mews by Lily Coombs, wouldn't have known that it was Digby who was waiting for him. Certainly, Maurice had gone from the Cortez Club to his death. And Digby was the only suspect who was connected with the Club.

But all this was no more than suspicion. Nowhere was there any proof. There was no evidence that Lil had directed Maurice here; even if she had, Lil was capable of an obstinate adherence to a good story that would have been commendable in a better cause. It would need stronger measures than any English police force would tolerate to persuade Lil to talk. There was no proof that Maurice had been in the Mews. Dalgliesh couldn't get into the locked cottage but Reckless or his men would have been over it; if there had been anything to find they would have found it. There wasn't even any proof that Maurice had been murdered. Reckless didn't believe it, the Chief Constable didn't believe it and probably no one else did except Adam Dalgliesh, stupidly persistent, blindly following his hunch in the teeth of the evidence. And, if Maurice had been murdered, the biggest problem remained. He had died at midnight when Digby Seton and indeed most of the other suspects, had an unbreakable alibi. Until one could discover the "how" it was pointless to concentrate on the "who".

Dalgliesh shone his torch for the last time round the deserted yard, over the stacked timber under its tarpaulin cover, the piles of new bricks, the garage doors with their peeling notices. Then he passed under the arch as silently as he had entered and made his way to Lexington Street and his car.

It was just outside Ipswich that the tiredness hit him and he knew that it wouldn't be safe to drive much further. He needed food. It had been a long time since his substantial lunch with Max and he had eaten nothing since. He was perfectly happy to spend the night in a lay-by but not to wake in the early hours with a gnawing hunger and no chance of an early breakfast. But the problem was that it was too late for a pub and he had no intention of stopping at a country club or small hotel to do battle with the proprietor's fixed determination to serve meals only at regulated hours and at a price and quality to deter all but the starving. After a mile or two, however, he found an all night transport cafe, advertised by the black phalanx of lorries parked around its doors and the blaze of light from its low windows. The place was full, the air thick with smoke and jangling with talk and the cacophony of the juke box, but he sat undisturbed at a corner table, bare-topped but clean, and was served with a plate of eggs, sausages and crisply fried chips and a pint mug of hot, sweet tea.

Afterwards he went in search of the telephone, inconveniently placed in a narrow passage between the kitchen and the parking yard, and put through a call to Pentlands. There was no need to telephone. His aunt wasn't expecting him back at any particular time. But he was suddenly uneasy about her and determined if there were no reply to drive on. He told himself that it was an irrational anxiety. She might well be dining at Priory House or even be taking a solitary walk along the beach. He had discovered nothing to suggest that she was in any danger; but still there was this sense that all was not well. It was probably only the result of weariness and frustration, but he had to know.

It seemed an unusually long time before she answered and he heard the quiet, familiar voice. If she was surprised at his call she didn't say so. They spoke briefly against the clatter of washing-up and the roar of departing lorries. When he replaced the receiver he felt happier but still uneasy. She had promised him to bolt the cottage door tonight—thank God she wasn't the woman to argue, question or laugh over a simple request—and he could do no more. He was half irritated by this worry which he knew to be unreasonable; otherwise, whatever his tiredness, he must have driven on.

Before leaving the telephone booth a thought struck him and he searched in his pocket for a further supply of coins. It took longer to get through this time and the line wasn't clear. But eventually he heard Plant's voice and asked his question. Yes, Mr. Dalgliesh was quite right. Plant had telephoned Seton House on Wednesday night. He was sorry that he hadn't thought to mention it. Actually he had been phoning about every three hours that evening in the hope of getting Mr. Seton. About what time? Well, as far as he could remember at about six, nine and twelve o'clock. Not at all. Plant was only too glad to have been of help.

Was it any help? Dalgliesh wondered. It proved nothing except that Plant's unanswered call could have been the ringing telephone heard by Elizabeth Marley when she left Digby at Seton House. The time was about right and Reckless hadn't been able to trace the other call. But that didn't mean that no one had made it. He would need stronger evidence than this to prove Digby Seton a liar.

Ten minutes later Dalgliesh parked under the shelter of the hedge at the next lay-by and settled himself in the car as comfortably as was possible for a man of his height. Despite the pint of tea and the indigestible supper sleep came almost immediately and for a few hours it was deep and dreamless. He was awoken by a spatter of gravel against the car windows and the high keening of the wind. His watch showed three-fifteen. A gale was blowing and, even in the shelter of the hedge, the car was rocking gently. The clouds were scudding across the moon like black furies and the high branches of the hedge, dark against the sky, were groaning and curtseying like a chorus row of demented witches. He eased himself out of the car and took a short walk down the deserted road. Leaning against a gate he gazed out over the dark flat fields, taking the force of the wind full in his face so that it was difficult to breathe. He felt as he had as a boy on one of his solitary cycling trips when he would leave his small tent to walk in the night. It had been one of his greatest pleasures, this sense of complete loneliness, of being not only without a companion but with the knowledge that no one in the world knew exactly where he was. It was a solitude of spirit as well as of the body. Shutting his eyes and smelling the rich dampness of grass and earth, he could imagine himself back in childhood, the smells were the same, the night was familiar, the pleasure was as keen.

Half an hour later he settled himself to sleep again. But before he dropped into the first layer of unconsciousness, something happened. He had been thinking drowsily and without effort of Seton's murder. It had been no more than the mind's slow recapitulation of the past day. And suddenly, inexplicably, he knew how it could have been done.

Book Three

CHAPTER ONE

It was just after nine o'clock when Dalgliesh got back to Pentlands. The cottage was empty, and for a moment, he felt again the foreboding of the night. Then he saw the note on the kitchen table. His aunt had breakfasted early and was walking along the shore towards Sizewell. There was a jug of coffee ready to be reheated and the breakfast table was laid for one. Dalgliesh smiled. This was typical of his aunt. It was her habit to take a morning walk along the beach and it would never occur to her to vary the routine merely because her nephew was flying backwards and forwards between London and Monksmere in chase of a murderer and might wish her to be immediately available to hear his news. Nor would she imagine that a healthy male was incapable of getting his own breakfast. But, as always at Pentlands, the essential comforts were there, the kitchen was warm and welcoming, the coffee strong, and there was a blue bowl of new laid eggs and a batch of home-baked rolls still warm from the oven. His aunt had obviously been up early. Dalgliesh breakfasted quickly, then decided to stretch his car cramped legs by walking along the shore to meet her.

He jumped his way down the uneven path of sand and rock which led from Pentlands to the beach. The leaping sea was white capped to the horizon, a brown-grey waste of heaving water, empty of sails and with only the sturdy silhouette of a coaster against the skyline. The tide was coming in fast. Lurching over the stones of the upper beach, he found the ridge of fine shingle which ran half-way between the sea's edge and the plateau of marram grass which fringed the marshes. Here walking was easier although, from time to time, he was forced to turn his back to the wind and fight for breath. Buffetted and foam-flecked, he squelched onward over the shingle finding the occasional and welcome stretch of firm serrated sand, and pausing from time to time to watch the smooth green underbelly of the waves as they rose in their last curve before crashing at his feet, in a tumult of flying shingle and stinging spray. It was a lonely shore, empty and desolate, like the last fringes of the world. It evoked no memories, cosily nostalgic, of the enchantments of childhood holidays by the sea. Here were no rockpools to explore, no exotic shells, no breakwaters festooned with sea weed, no long stretches of yellow sand sliced by innumerable spades. Here was nothing but sea, sky and marshland, an empty beach with little to mark the miles of outspate shingle but the ocasional tangle of tar splotched drift wood and the rusting spikes of old fortifications. Dalgliesh loved this emptiness, this fusion of sea and sky. But today the place held no peace for him. He saw it suddenly with new eyes, a shore alien, eerie, utterly desolate. The unease of the night before took hold of him and he was glad to see, rising from the sand dunes, the familiar figure of his aunt braced like a flag staff against the wind, the edges of her red scarf flying.

She saw him almost immediately and came towards him. As they met and stood together, fighting for breath against a sudden gust of wind, there was a harsh "kraaank" and two heron flew low overhead, pounding the air with heavy, laborious wings. Dalgliesh watched their flight. Their long necks were drawn in, their delicate brown legs stretched straight behind them like a slipstream.

"Heron," he said with mock triumph.

Jane Dalgliesh laughed and handed him her field glasses. "But what do you make of these?"

A small flock of grey-brown waders was twittering on the edge of the shingle. Before Dalgliesh had time to note more than their white rumps and blackish, down-turned beaks, the birds rose in one swift direct flight and faded into the wind like a wisp of thin white smoke.

"Dunlin?" he hazarded.

"I thought you might say dunlin. They're very similar. No, those were curlew-sandpipers."

"But the last time you showed me a curlew-sandpiper it had pink plumage," protested Dalgliesh.

"That was last summer. In the autumn they take on the buffish plumage of the young birds. That's why they look so like the dunlin. . . . Did you have a successful time in London?"

Dalgliesh said:

"Most of the day I spent following rather ineffectually in Reckless's footsteps. But during the course of a too-large lunch with Max Gurney at the Cadaver Club I learnt something new. Seton was proposing to use virtually all his capital to endow a literary prize. Having given up hope of personal fame he was proposing to buy a vicarious immortality. He wasn't skimping the price, either. Incidentally I have an idea now how Seton was killed but as it's going to be virtually impossible to prove, I don't think Reckless will thank me for it. I suppose I'd better phone him as soon as we get back."

He spoke without enthusiasm. Jane Dalgliesh cast a glance at him but asked no questions, and quickly turned her face away in case he should see, and be irritated by, her obvious concern.

"Did Digby know that he was likely to be done out of his inheritance?" she asked.

"Apparently no one knew except Max. The odd thing is that Seton wrote to him about it and typed the letter himself by the look of it. Yet Reckless didn't find the carbon at Seton House. He would certainly have mentioned it if he had. And he would certainly have questioned Sylvia Kedge and Digby to find out whether they knew."

"If Maurice wanted to keep his intention secret, wouldn't he have typed the letter without taking a carbon?" suggested Miss Dalgliesh.

"He took a carbon, all right. The bottom edge of the carbon got turned in when he put the paper into the machine and the last few words appear on the back of the letter. There's also a faint smear of carbon on the top edge. He might have decided later to destroy the copy but he was meticulous about his affairs and it doesn't seem likely. Incidentally, this isn't the only mystery about carbons. Seton is supposed to have typed that passage about his hero's visit to the Cortez Club while he was staying in London. But the servant at the Cadaver Club says that there were no carbon copies found in his room. So what happened to them?"

His aunt thought for a moment. This was the first time

he had ever discussed a case with her and she was intrigued and a little flattered until she remembered that it wasn't, of course, his case. Reckless was the one responsible. It was Reckless who would have to decide the significance, if any, of those missing carbons at the Cadaver. But she was surprised at her own interest in the problem. She said:

"There are several possibilities, I suppose. Perhaps Seton didn't take carbons. In view of his meticulous habits I think that unlikely. Or perhaps he, or someone who had access to his room, destroyed them. Or perhaps the manuscript which Sylvia produced wasn't the one Seton actually sent her. I expect that Reckless has checked with the postman that a long buff envelope was delivered to her but we've only her word that it contained the manuscript. And, if it did, presumably someone who knew that Seton was staying at the Club could have substituted one set of papers for another sometime between the sticking down of the envelope and its posting. Or could they? Do we know if Seton put the envelope out for posting where other people could see it? Or did he take it immediately to the post himself?"

"This was one of the things I asked Plant. No one at the Cadaver posted anything for Seton. But the envelope could have been left in his room long enough for someone to get at it. Or he could have handed it to someone else to post. But surely no one could have relied on that? And we know that this wasn't an unpremeditated killing. At least, I know it. I've yet to convince Reckless that it was a killing at all."

His aunt said: "Isn't there another possibility? We know that Seton couldn't have posted the second manuscript, the one describing the body drifting to shore. He was dead by then. And we've no reason to suppose that he even wrote it. We've only got Sylvia Kedge's word that it was his work."

"I think he wrote it," said Dalgliesh. "When Max Gurney showed me Seton's letter I recognised the typing. The same man typed the second manuscript."

As he spoke they were moving instinctively out of the bite of the wind into the shelter of the sunken lane which ran between the sand dunes and the bird sanctuary. Some twenty yards further on was the third in a series of small observation hides which overlooked the sanctuary. This particular hide made a natural turning point to their beach walks and Dalgliesh did not need to ask his aunt whether they should go in. To spend ten minutes scanning the reed beds through his aunt's binoculars and sheltering from the bitter east coast winds had become one of those rituals which were part of an autumn visit to Monksmere. The hide was typical of its kind, a rough wooden shelter, reed thatched, with a bench high enough to support tired thighs along the back wall and a slit at eye-level giving a wide view over the marshes. In summer it smelt strongly of sun-baked wood, moist earth and lush grasses. Even in the cold months, this warmth lingered, as if all the heat and smells of summer were trapped within its wooden walls.

They had reached the hide and Miss Dalgliesh was about to step first through the narrow entrance when Dalgliesh suddenly said:

"No! Wait!" A minute earlier he had been strolling along almost in a dream. Now, suddenly, his brain awoke to the significance of the signs which his trained senses had subconsciously noted: the single line of male footprints leading from the sand-dusted lane to the hide entrance, a trace on the wind of a sick stench which had nothing to do with the smell of earth or grasses. As his aunt paused he slipped in front of her and stood in the entrance of the hide.

His tall body blocked most of the light from the narrow entrance so that he smelt death before he saw it. The stench of sour vomit, blood and diarrhoea stung his nostrils as if the air of the little hut was saturated with corruption and evil. The smell was not unfamiliar to him but, as always, he had to fight against a momentary and intolerable urge to be sick. Then he bent down, the light streamed in behind him and he saw the body clearly for the first time.

Digby Seton had crawled like a dog into the corner of the hut to die and he had not died easily. The pathetic body, rigid and cold, was huddled along the far wall, the knees drawn up almost to the chin, the head twisted upwards as if the glazed eyes had made one last despairing effort to catch the light. In his agony he had bitten his bottom lip almost in two and a stream of blood, blackened now, had mixed with the vomit which encrusted his chin and the lapels of the once smart Melton overcoat. He had dug in the earth of the hut with torn and bleeding hands, smearing it over his face and hair and stuffing it even into his mouth as if in a last delirious craving for coolness and water. Six inches from his body lay his hip flask, the top unscrewed.

Dalgliesh heard his aunt's calm voice.

"Who is it, Adam?"

"Digby Seton. No, don't come in. There's nothing we can do for him. He's been dead for twelve hours at least; from some irritant poison by the look of it, poor devil."

He heard her sigh and she muttered something that he could not catch. Then she said:

"Shall I go for Inspector Reckless or would you rather I stayed here?"

"You go, if you will. I'll keep an eye on this place."

It was possible that he could have saved ten or fifteen minutes by going himself but there was nothing that anyone could do now to help Seton and he had no intention of leaving her alone in this stinking place of death. And she was a fast and strong walker; there would be little time wasted.

She set off at once and he watched her until a turn in the lane hid her from sight. Then he made his way to the top of the sand dunes and found a sheltered hollow in which to sit, his back wedged against a clump of marram grass. From this point of vantage he could keep the hide under observation and could see on his right the whole sweep of the beach and on his left the sunken lane. From time to time he caught a glimpse of his aunt's tall striding figure. She seemed to be making excellent time but it would be at least three quarters of an hour before Reckless and his men, laden with stretcher and their paraphernalia, came into view. There was no spot closer to the beach to bring an ambulance than Pentlands and no shorter way to the hide than by the lane. Burdened with their equipment, they would have a hard time of it against the wind.

Dalgliesh had spent only a few minutes in the hide but every detail was sharp and clear in his mind. He had no doubt that Digby Seton had been murdered. Although he had not searched the body—that was a job for Reckless—nor even touched it except to verify briefly that it was cold and that rigor mortis was well established, he had little doubt that no suicide note would be found. Digby Seton, that facile, uncomplicated, rather stupid young man, as pleased with his fortune as a child with a new toy and full of happy plans for bigger and brighter night clubs, was hardly a likely suicide risk. And even Digby had sense enough to know that there were easier ways of dying than to have one's stomach and guts burnt away with poison. There had been no bottle near the body except the hip flask. Almost certainly that had contained the stuff. The dose must have been very large. Dalgliesh's mind ranged over the possibilities. Arsenic? Antimony? Mercury? Lead? All could produce those signs. But this was mere speculation. In time the pathologists would have all the answers; the name of the poison, the dose, the time it had taken for Seton to die. And the rest would be for Reckless.

But assuming that the stuff had been put in the hip flask, who was a likely suspect? Someone who had access both to the poison and the flask. That was obvious. Someone who knew the victim well; knew that Digby, alone and bored, wouldn't be able to resist taking a pull at the flask before facing the bitter wind and the long walk home. And that implied someone who could persuade him to a rendezvous at the hide. Why else should he have gone there? No one at Monksmere had ever known Digby Seton to be interested in bird watching or in walking. And he had not been dressed for either activity. Nor had he carried binoculars. This was murder all right. Even Reckless would hardly suggest that Digby Seton had died naturally or that someone with a perverted sense of humour had put his corpse in the hide with the object of inconveniencing Adam Dalgliesh and his aunt.

Dalgliesh had no doubt that the two murders were related but he was struck with their dissimilarity. It was as if two different minds were at work. The killing of Maurice Seton had been almost unnecessarily complicated. Although it might still be difficult to prove that the crime was indeed murder in face of the pathologist's report of death from natural causes, there was little else natural about it. The difficulty was not lack of clues. There were too many. It was as if the murderer had needed to demonstrate his cleverness as much as he had needed to kill Seton. But this new killing was simpler, more direct. There could be no possibility here of a verdict of death from natural causes. This murderer was not trying any double bluff. There hadn't even been an attempt to make it look like suicide, to suggest that Digby had killed himself in a fit of remorse over his brother's death. Admittedly it wouldn't have been easy to fake a suicide but Dalgliesh thought it significant that no attempt had been made. And he was beginning to understand why. He could think of one vital reason why this killer should want to avoid any suggestion that Digby had killed himself through remorse or had been in any way concerned in his brother's death.

Dalgliesh was surprisingly warm and comfortable in the shelter of the marram grass. He could hear the wind whistling in the dunes and the insistent thudding of the tide. But the tall clumps of grass shielded him so effectively that he had an odd sense of isolation as if the roar of wind and sea was coming from far away. Through the thin screen of grasses he could see the hide, a familiar, ordinary, primitive hut outwardly no different from half a dozen others which fringed the bird sanctuary. He could almost persuade himself that it was no different. Touched by this sense of isolation and unreality he had to resist an absurd impulse to see if Seton's body were really there.

Jane Dalgliesh must have made good time. It was less than forty-five minutes before he caught the first glimpse of approaching figures in the lane. The straggling group came briefly into view and then they were hidden again behind the dunes. The second time he glimpsed them they seemed no nearer. Then, unexpectedly, they turned the last bend in the lane and were with him. He saw a windblown, incongruous little group, burdened with equipment and having the air of a badly organised and slightly demoralised expedition. Reckless was there, of course, grim-faced and rigid with anger, the ubiquitous raincoat buttoned to his chin. He had with him his sergeant, the police surgeon, a photographer and two young detective constables, carrying a stretcher and a rolled canvas shield. Few words were exchanged. Dalgliesh bellowed his report in the Inspector's ear and then went back to his shelter in the dunes and left them to it. This wasn't his job. There was no sense in having an extra pair of feet churning up the moist sand around the hide. The men got to work. There was much shouting and gesticulating. The wind, as if in spite, had risen to a crescendo on their arrival and even in the comparative shelter of the lane, it was hard to make oneself heard. Reckless and the doctor disappeared into the hide. There at least, thought Dalgliesh, it would be sheltered enough. Sheltered, airless and stinking of death. They were welcome to it. After about five minutes they reappeared and the photographer, tallest of the group, bent nearly double and edged his equipment through the opening. Meanwhile the two constables were making ineffective efforts to get up a screen around the hide. The canvas leaped and whirled in their hands and whipped around their ankles with every gust of wind. Dalgliesh wondered why they bothered. There were hardly likely to be many sightseers on this lonely shore nor were the sandy approaches to the hide likely to yield further clues. There were only three sets of prints leading to the door; his own, those of his aunt, and the third set which were presumably Digby Seton's. They had already been measured and photographed and soon, no doubt, the flying sand would obliterate them completely.

It was half an hour before they got the corpse out of the hide and placed on the stretcher. As the constables struggled to hold down the mackintosh covers while the straps were applied, Reckless came over to Dalgliesh. He said:

"A friend of yours telephoned me yesterday afternoon. A Mister Max Gurney. It appears he's been keeping to himself some intresting information about Maurice Seton's Will."

It was an unexpected opening. Dalgliesh said:

"I lunched with him and he asked me whether he ought to get in touch with you."

"So he said. You'd imagine he would be capable of thinking it out for himself. Seton was found dead with marks of violence on the body. It stands to reason we'd be interested in the money side."

"Perhaps he shares your view that it was a natural death," suggested Dalgliesh.

"Maybe. But that's hardly his business. Anyway, he's told us now and it was news to me. There was no record of it at Seton House."

Dalgliesh said:

"Seton took a carbon of the letter. Gurney will be posting the original to you and you'll find the carbon markings on the back. Someone destroyed the copy, presumably."

Reckless said gloomily:

"Someone. Perhaps Seton himself. I haven't changed my mind yet about that killing, Mr. Dalgliesh. But you could be right. Especially in view of this." He jerked his head towards the stretcher which the two policemen squatting at the poles, were now bracing themselves to raise. "There's no doubt about this one. This is murder, all right. So we take our choice. One murderer and one unpleasant practical joker. Or one murderer and two crimes. Or two murderers."

Dalgliesh suggested that this last was unlikely in such a small community.

"But possible, Mr. Dalgliesh. After all, the two deaths haven't much in common. There's nothing particularly subtle or ingenious about this killing. Just a whacking great dose of poison in Seton's hip flask and the knowledge that, sooner or later, he'd take a swig at it. All the murderer had to do was ensure that he wasn't too close to medical help when it happened. Not that it would have done him much good by the look of it."

Dalgliesh wondered how the killer had succeeded in luring Seton to the hide. Had it been done by persuasion or by threats? Was Seton expecting to meet a friend or an enemy? If the latter, was he the sort of man to go alone and undefended? But suppose it were a different kind of assignation? For how many people at Monksmere would Digby Seton have been ready to walk two miles over rough ground on a cold autumn day and in the teeth of a rising gale?

The stretcher was moving forward now. One of the constables had apparently been instructed to stay on guard at the hide. The rest of the party fell into line behind the corpse like an escort of shabby and ill-assorted mourners. Dalgliesh and Reckless walked together and in silence. Ahead, the shrouded lump on the stretcher swayed gently from side to side as the bearers picked their way over the ridges in the lane. The edges of the canvas flapped rhythmically like a sail in the wind and overhead a sea bird hovered over the corpse, screaming like a soul in pain, before rising in a wide curve to disappear over the marshes.

CHAPTER TWO

It was early evening before Dalgliesh saw Reckless alone. The Inspector had spent the afternoon interviewing his suspects and checking on Digby Seton's movements during the past few days. He arrived at Pentlands just before six o'clock, ostensibly to ask Miss Dalgliesh again if she had seen anyone walking along the shore towards Sizewell on the previous day and whether she had any idea what could have induced Digby Seton to visit the hide. Both questions had been answered earlier when Dalgliesh and his aunt had met Reckless at the Green Man to give their formal account of the finding of the body. Jane Dalgliesh had stated that she had spent the whole of Monday evening at Pentlands and had seen no one. But then, as she had pointed out, it would be possible for Digby—or indeed, anyone else—to have walked to the hide by the sunken lane behind the sand dunes or by way of the beach, and this path for most of its length wasn't visible from Pentlands.

"All the same," said Reckless obstinately, "he must have come past your cottage to get into the lane. Would that really be possible without you seeing him?"

"Oh perfectly, provided he kept close in to the cliffs. There is a strip of about twenty yards between my access to the beach and the beginning of the lane when I might have glimpsed him. But I didn't. Perhaps he wanted to avoid notice and chose his moment to slip past."

Reckless muttered as if thinking aloud.

"And that suggests a secret assignation. Well, we suspect that. He wasn't the man to go bird watching on his own. Besides, it must have been dusk before he set off. Miss Kedge said that he got his own tea at Seton House yesterday. She found the dirty tea things waiting for her to wash up this morning."

"But no supper?" enquired Miss Dalgliesh.

"No supper, Miss Dalgliesh. It looks as if he died before

he had his evening meal. But the P.M. will tell us more, of course."

Jane Dalgliesh made her excuses and went into the kitchen to prepare dinner. Dalgliesh guessed that she thought it tactful to leave him alone with Reckless. As soon as the door closed behind her, he asked:

"Who saw him last?"

"Latham and Bryce. But nearly everyone admits to having spent some time yesterday with him. Miss Kedge saw him shortly after breakfast when she went up to the house to do her chores. He has kept her on as a kind of secretary-housemaid. Making use of her rather as his half-brother did, I imagine. Then he lunched with Miss Calthrop and her niece at Rosemary Cottage and left shortly after three. He called in on Bryce on his way home to Seton House to gossip about the return of your aunt's chopper and to try to find out what you were doing in London. That little trip seems to have aroused general interest. Latham was with Bryce at the time and the three of them were together until Seton left shortly after four."

"What was he wearing?"

"The clothes he was found in. He could have carried his flask in his jacket, trousers or overcoat pocket. He took the coat off, of course, at Rosemary Cottage and Miss Calthrop hung it in the hall cupboard. At Bryce's place he slung it over a chair. No one admits to seeing the flask. As I see it, any of them could have put in the poison, Kedge, Calthrop, Marley, Bryce or Latham. Any of them. And it needn't have been yesterday." He did not, Dalgliesh noted, add Miss Dalgliesh's name; but that didn't mean that she wasn't on the list. Reckless went on:

"I can't make much headway, of course, until I get the P.M. and know what the poison was. Then we shall get moving. It shouldn't be too difficult to prove possession. This wasn't the kind of stuff you get prescribed on E.C.10 or buy over the chemist's counter."

Dalgliesh thought he could guess what the poison was and where it had come from. But he said nothing. There had already been too much theorising in advance of the facts and he judged it wiser to wait for the post-mortem. But if he were right, Reckless wasn't going to find it so easy to prove possession. Nearly everyone at Monksmere had access to this particular source. He began to feel rather sorry for the Inspector.

They sat together in silence for a minute. It wasn't a companionable silence. Dalgliesh could sense the stress between them. He couldn't guess what Reckless was feeling, he could only recognise with a kind of hopeless irritation his own awkwardness and dislike. He looked across at the Inspector's face with detached interest, building up the features in his mind as he might an identikit picture, observing the flatness of the wide cheekbones, the patch of white smooth-looking skin at each side of the mouth, the downward fold at the corners of the eyes and the little rhythmic twitch at the upper lid which was the only sign that the man had nerves. The face was uncompromising in its ordinariness, its anonymity. And yet, sitting there in that grubby raincoat, his face grey with tiredness, he still had force and personality. It might not be a personality which others found appealing. But it was there.

Suddenly Reckless, as if making up his mind to something, said harshly. "The Chief Constable wants to call in the Yard. He's sleeping on it. But I think he's already made up his mind. And there are those who will say it's none too soon."

Dalgliesh could find nothing appropriate to say to this. Reckless, still not looking at him, added:

"He seems to take your view, that the two crimes are connected."

Dalgliesh wondered whether he was being accused of trying to influence the Chief Constable. He couldn't recall expressing this view to Reckless but it seemed to him obvious. He said so and added:

"When I was in London yesterday it came to me how Maurice Seton could have been killed. It's little more than conjecture at present and God knows how you'll be able to prove it. But I think I know how it was done."

Briefly he outlined his theory, morbidly sensitive to every inflection in his own voice which the Inspector might interpret as criticism or self-congratulation. His story was received in silence. Then Reckless said:

"What put you on to that, Mr. Dalgliesh?"

"I'm not altogether sure. A number of small things I suppose. The terms of Seton's Will; the way he behaved at that basement table in the Cortez Club, his insistence on having one particular room whenever he stayed at the Cadaver Club; the architecture of his house even."

Reckless said:

"It's possible, I suppose. But without a confession I'll never prove it unless someone panics."

"You could look for the weapon."

"A funny kind of weapon, Mr. Dalgliesh."

"But a weapon and a lethal one."

Reckless drew an ordnance map from his pocket and spread it out on the table. Together they bent their heads over it, the Inspector's pencil hovering above the twenty mile radius around Monksmere.

"Here?" he asked.

"Or here. If I were the killer I'd look for deep water."

Reckless said:

"Not the sea, though. It might get washed up while we could still identify it. Not that I think it likely anyone would have connected it with the crime."

"But you might have. And the murderer couldn't risk that. Better get rid of it where there was every chance it wouldn't be found, or would be found too late. Failing an old mine shaft I'd have looked for a sluice or river."

The pencil came down and Reckless made three small crosses.

"We'll try here first Mr. Dalgliesh. And I hope to God you're right. Otherwise with this second death on our hands, it's all going to be a waste of time."

Without another word, he folded the map and was gone.

CHAPTER THREE

After dinner there was more company. Celia Calthrop, her niece, Latham and Bryce arrived within a short time of each other, driving or fighting their way through the rising storm to seek a spurious safety at Jane Dalgliesh's fireside. Perhaps, thought Dalgliesh, they could neither bear their own company nor feel at ease with each other. This at least was neutral ground, offering the comforting illusion of normality, the age-old protection of light and a warm fire against the darkness and enmity of the night. It certainly wasn't a time for the nervous or imaginative to be alone. The wind was alternately howling and moaning across the headland and a fast running tide was thundering up the beach driving the shingle in ridges before it. Even from the sitting room at Pentlands he could hear its long withdrawing sigh. From time to time a fitful moon cast its dead light over Monksmere so that the storm became visible and he could see, from the cottage windows, the stunted trees writhing and struggling as if in agony and the whole wilderness of sea lying white and turbulent under the sky.

The uninvited guests, their heads down, fought their way up the path to Miss Dalgliesh's door with the desperation of a fugitive band.

By half past eight they had all arrived. No one had troubled to fetch Sylvia Kedge, but apart from her the little company of five nights earlier was met again. And Dalgliesh was struck by the difference in them. Analysing it, he realised that they looked ten years older. Five nights ago they had been only mildly concerned and a little intrigued by Seton's disappearance. Now they were anxious and shaken, possessed by images of blood and death from which they had little hope of shaking free. Behind the brave assumptions of ease, the rather desperate attempts at normality, he could smell fear.

Maurice Seton had died in London and it was still theoretically possible to believe that he had died naturally or that someone in London was responsible for his murder if not for the mutilation of his body. But Digby's death was on home ground and no one could pretend that there had been anything natural about it. But Celia Calthrop, apparently, was still prepared to try. She was squatting in the fireside chair, knees gracelessly splayed, her hands restless in the heavy lap.

"It's the most terrible tragedy. Poor boy! I don't suppose we shall ever know what drove him to it. And he had everything to live for: youth, money, talent, looks, charm."

This startlingly unrealistic assessment of Digby Seton was received in silence. Then Bryce said:

"I grant you he had money, Celia. Or the prospect of

it anyway. Otherwise one did tend to think of poor Digby as a whey-faced, ineffectual, conceited, vulgar little twit. Not that one bore him the least ill-will. Nor, incidentally, does one believe that he killed himself."

Latham burst out impatiently:

"Of course he didn't! And Celia doesn't even believe it either! So why not be honest for a change, Celia? Why not admit that you're as scared as the rest of us?"

Celia said with dignity:

"I'm not in the least scared!"

"Oh, but you ought to be!" Bryce's gnome-like face was creased with mischief, his eyes sparkled up at her. He looked suddenly less harassed, less like a tired old man.

"After all, you're the one who gains by his death. There should be a nice little sum left even after double death duties. And Digby's been a fairly regular visitor to you recently hasn't he? Didn't he lunch with you yesterday? You must have had plenty of opportunities to slip a little something into his flask. You were the one who told us that he always carried it. In this very room. Remember?"

"And where am I supposed to have got hold of arsenic?"

"Ah—but we don't know yet that it was arsenic Celia! That's exactly the kind of remark that you shouldn't make. It doesn't matter in front of Oliver and me but the Inspector may get wrong ideas. I do hope you haven't been talking to him about arsenic!"

"I haven't been talking to him about anything. I've merely answered his questions as fully and honestly as I can. I suggest you and Oliver do the same. And I don't know why you're so keen to prove Digby was murdered. It's this morbid love you both have for looking on the dark side."

Latham said dryly:

"Just a morbid love of looking facts in the face."

But Celia was undaunted:

"Well, if it were murder, all I can say it that Jane Dalgliesh was very lucky to have Adam with her when she found the body. Otherwise people might begin to think. But a C.I.D. Superintendent—well, naturally he knows how important it is not to disturb anything or tamper with the evidence."

Dalgliesh, too fascinated by the enormity of the remark

and Celia's capacity for self-deception to make his protest, wondered whether she had forgotten that he was there. The others seemed to have forgotten too.

"What might people begin to think?" asked Latham quietly; Bryce laughed.

"You can't seriously suspect Miss Dalgliesh, Celia! If so you're shortly going to be faced with the delicate problem of etiquette. Your hostess is at this moment preparing coffee for you with her own hand. Do you drink it gracefully, or pour it surreptitiously into the flower vase?"

Suddenly Eliza Marley swung round at them:

"For God's sake shut up, both of you! Digby Seton's dead and he died horribly. You may not have liked him but he was a human being. What's more he knew how to enjoy life in his own way. It may not have been your way but what of it? He was happy planning his horrible night-clubs and deciding how to spend his money. You may despise that but he wasn't doing you any harm. And now he's dead. And one of us murdered him. I don't happen to find that amusing."

"My dear, don't distress yourself." Celia's voice had taken on the vibrant, emotional tone which she now almost unconsciously assumed when dictating the more highly charged passages in her novels.

"We're all used to Justin by now. Neither he nor Oliver cared one whit for Maurice or Digby so it's no use expecting them to behave with ordinary decency, let alone respect. I'm afraid they care for no one but themselves. It's pure selfishness, of course. Selfishness and envy. Neither of them has ever forgiven Maurice for being a creative writer when all they're fit for is to criticise other people's work and batten on other men's talent. You see it every day; the envy of the literary parasite for the creative artist. Remember what happened to Maurice's play. Oliver killed it because he couldn't bear to see it succeed."

"Oh that!" Latham laughed. "My dear Celia, if Maurice wanted to indulge in emotional catharsis he should have consulted a psychiatrist, not inflicted it on the public in the guise of a play. There are three essentials for any playwright, and Maurice Seton hadn't one of them. He must be able to write dialogue, he must understand what is meant by dramatic conflict, and he must know something about stage-craft."

This was no more than Latham's professional theme song and Celia was unimpressed.

"Please don't talk to me about craftsmanship, Oliver. When you have produced a work which shows the slightest sign of original creative talent there will be some point in discussing craftsmanship. And that goes for you too Justin."

"What about my novel?" demanded Bryce, affronted.

Celia cast him a long-suffering look and sighed deeply. She was obviously not prepared to comment on Bryce's novel. Dalgliesh recalled the work in question; a short exercise in sensitivity which had been well received but which Bryce had apparently never found the energy to repeat. He heard Eliza Marley's laugh.

"Isn't that the book the reviewers said had the intensity and the sensitivity of a short story? Hardly surprising when essentially that was all it was. Even I could keep the sensitivity going for a hundred and fifty pages."

Dalgliesh did not wait to hear more than Bryce's first protesting wail. Predictably the argument was degenerating into literary abuse. He wasn't surprised, having noticed this tendency before in his writing friends; but he had no wish to get involved. At any moment now they would be canvassing his opinion and his own verse no doubt would be subject to the devastating candour of the young. True, the argument appeared to be taking their minds from the subject of murder but there were more agreeable ways of getting through the evening.

Holding the door open for his aunt as she came in with the tray of coffee, he took the opportunity to slip away. It was perhaps a little unkind to abandon her just at this moment to the contentions of her guests but he didn't doubt her capacity to survive. He was less sure of his own.

His room was still and very quiet, insulated by sound building and oak boards from the jabber of the dissenting voices below. He unlatched the window and the seaward wall and forced it open with both hands against the blast of the gale. The wind rushed into the room swirling the bed cover into folds, sweeping the papers from his desk and rustling the pages of his bedside Jane Austen like a giant hand. It took his breath away so that he leaned gasping against the window ledge, welcoming the sting of spray on his face and tasting the salt drying on his lips. When he closed the window the silence seemed absolute. The thundering surf receded and faded like the far-away moaning on another shore.

The room was cold. He hitched his dressing gown around his shoulders and switched on one bar of the electric fire. Then he gathered up the scattered sheets of paper and replaced them with obsessive care, sheet on sheet, on the small writing table. The square white pages seemed to reproach him and he remembered that he hadn't written to Deborah. It wasn't that he had been too indolent, too busy or too preoccupied with the problem of Seton's murder. He knew perfectly well what had held him back. It was a cowardly reluctance to commit himself further by even one word until he had made up his mind about the future. And he was no nearer that tonight than he had been on the first day of the holiday. He had known when they said goodbye on his last evening that she understood and accepted that this break was in some way crucial for them, that he wasn't driving alone to Monksmere solely to escape from London or recover from the strain of his last case. There was no reason, otherwise, why she shouldn't have come with him. She wasn't as tied to her job as all that. But he hadn't suggested it and she had said nothing except that last "Remember me at Blythburgh". She had been at school near Southwold and knew and loved Suffolk. Well, he had remembered, and not only at Blythburgh. Suddenly he longed for her. The need was so intense that he no longer cared whether it were wise to write. In the face of this craving to see her again, to hear her voice, all his uncertainties and self-distrust seemed as unimportant and ludicrously unreal as the morbid legacy of a nightmare, fading in the light of day. He longed to talk to her, but with the sitting room filled with people there would be no chance of telephoning tonight. Switching on the desk lamp he sat at the table and unscrewed his pen. The words, as sometimes happened, came simply and easily. He wrote them down without pausing to think too much or even to wonder whether he was being sincere.

Remember me, you said, at Blythburgh,
As if you were not always in my mind
And there could be an art to bend more sure
A heart already wholly you inclined.
Of you, the you enchanted mind bereave
More clearly back your image to receive,
And in this unencumbered holy place
Recall again an unforgotten grace.
I you possessed must needs remember still
At Blythburgh my love, or where you will.

"This metaphysical conceit, like most minor verse, comes to you with an ulterior motive. I don't need to tell you what. I won't say that I wish you here. But I wish I were with you. This place is full of death and disagreeableness and I don't know which is worse. But God and the Suffolk C.I.D. willing I shall be back in London by Friday evening. It would be good to know that you might be at Queenhithe."

Writing this note must have taken longer than he thought for his aunt's knock on the door surprised him. She said:

"They're going, Adam. I don't know whether you feel the need to say goodnight."

He went down with her. They were, indeed, going and he was surprised to see that the clock said twenty past eleven. No one spoke to him and they seemed as unconcerned at his reappearance as they had been at his going. The fire had been let die and was now little more than a heap of white ash. Bryce was helping Celia Calthrop into her coat and Dalgliesh heard her say:

"It's naughty of us to be so late. And I've got to be up so early. Sylvia phoned me from Seton House late this afternoon and asked me to drive her to the Green Man first thing tomorrow. There's something urgent she has to tell Reckless."

Latham, already at the door, spun round.

"What does she mean—something urgent to tell him?"

Miss Calthrop shrugged.

"My dear Oliver, how can I know? She more or less hinted that she knew something about Digby but I imagine it's just Sylvia trying to make herself important. You know how she is. But one can hardly refuse to take her."

"But didn't she give you any idea what it's all about?" Latham was sharply insistent.

"No she didn't. And I certainly wasn't going to give her the satisfaction of asking. And I'm not going to hurry myself. If this wind continues I shall be lucky to get much sleep tonight."

Latham looked as if he would like to have questioned further but Celia had already pushed past him. Murmuring a final and abstracted goodnight to his hostess, he followed the others into the storm. A few minutes later straining his ears against the howling of the wind, Dalgliesh heard the slamming of doors and the faint row of the departing cars.

CHAPTER FOUR

The wind woke Dalgliesh just before three o'clock. As he drifted into consciousness he heard the three chimes of the sitting room clock and his first waking thought was a drowsy wonder that so sweet and uninsistent a sound could strike so clearly through the bedlam of the night. He lay awake and listened. Drowsiness gave way to pleasure, then to a faint excitement. He had always enjoyed a storm at Monksmere. The pleasure was familiar and predictable; the frisson of danger; the illusion of being poised on the very edge of chaos; the contrast between the familiar comfort of his bed and the violence of the night. He wasn't worried. Pentlands had stood for four hundred years against the Suffolk seas. It would stand tonight. The sounds he was hearing now hadn't changed with the years. For over four hundred years men had lain awake in this room and listened to the sea. One storm was very like another, all impossible to describe except in clichés. He lay still and listened to the familiar noises; the wind hurling itself against the walls like a demented animal; the perpetual background surge of the sea, the hiss of rain heard as the gusts abated; and, in the momentary calm, the trickle of falling shingle from roof and window sills. At about twenty to four the storm seemed to be dying away. There was one moment of complete peace in which Dalgliesh could hear his own breathing. Shortly afterwards he must have drifted again into sleep.

Suddenly he woke again to a gust so violent that the cottage seemed to rock, the sea roared as if it were about to break over the roof. He had never known anything like this before, even at Monksmere. It was impossible to sleep through such fury. He had an uncomfortable urge to be up and dressed.

He switched on his bedside lamp and, at that moment, his aunt appeared in the doorway, close buttoned into her old plaid dressing gown and with one heavy plait of hair hanging over her shoulder. She said:

"Justin is here. He thinks we ought to see if Sylvia Kedge is all right. We may have to get her out of that cottage. He says that the sea's coming in fast."

Dalgliesh reached for his clothes.

"How did he get here? I didn't hear him."

"Well, that isn't surprising, is it? You were probably asleep. He walked. He says we can't get the car to the road because of flooding. So it looks as if we'll have to go across the headland. He tried to telephone the coastguards but the line is down."

She disappeared and Dalgliesh hurriedly pulled on his clothes, cursing gently.

It was one thing to lie in warm security analysing the noises of the storm; it was another to fight one's way over the highest point of the headland on an adventure which could appeal only to the young, the energetic or the incurably romantic.

He felt unreasonably irritated with Sylvia Kedge as if she were somehow responsible for her own danger. Surely to God the girl knew whether the cottage was safe in a storm! It might, of course, be that Bryce was fussing unnecessarily. If Tanner's Cottage had stood through the 1953 flood disaster it would stand tonight. But the girl was a cripple. It was right to make sure. All the same it was hardly an enterprise to be welcomed. At best it would be uncomfortable, exhausting and embarrassing. At worst, especially with Bryce in tow, it had all the elements of farce.

His aunt was already in the sitting room when he went

down. She was packing a thermos and mugs into a rucksack and was fully dressed. She must have been wearing most of her clothes under her dressing gown when she called him. It struck Dalgliesh that Bryce's call was not altogether unexpected and that Sylvia Kedge's danger might be more real than he knew. Bryce, wearing a heavy oilskin which reached to his ankles topped with an immense sou'wester, stood dripping and glistening in the middle of the room, like an animated advertisement for sardines. He was clutching a coil of heavy rope with every appearance of knowing what to do with it and had the air of a man dedicated to action.

He said:

"If there's any swimming to be done, my dear Adam, one must leave it to you. One has one's asthma, alas." He gave Dalgliesh a sly elliptical glance and added deprecatingly, "Also, one cannot swim."

"Of course," said Dalgliesh faintly. Did Bryce seriously believe that anyone could swim on a night like this? But there was no point in arguing. Dalgliesh felt like a man committed to an enterprise which he knows to be folly but which he can't summon up the energy to resist.

Bryce went on:

"I didn't call for Celia or Liz. No point in having a crowd. Besides, the lane is flooded so they wouldn't be able to get through. But I did try to get Latham. However, he wasn't at home. So we must just manage on our own." He was apparently unconcerned at Latham's absence. Dalgliesh bit back his questions. There was enough on hand without taking on fresh problems. But what on earth could Latham be doing on a night like this? Had the whole of Monksmere gone mad?

Once they had climbed out of the shelter of the lane and had mounted the headland there was energy for nothing but the effort of moving forward and Dalgliesh let the problem of Latham drop from his mind. It was impossible to walk upright and they clawed onwards like crouched beasts until aching thighs and stomach muscles forced them to kneel, palms pressed against the turf, to recover breath and energy. But the night was warmer than Dalgliesh had expected and the rain, less heavy now, dried softly on their faces. From time to time they gained the shelter of scrub and bushes and, released from the weight of the wind, trod lightly as disembodied spirits through the warm, green-smelling darkness.

Emerging from the last of these refuges they saw Priory House to sea-ward, the windows ablaze with light so that the house looked like a great ship riding the storm. Bryce drew them back into the shelter of the bushes and shouted:

"I suggest that Miss Dalgliesh calls Sinclair and his housekeeper to help. By the look of it they're up and about. And we shall need a long stout ladder. Our best plan is for you, Adam, to wade across Tanner's Lane if the water isn't too high and get to the house as soon as possible. The rest of us will move inland until we can cross the lane and approach the house from the north bank. We ought to be able to reach you with the ladder from that side."

Before he had finished expounding this unexpectedly lucid and positive plan Miss Dalgliesh without a word set off towards Priory House. Dalgliesh, cast without his consent in the role of hero, was intrigued by the change in Bryce. The little man obviously had a concealed passion for action. Even his affectations had fallen away. Dalgliesh had the novel and not disagreeable sensation of being under command. He was still unconvinced that there was any real danger. But if there were, Bryce's plan was as good as any.

But when they reached Tanner's Lane and stood sheltering in the slope of the south bank and looking down on Tanner's Cottage, the danger was apparent. Under a racing moon the lane shone white, a turbulent sheet of foam which had already covered the garden path and was sucking at the cottage door. The downstairs lights were on. From where they stood the squat, ugly doll's house looked strangely lonely and threatened. But Bryce apparently found the situation more hopeful than he had expected. He hissed in Dalgliesh's ear:

"It's not very high. You ought to be able to get across with the rope. Funny, I thought it would be well up by now. This may be as far as it will get. Not much danger really. Still, you'd better go in, I suppose." He sounded almost disappointed.

The water was incredibly cold. Dalgliesh was expecting it but the shock still took his breath away. He had stripped off his oilskin and jacket and was wearing only his slacks and jersey. One end of the rope was around his waist. The other, hitched around the trunk of a sapling, was being plied out inch by inch through Bryce's careful hands. The swift current was already armpit high and Dalgliesh had to fight hard to keep upright. Occasionally his feet stumbled into a rut in the lane's surface and he lost his footing. Then, for a desperate moment, it was a struggle to keep his head above water as he fought on the end of the rope like a hooked fish. It was hopeless to try to swim against this tide. The cottage lights were still on as he gained the door and braced his back against it. The sea was boiling around his ankles, each wave carrying it higher. Panting to get back his breath he signalled to Bryce to release the rope. In response the bulky little figure on the far bank flailed its arms enthusiastically but made no move to unhitch the rope from the tree. Probably his exuberant gestures were no more than a congratulatory acknowledgement that Dalgliesh had gained his objective. Dalgliesh cursed his folly in having agreed with Bryce who should keep the rope before plunging to his task with such spectacular fervour. Any shouted communication between them was impossible. If he were not to remain tethered to the tree indefinitely—and his situation was already uncomfortably close to burlesque—he had better let Bryce have the rope. He released the bowline and the rope whipped free from his waist. Immediately Bryce began to coil it in with wide sweeps of his arms.

The wind had dropped a little but he could hear no sounds from inside the cottage and there was no answer to his shout. He pushed against the door but it was stuck. Something was wedged against it. He pushed harder and felt the obstruction shift as if a heavy sack were sliding across the floor. Then there was a gap wide enough for him to squeeze through and he saw that the sack was the body of Oliver Latham.

He had fallen across the narrow hall, his body blocking the sitting room doorway and his head resting face upward on the first stair. It looked as if he had struck the banister. There was a gash behind the left ear from which the blood was still oozing and another over the right eye. Dalgliesh knelt over him. He was alive and already regaining consciousness. At the feel of Dalgliesh's hand he groaned, twisted his head to one side and was neatly sick. The grey eyes opened, tried to focus, then closed again.

Dalgliesh looked across the brightly lit sitting room to the still figure sitting bolt upright on the divan bed. The face was an oval, deathly pale against the heavy swathes of hair. The black eyes were immense. They stared across at him, watchful, speculative. She seemed utterly unaware of the swirling water spreading now in waves across the floor.

"What happened?" Dalgliesh asked.

She said calmly:

"He came to kill me. I used the only weapon I had. I threw the paper weight at him. He must have caught his head when he fell. I think I've killed him."

Dalgliesh said briefly:

"He'll live. There's not much wrong with him. But I've got to get him upstairs. Stop where you are. Don't try to move. I'll come back for you."

She gave a little shrug of the shoulders and asked:

"Why can't we get across the lane? You came that way."

Dalgliesh answered brutally:

"Because the water's already up to my armpits and running in a torrent. I can't swim across burdened with a cripple and a semi-conscious man. We'll get upstairs. If necessary we'll have to get on the roof."

He edged his shoulder under Latham's body and braced himself for the lift. The staircase was steep, ill-lit and narrow but its very narrowness was an advantage. Once he had Latham balanced across his shoulders it was possible to pull himself up by both banisters. Luckily there were no corners. At the top he felt for the switch and the top landing was flooded with light. He paused for a moment recalling where the skylight was. Then he pushed open the door to his left and groped round again for a light. It took him a few seconds to find. As he stood in the doorway grasping Latham's body with his left hand and running his right over the wall the smell of the room came out at him, musty, airless and sickly sweet like a faint stench of decay. Then his fingers found the switch and the room became visible, lit by a single unshaded bulb hanging from the centre of the ceiling. It had obviously been Mrs. Kedge's bedroom and looked he thought as it must have done when she last slept in it. The furniture was heavy and ugly. The great bed, still made up, occupied almost all the back of the room. It smelt of damp and decay. Dalgliesh dumped Latham gently on it and looked up at the slope of the roof. He had been right about the skylight. But there was only the one tiny square window and this faced the lane. If they were to get out of the cottage it would have to be by the roof.

He went back to the sitting room to fetch the girl. The water was waist high and she was standing on the divan bed and holding on to the mantelshelf for support. Dalgliesh noticed that she had a small plastic sponge bag hanging around her neck. Presumably it contained such valuables as she possessed. As he entered she gazed round the room as if to ensure that there was nothing else which she wished to take. He fought his way over to her, feeling the strength of the tide even in this tiny confined space and wondering how long the foundations of the cottage could stand against it. It was easy to comfort oneself with the thought that the cottage had survived earlier floods. But the tide and the wind were unpredictable. The water may have risen further in earlier years but it could hardly have burst in with greater force. Even as he struggled across to the waiting figure he thought he could hear the walls shake.

He came up to her and without a word, lifted her in his arms. She was surprisingly light. True, he could feel the downward drag of the heavy leg irons but the upper part of her body was so buoyant that it might have been boneless, sexless even. He was almost surprised to feel the rib cage under his hands and the firmness of her high breasts. She lay passively in his arms as he carried her sideways up the narrow stairs and into her mother's room. It was only then that he remembered her crutches. He felt a sudden embarrassment, a reluctance to speak of them. As if reading his thoughts she said:

"I'm sorry. I should have remembered. They're hitched on to the end of the mantelshelf."

That meant another trip downstairs but it was hardly

avoidable. It would have been difficult to manage both the girl and her crutches in one journey up those narrow stairs. He was about to carry her over to the bed when she looked at Latham's writhing body and said with sudden vehemence. "No! Not there! Leave me here." He slid her gently from his arms and she leaned back against the wall. For a moment their eyes were level and they gazed at each other, wordlessly. It seemed to Dalgliesh that in that moment some kind of communication passed but whether those black eyes held a warning or an appeal he was never afterwards able to decide.

He had no difficulty in retrieving the crutches. The water in the sitting room had now covered the mantelshelf and as Dalgleish reached the bottom of the stairs they floated through the sitting room door. He grasped them by the rubber grips of the hand pieces and drew them over the banisters. As he retreated again up the stairs a great wave broke through the shattered front door and hurled them to his feet. The pedestal of the banisters broke free, spun as if in a whirlpool and was dashed into splinters against the wall. And this time there could be no doubt about it: he felt the cottage shake.

The skylight was about ten feet above the floor, impossible to reach without something to stand on. It was useless to try shifting the heavy bed, but there was a square substantial looking commode by the side of it and he dragged this across and positioned it under the skylight.

The girl said: "If you can push me through first I'll be able to help with . . . him."

She looked across at Latham who had now dragged himself upright and was sitting, head in hands, on the edge of the bed. He was groaning audibly.

She added: "I've got strong hands and shoulders."

And she held out the ugly hands towards him like a suppliant. This in fact had been Dalgliesh's plan. Getting Latham on to the roof was the trickiest part of the business. Without her help he doubted whether it would be possible.

The skylight, encrusted with dirt and festooned with grey cobwebs, looked as if it might be hard to shift. But when Dalgliesh punched at the frame he heard the splinter of rotting wood. The skylight was jerked upwards and was immediately whirled away into the storm. Night came bursting into the close little room sweeping it with welcome gusts of cold, sweet air. At that moment the lights failed and they saw as from the bottom of a pit the small grey square of turbulent sky and the reeling moon.

Latham came lurching across the room towards them. "What the hell . . . ? Someone's put out the bloody light."

Dalgliesh guided him back to the bed.

"Stay here and save your strength. You're going to need it. We've got to get out on the roof."

"You can. I'm staying here. Get me a doctor. I want a doctor. Oh God, my head!"

Dalgliesh left him rocking in lachrymose self-pity on the edge of the bed and went back to the girl.

Jumping from the chair he grasped the outer frame of the skylight and drew himself up. As he had recalled, the crown of the slated roof was only a few feet away. But the slope was steeper than he had expected and the chimney stack, which would afford them some shelter and support, was at least five feet to the left. He dropped again to the floor and said to the girl:

"See if you can get astride the roof and work your way back to the chimney. If you're in trouble, stay absolutely still and wait for me. I'll manage Latham once we're both out but I shall need you to help pull him up. But I won't shove him through until you're properly balanced. Give me a shout when you're ready. Do you want your crutches?"

"Yes," she said calmly. "I want my crutches. I can hook them on to the roof top and they may be useful."

He hoisted her through the skylight by the irons which braced both her legs from thigh to ankles. Their rigid strength made it easy for him to push her high on the crown of the roof. She grasped it and swung one leg to the other side then crouched down low against the fury of the storm, her hair streaming in the wind. He saw her nod vigorously as a sign that she was ready. Then she leaned towards him and held out both her hands.

It was at that moment that he sensed a warning, the unmistakable instinct for danger. It was as much part of his detective's equipment as his knowledge of firearms, his nose for an unnatural death. It had saved him time and time again and he acted on it instinctively. There was no time now for argument or analysis. If the three of them were to survive they had to get out on that roof. But he knew that Latham and the girl mustn't be up there alone together.

It wasn't easy getting Latham through the skylight. He was only just conscious and even the swirls of water spreading now over the bedroom floor couldn't rouse him to a sense of danger. He craved only to be allowed to sink on to the pillows of the bed and fight his nausea in comfort. But at least he could cooperate to some extent. He wasn't yet a dead weight. Dalgliesh took off his own and Latham's shoes then urged him on to the chair and hoisted him through the skylight. Even when the girl's hands had caught Latham under his armpits he didn't let go but immediately swung himself through the hole bracing himself against the wind, his back to the flooded lane and his legs dangling into the room. Together they pulled and pushed the half-conscious man until his hands grasped the roof top and he pulled himself up and lay astride it, motionless. The girl released her hands and taking up her elbow crutches, edged herself backward until she was leaning against the chimney stack. Dalgliesh swung himself up to join Latham.

It was then that it happened. In the second when Dalgliesh weakened his hold on Latham she struck. It was so instantaneous that he hardly saw the vicious kick of the armoured legs. But the irons caught Latham's hands and, immediately, they loosed their hold of the roof and his body slipped. Dalgliesh shot out his hands and caught Latham's wrists. There was a sudden intolerable jerk and he took the full weight of Latham's body as it hung spread-eagled over the roof. Then she struck again and again. And now it was Dalgliesh's hands. They were too numb to feel the pain but he experienced the sudden scalding gush of blood and knew that it couldn't be long before the wrists were fractured and Latham slid out of his powerless hands. And then it would be his turn. She was braced securely against the chimney stack and armed with her crutches and those deadly irons. No one on the bank could see them. They were the wrong side of the roof and the night was dark. To those anxious watchers if indeed they were there they could be nothing more than crouched silhouettes against the sky. And when his and Latham's bodies were found there would be no injuries which couldn't be explained by the fury of the rocks and sea. There was only one chance for him and that was to let Latham go. Alone he could probably wrest the crutches from her. Alone he would have more than an even chance. But she knew of course that he wouldn't let Latham go. She had always known just how her adversary would act. He hung on doggedly; and still the blows fell.

They had both discounted Latham. Perhaps the girl thought he was unconscious. But suddenly a slate, dislodged by his fall, fell from the roof and his feet found a hold. Some desperate instinct for survival awoke in him. He lurched forward twisting his left hand from Dalgliesh's weakening hold and clutched with sudden force at her leg irons. Surprised she lost her balance and, at that moment, a gust of wind tore at the roof. Latham pulled again and she fell. Dalgliesh shot out his hand towards her and caught at the string of the little bag around her neck. The cord snapped and the body rolled past him. The clumsy surgical boots could find no hold and the rigid legs, powerless in their heavy irons rolled her over and over inexorably towards the edge. Then she hit the gutter and bounced into space, turning like a mechanical doll, her legs splayed against the sky. They heard the one wild cry and then nothing. Dalgliesh stuffed the little bag into his pocket and then lay motionless, his head resting on his bleeding hands. And it was then that he felt the ladder nudging his back.

Uninjured, the journey to the bank would have been relatively easy. But Dalgliesh's hands were now almost useless. The pain had started and he could hardly bear to flex the fingers. And there was no grip left. Latham's last effort seemed to have exhausted him. He seemed about to laps again into unconsciousness. It took some minutes before Dalgliesh, shouting in his ear, could urge him on the ladder.

Dalgliesh went first, working his way backward and supporting Latham as best as he could with his hooked arms. Latham's face, beaded with sweat, was within inches of his own. Dalgliesh could smell his breath, the sweet-sour trace of too much drinking, too much high living. He wondered bitterly whether his last conscious discovery before they were hurled into the vortex was to be this realisation that Latham had mild halitosis. There were more significant discoveries and there were pleasanter ways of dying. Surely Latham could make some effort! Why the hell couldn't the man keep himself in decent physical condition? Dalgliesh muttered alternate curses and encouragement under his breath and Latham, as if catching them, roused himself to a fresh effort, grasped the next rung with both hands and drew himself forward a few painful inches. Suddenly the rung bent, then snapped from the ladder. It spun from Latham's hand in a wide arch and disappeared, soundlessly, below the waves. For a sickening moment both their heads dropped through the gap and hung, wide-eyed above the boiling water only twenty feet below. Then Latham lifted his head to rest it on the edge of the ladder and grunted at Dalgliesh:

"You'd better get back. This ladder won't stand two. No sense in both of us getting wet."

"Save your breath," said Dalgliesh. "And keep moving."

He braced his elbows under Latham's armpit and lifted him forward a few rungs. The ladder creaked and bent. They lay immobile after the effort then tried again. This time Latham managed to grip a rung with his feet and lurched forward with such unexpected force that Dalgliesh was nearly thrown off his balance. The ladder, caught by a sudden gust, swung sideways. They could feel it shift on the roof. Neither dared move until the wild swing steadied. Then they inched forward again. They were nearing the bank now. Below they could see the dark shapes of tangled trees. Dalgliesh thought that they must be within earshot of the headland but there was no sound except the howling of the storm. He guessed that the little group was waiting in silence, terrified to break their fearful concentration even with shouts of encouragement. Suddenly it was all over. He felt a strong grip on his ankles. Someone was pulling him to safety.

He wasn't conscious of relief, only of intense weariness and self-disgust. There was no strength left in his body but his mind was clear enough and his thoughts were bitter. He had underestimated the difficulties, had allowed himself to be drawn by Bryce into the amateurish farce in a tolerant contempt of the danger, had behaved like an impulsive fool. They had set out like a couple of Boy Scouts to save the girl from drowning. And, as a result, the girl had drowned. All that had been necessary was to wait quietly in that upstairs bedroom until the water began to drop. The storm was already abating. By morning they could have been rescued in comfort, cold possibly, but unharmed.

And then, as if in answer to his thought, he heard the rumbling. It grew into a roar and the little group on the bank watched fascinated as the cottage with a kind of awkward grace curtseyed slowly into the sea. The roar reverberated around the headland and the waves, dashing against the dam of bricks, leaped and thundered. The spume rose dancing into the night sky, and floated into their eyes. And then the rumbling died away. The last Tanner's Cottage was under the sea.

The headland was peopled with black shapes. They crowded around him blotting out the storm. Their mouths opened and shut but he could hear nothing they said. He had one vivid picture of R. B. Sinclair's white hair streaming against the moon and he could hear Latham demanding a doctor with the querulous insistence of a child. Dalgliesh longed intolerably to sink down to the soft turf and lie there quietly until the pain had gone from his hands and this dreadful aching from his body. But someone was holding him up. He supposed it must be Reckless. The hands braced under his armpits were unexpectedly firm and he could smell the strong pungent smell of wet gaberdine and feel its harshness against his face. Then the mouths, opening and shutting like the jaws of puppets, began to make sounds. They were asking if he was all right and someone, he thought it was Alice Kerrison, was suggesting that they all go back to Priory House. Someone else mentioned the Landrover. It could probably get through the lane to Pentlands if Miss Dalgliesh would prefer to take Adam home. For the first time Dalgliesh noticed the Landrover, a dark shape on the outskirts of the group. It must be the one belonging to Bill Coles and that bulky figure in yellow oilskins must be Coles himself. How in the devil had he got here? The white blur of faces seemed to be expecting him to make up his mind to something. He said: "I want to go home."

He shook off their helping hands and hoisted himself by his elbows into the back of the Landrover. On the floor was a cluster of storm lanterns which cast their yellow light on the row of sitting figures. For the first time he saw his aunt. She had one arm round Latham's shoulders and he was leaning against her. He looked, thought Dalgliesh, like the romantic lead in a Victorian melodrama with his long pale face, his closed eyes, and the white handkerchief which someone had bound around his brow already showing a stain of blood. Reckless got in last and sat against Dalgliesh. As the Landrover lurched off across the headland Dalgliesh held out his torn hands like a surgeon waiting to be gloved. He said to Reckless:

"If you can get your hand into my pocket there's a plastic bag there which will interest you. I tore it from Sylvia Kedge's neck. I can't touch anything myself."

He shifted his body so that Reckless, bouncing violently with the shaking of the Landrover, could slide his hand into the pocket. He drew out the little bag, untied the cord and edging his thumb into the neck worked it open. Then he spilled the contents out on to his lap. There was a small faded photograph of a woman in an oval silver frame, a reel of recording tape, a folded wedding certificate and a plain gold ring.

CHAPTER FIVE

Brightness was pressing painfully against Dalgliesh's eyeballs. He swam up through a kaleidoscope of whirling reds and blues and forced open his eyelids, gummed with sleep, to blink at the bright day. It must be long after his normal waking hour; already shafts of sunlight lay warm across his face. He lay for a moment, cautiously stretching his legs and feeling the ache return almost pleasurably to his sore muscles. His hands felt heavy. Drawing them from under the bedclothes he turned the two white cocoons slowly before his eyes, focussing on them with the strained intentness of a child. Presumably these professional looking bandages had been applied by his aunt but he had no clear recollection of her doing so. She must have used some ointment too. He could feel a disagreeable slipperiness inside the encasing gauze. He was becoming aware now that his hands still hurt but he could move the joints, and the tips of his three middle fingers, the only parts visible, looked normal enough. Apparently no bones were broken.

He wriggled his arms into his dressing gown and walked across to the window. Outside the morning was calm and bright, bringing an immediate memory of the first day of his holiday. For a moment the fury of the night seemed as remote and legendary as any of the great storms of the past. But the evidence was before him. The tip of headland visible from his eastward window was ravaged and raw as if an army had clumped across it littering its way with torn boughs and uprooted gorse. And, although the wind had died to a breeze so that the litter of the headland scarcely stirred, the sea was still turbulent, slopping in great sluggish waves to the horizon as if weighted with sand. It was the colour of mud, too turbid and violent to reflect the blue translucence of the sky. Nature was at odds with itself, the sea in the last throes of a private war, the land lying exhausted under a benign sky.

He turned from the window and looked round the room as if seeing it for the first time. There was a folded blanket across the back of the easy chair by the window and a pillow resting on the arm. His aunt must have spent the night sleeping there. It could hardly have been because of concern for him. He remembered now. They had brought Latham back to Pentlands with them; his aunt must have given up her room. The realisation irritated him and he wondered whether he was being petty enough to resent his aunt's concern for a man he had never liked. Well, what of it? The dislike was mutual if that were any justification and the day threatened to be traumatic enough without beginning it in a mood of morbid self-criticism. But he could have done without Latham. The events of the night were too raw in the memory to relish the prospect of exchanging small talk over breakfast with his partner in folly.

As he made his way downstairs he could hear a murmur of voices from the kitchen. There was the familiar morning smell of coffee and bacon but the sitting room was empty. His aunt and Latham must be breakfasting together in the kitchen. He could hear Latham's high arrogant voice more clearly now although his aunt's softer replies were inaudible. He found himself treading softly so that they might not hear him, tiptoeing across the sitting room like an intruder. Soon, inevitably, he would have to face Latham's excuses and explanations, even—horrible thought —his gratitude. Before long the whole of Monksmere would arrive to question, argue, discuss and exclaim. Little of the story would be news to him, and he had long outgrown the satisfaction of being proved right. He had known who for a long time now and since Monday night he had known how. But to the suspects the day would bring a gratifying vindication and they could be expected to make the most of it. They had been frightened, inconvenienced and humiliated. It would be churlish to grudge them their fun. But for the moment he trod warily, as if reluctant to waken the day.

There was a small fire burning in the sitting room, its thin flame flickering wanly in the brightness of the sun. He saw that it was after eleven o'clock and the post had already arrived. There was a letter for him propped on the mantelpiece. Even across the room he could recognise Deborah's large, sloping handwriting. He felt in his dressing gown pocket for his own unposted letter to her, and with difficulty propped it up beside that other envelope, his small and upright hand looking obsessionally neat beside her generous scrawl. Hers was a thin envelope. That meant one page at the most. Suddenly he knew just what Deborah could have written on no more than one quarto page and the letter became infected with the menace of the day, opening it a chore which could reasonably be postponed. As he stood there, angry at his own indecision and trying to force himself to that one simple action he heard the approaching car. So they were coming already, avid no doubt with curiosity and pleasurable anticipation. But when the car drew nearer he recognised the Ford which Reckless used and, moving to the window, could see that the Inspector was alone. A minute later the car door slammed and Reckless paused, as if bracing himself to approach the cottage. Under his arm he carried Celia Calthrop's tape recorder. The day had begun.

Five minutes later the four of them listened together to the murderer's confession. Reckless sat beside the tape recorder frowning at it constantly with the anxious, slightly peeved look of a man who expects it at any moment to break down. Jane Dalgliesh sat in her usual chair on the left of the fire, motionless, hands folded in her lap, listening as intently as if to music. Latham displayed himself against the wall, one arm drooping from the chimney piece, his bandaged head resting against the grey stones. He looked, thought Dalgliesh, like a slightly passé actor posing for a publicity photograph. He, himself, sat opposite his aunt balancing a tray on his knees, spearing with a fork the small cubes of buttered toast which she had prepared for him or cupping his hands, comfortably insulated, round a steaming beaker of coffee.

The voice of the dead girl spoke to them, not with the familiar irritating submissiveness, but clear, confident and controlled. Only from time to time was there a trace of excitement quickly restrained. This was her paean of triumph, yet she told her dreadful story with assurance and detachment of a professional broadcaster reading a book at bedtime.

"This is the fourth time I've dictated my confession and it won't be the last. The tape can be used over and over again. One can always improve. Nothing need be final. Maurice Seton used to say that, working away at his pathetic books as if they were worth writing, as if anyone cared what word be used. And as likely as not it would be my word in the end, my suggestion, breathed oh so tentatively and quietly so that he wouldn't notice that it was a human being who spoke. I wasn't ever that to him. Just a machine who could take shorthand, type, mend his clothes, wash up, even do a little cooking. Not a really efficient machine, of course, I hadn't the use of my legs. But that made it easier for him in some ways. It meant that he didn't even have to think of me as female. He never saw me as a woman, of course. That was to be expected. But after a time I wasn't even female. I could be asked to work late, stay the night, share his bathroom. No one would talk. No one would care. There was never any scandal.

Why should there be? Who would want to touch me? Oh, he was safe enough with me in the house. And, God knows, I was safe enough with him.

"He would have laughed if I had told him that I could make him a good wife. No, not laughed. He would have been disgusted. It would have seemed like mating with a half-wit, or an animal. Why should deformity be disgusting? Oh, he wasn't the only one. I've seen that look in other faces. Adam Dalgliesh. Why should I instance him? He can hardly bear to look at me. It's as if he's saying, 'I like women to be lovely. I like women to be graceful. I'm sorry for you but you offend me'. I offend myself Superintendent. I offend myself. But I mustn't waste tape on preliminaries. My first confessions were too long, imperfectly balanced. By the end they even bored me. But there will be time to get the story right, to tell it perfectly so that I can play the tape over and over for the rest of my life and yet feel the first keen pleasure. Then, perhaps, one day I shall clean it all away. But not yet. Perhaps never. It would be amusing to leave it for posterity. The only drawback to planning and carrying out a perfect murder is that no else can appreciate it. I may as well have the satisfaction, however childish, of knowing that I shall make the headlines after my death.

"It was a complicated plot, of course, but that made it all the more satisfying. After all, there is nothing difficult about killing a man. Hundreds of people do it every year and have their brief moment of notoriety before they are as forgotten as yesterday's news. I could have killed Maurice Seton any day I chose, especially after I got my hands on those five grains of white arsenic. He took them from the Cadaver Club museum, substituting a bottle of baking powder, at the time he was writing *Death in the Pot.* Poor Maurice, he was obsessed by this urge for verisimilitude. He couldn't even write about an arsenical poisoning without handling the stuff, smelling it, seeing how quickly it would dissolve, enjoying the thrill of playing with death. This absorption in detail, this craving for vicarious experience, was central to my plot. It led him, the predestined victim, to Lily Coombs and the Cortez Club. It led him to his murderer. He was an expert in vicarious death. I should like to have been there to see how he enjoyed the real thing. He meant to put the stuff back, of course; it was only borrowed. But before he could do so I did some substituting of my own. The baking powder in the show case at the Club was replaced by Maurice with baking powder—again. I thought that the arsenic might come in handy. And it will. It will shortly come in very handy indeed. There will be no problem for me in putting it into that flask which Digby always carries. And then what? Wait for the inevitable moment when he is alone and can't face the next minute without a drink? Or tell him that Eliza Marley has discovered something about Maurice's death and wants to meet him secretly far along the beach? Any method will do. The end will be the same. And once he is dead, what can anyone prove? After a little time I shall ask to see Inspector Reckless and tell him that Digby has been complaining recently about indigestion and that I have seen him at Maurice's medicine chest. I shall explain how Maurice borrowed some arsenic once from the Cadaver Club but he assured me that he had replaced it. But suppose he didn't? Suppose he couldn't bring himself to part with it? That would be typical of Maurice. Everyone will say so. Everyone will know about *Death in the Pot*. The powder in the museum show case will be tested and found to be harmless. And Digby Seton will have died by a tragic accident but through his half-brother's fault. I find that very satisfying. It is a pity that Digby, who despite his stupidity, has been very appreciative of so many of my ideas, has to be kept ignorant of this final part of the plan.

"I could have used that arsenic for Maurice just as easily and seen him die in agony any day I chose. It would have been easy. Too easy. Easy and unintelligent. Death by poison wouldn't have satisfied any of the necessary conditions of Maurice's murder. It was those conditions which made the crime so interesting to plan and so satisfying to execute. Firstly, he had to die from natural causes. Digby, as his heir, would be the natural suspect and it was important to me that nothing should jeopardise Digby's inheritance. Then he had to die away from Monksmere; there must be no danger of anyone suspecting me. On the other hand I wanted the crime to be connected with the Monksmere community; the more they were harassed, suspected and frightened the better, I had plenty of old scores to be settled. Besides, I wanted to watch the investigation. It wouldn't have suited me to have it treated as a London crime. Apart from the fun of watching the reactions of the suspects I thought it important that the police work should be under my eye. I must be there to watch and, if necessary, to control. It didn't work out altogether as I had planned, but on the whole very little has happened which I haven't known about. Ironically, I have been less skilful at times than I hoped at controlling my own emotions, but everyone else has behaved strictly according to my plan.

"And then there was Digby's requirement to be met. He wanted the murder to be associated with L. J. Luker and the Cortez Club. His motive was different, of course, He didn't particularly want Luker to be suspected. He just wanted to show him that there were more ways than one of committing murder and getting away with it. What Digby wanted was a death which the police would have to accept as natural—because it would be natural—but which Luker would know had been murder. That's why he insisted on sending Luker the severed hands. I took most of the flesh off them first with acid—it was an advantage to have a dark room in the cottage and the acid available—but I still didn't like the idea. It was a stupid, an unnecessary risk. But I gave in to Digby's whim. A condemned man, by tradition, is pampered. One tries to gratify his more harmless requests.

"But before I describe how Maurice died there are two extraneous matters to get out of the way. Neither of them is important but I mention them because both had an indirect part in Maurice's murder and both were useful in throwing suspicion on Latham and Bryce. I can't take much credit for Dorothy Seton's death. I was responsible, of course, but I didn't intend to kill her. It would have seemed a waste of effort to plan to kill a woman so obviously bent on self destruction. It couldn't, after all, have been long. Whether she took an overdose of her drugs, fell over the cliff on one of her half-doped nocturnal wanderings, got killed with her lover on one of their wild drives around the country, or merely drank herself to death, it could only be a matter of time. I wasn't even particularly interested. And then, soon after she and Alice Kerrison had left for that last holiday at Le Toucquet I found the manuscript. It was a remarkable piece of prose. It's a pity that people who say that Maurice Seton couldn't write will never have the chance to read it. When he cared, he could write phrases that scorched the paper. And he cared. It was all there; the pain, the sexual frustration, the jealousy, the spite, the urge to punish. Who better than I could know how he felt? It must have given him the greatest satisfaction to write it all down. There could be no typewriter, no mechanical keys between this pain and its expression. He needed to see the words forming themselves under his hand. He didn't mean to use it, of course. I did that; merely steaming open one of his weekly letters to her and including it with that. Looking back, I'm not even sure what I expected to happen. I suppose it was just that the sport was too good to miss. Even if she didn't destroy the letter and confronted him with it he could never be absolutely sure that he himself hadn't inadvertently posted it. I knew him so well, you see. He was always afraid of his own subconscious, persuaded that it would betray him in the end. Next day I enjoyed myself watching his panic, his desperate searching, his anxious glances at me to see whether I knew. When he asked whether I had thrown away any papers I answered calmly that I had only burnt a small quantity of scrap. I saw his face lighten. He chose to believe that I had thrown away the letter without reading it. Any other thought would have been intolerable to him so that was what he chose to believe until the day he died. The letter was never found. I have my own idea what happened to it. But the whole of Monksmere believes that Maurice Seton was largely responsible for his wife's suicide. And who could have a better motive for revenge in the eyes of the police than her lover, Oliver Latham?

"It is probably unnecessary to explain that it was I who killed Bryce's cat. That would have been obvious to Bryce at the time if he hadn't been so desperate to cut down the body that he failed to notice the slip knot. If he had been in any condition to examine the rope and the method he would have realized that I could have strung up Arabella without lifting myself more than an inch or two in my chair. But, as I had anticipated, he neither acted rationally nor thought coolly. It never occurred to him for a second that Maurice Seton might not be the culprit. It may seem strange that I waste time discussing the killing of a cat but Arabella's death had its place in my scheme. It ensured that the vague dislike between Maurice and Bryce hardened into active enmity so that Bryce, like Latham, had a motive for revenge. The death of a cat may be a poor motive for the death of a man and I thought it unlikely that the police would waste much time with Bryce. But the mutilation of the body was a different matter. Once the post-mortem showed that Maurice had died from natural causes the police would concentrate on the reasons for hacking off the hands. It was, of course, vital that they should never suspect why this mutilation was necessary and it was convenient that there should be at least two people at Monksmere, both spiteful, both aggrieved, both with an obvious motive. But there were two other reasons why I killed Arabella. Firstly I wanted to. She was a useless creature. Like Dorothy Seton she was kept and petted by a man who believed that beauty has a right to exist, however stupid, however worthless, because it is beauty. It took only two twitching seconds on the end of a clothes line to dispose of that nonsense. And then, her death was to some extent a dress rehearsal. I wanted to try out my acting ability, to test myself under strain. I won't waste time now describing what I discovered about myself. I shall never forget it; the sense of power, the outrage, the heady mixture of fear and excitement. I have felt that again many times since. I am feeling it now. Bryce gives a graphic account of my distress, my tiresomely uncontrolled behaviour after the body was cut down, and not all of it was acting.

"But to return to Maurice. It was by a lucky chance that I discovered the one fact about him that was crucial for my purpose—that he suffered badly from claustrophobia. Dorothy must have known of course. After all there were nights when she condescended to let him share her bedroom. He must have woken her sometimes with his recurring nightmare just as he woke me. I often wonder how much she knew and whether she told Oliver Latham before she died. That was a risk I had to take. But what if she did? No one can prove that I knew.

Nothing can change the fact that Maurice Seton died from natural causes.

"I remember that night, over two years ago, very clearly. It was a wet, blustery day in mid-September and the evening grew wilder as darkness fell. We had been working together since ten o'clock that morning and it wasn't going well. Maurice was trying to finish a series of short stories for an evening paper. It wasn't his métier and he knew it; he was working against time and he hated that. I had broken off only twice, to cook us a light lunch at one-thirty and again at eight o'clock when I prepared sandwiches and soup. By nine o'clock when we had finished our meal, the wind was howling around the house and I could hear a high tide pounding on the beach. Even Maurice could hardly expect me to get home in my wheelchair once darkness had fallen and he never offered to drive me home. That, after all, would put him to the trouble of fetching me again next day. So he suggested that I should stay the night. He didn't ask me if I were willing. It didn't occur to him that I might object or that I might perhaps prefer my own toothbrush or toilet things or even my own bed. The ordinary courtesies of life didn't apply to me. But he told me to put sheets on the bed in his wife's old room and he came himself to look for a nightdress for me. I don't know why. I think it may have been the first time since her death that he had brought himself to open her drawers and cupboards and that my presence was both an opportunity for breaking a taboo and a kind of support. Now that I can wear any of her underclothes or can rip them to shreds just as the fancy takes me, I can bring myself to smile at the memory of that night. Poor Maurice! He hadn't remembered that those wisps of chiffon, those bright transparencies in nylon and silk would be so pretty, so delicate, so very unsuitable for my twisted body. I saw the look on his face as his hands hovered over them. He couldn't bear to think of her clothes against my flesh. And then he found what he wanted. It was there at the bottom of the drawer, an old woollen nightdress which had belonged to Alice Kerrison. Dorothy had worn it once at Alice's insistence when she had been ill with influenza and was sweating with rigor. And it was this nightdress which Maurice handed to me. Would his fate have been any different, I wonder, if he had acted otherwise that night? Probably not. But it pleases me to think that his hands, hesitating over the layers of gaudy nonsense, were choosing between life and death.

"It was shortly after three o'clock when I was awoken by his scream. At first I thought it was a sea bird screeching. Then it came again and again. I fumbled for my crutches and went in to him. He was leaning, half dazed, against the bedroom window and had the last disorientated look of a man who has been sleep walking. I managed to coax him back into bed. It wasn't difficult. He took my hand like a child. As I drew the sheets up under his chin he suddenly seized my arm and said, 'Don't leave me! Don't go yet! It's my nightmare. It's always the same. I dream I'm being buried alive. Stay with me till I'm asleep.' So I stayed. I sat there with his hand in mine until my fingers were stiff with cold and my whole body ached. There were a great many things which he told me in the darkness about himself, about his great consuming fear, before his fingers relaxed, the muttering ceased and he dropped into peaceful sleep. His jaw had fallen open so that he looked stupid and ugly and vulnerable. I had never seen him asleep before. I was pleased to see his ugliness, his helplessness and I felt a sense of power which was so pleasurable that it almost frightened me. And, sitting there beside him, listening to that quiet breathing, I pondered how I might use this new knowledge to my advantage. I began to plan how I might kill him.

"He said nothing to me next morning about the events of the night. I was never sure whether he had completely forgotten his nightmare and my visit to his room. But I don't think so. I believe he remembered well enough but put it out of his thoughts. After all, he didn't have to apologise or explain to me. One doesn't need to justify one's weakness either to a servant or an animal. That's why it is so satisfying, so convenient to have a tame one in the house.

"There was no hurry over the planning, no time limit in which he had to die, and this in itself added to the interest and allowed me to develop a more complicated and sophisticated murder than would have been possible were I working against the clock. I share Maurice's view here.

No one can do his best work in a hurry. Towards the end, of course, there was some urgency when I found, and destroyed, the carbon of the letter to Max Gurney announcing that Maurice was thinking of changing his Will. But, by then, my final plans had been ready for over a month.

"I knew from the beginning that I should need an accomplice and who that accomplice should be. The decision to use Digby Seton to destroy firstly his half-brother and then himself was so magnificent in its boldness that at times I was frightened at my own daring. But it wasn't as foolhardy as it appears. I knew Digby, I knew precisely his weaknesses and his strengths. He is less stupid and far greedier than people realise, more practical but less imaginative, not particularly brave but obstinate and persistent. Above all, he is fundamentally weak and vain. My plan made use of his abilities as well as his defects. I have made very few mistakes in my handling of him and if I underestimated him in some important respects this has proved less catastrophic than I might have feared. He is becoming a liability as well as a nuisance now, of course, but he won't be worrying me for long. If he had proved less irritating to me and more reliable I might have considered letting him live for a year or so. I should prefer to have avoided death duties on Maurice's estate. But I have no intention of letting greed trap me into folly.

"In the beginning I did nothing so crude as to present Digby with a plan for killing Maurice. What I suggested to him was no more than a complicated practical joke. He didn't, of course, believe this for long but then he wasn't required to. During all the preliminary planning, neither of us mentioned the word murder. He knew and I knew, but neither of us spoke. We conscientiously kept up the fiction that we were engaged in an experiment, not perhaps without some danger but completely without malice, to prove to Maurice that it was possible to transport a man from London to Monksmere secretly and without his knowledge or cooperation. That was to be our alibi. If the plot failed and we were discovered with the body on our hands our story was ready and no one would be able to disprove it. Mr. Seton had wagered us that we couldn't kidnap him and take him back to Monksmere without being discovered.

He wanted to introduce such a scheme into his new book. There would be plenty of witnesses to testify that Maurice loved to experiment, that he was meticulous about detail. And if he should unexpectedly die of a heart attack during the journey, how could we be blamed? Manslaughter? Possibly. But murder, never.

"I think that Digby almost believed the fiction for a time. I did my best to keep it going. There are few men with the courage or the strength of mind to plan murder in cold blood and Digby certainly isn't one of them. He likes his unpleasant facts gift-wrapped. He prefers to shut his eyes to reality. He has always shut his eyes to the truth about me.

"Once he had convinced himself that it was all a cosy little game with easy rules, no personal risk and a prize of £200,000, he quite enjoyed planning the details. I gave him nothing to do which wasn't well within his peculiar capabilities and he wasn't pressed for time. Firstly, he had to find a second-hand motor cycle and long torpedo-shaped side car. He had to buy them separately and for cash in a part of London where he wasn't known. He had to rent or buy a flat with reasonable privacy and access to a garage, and keep his new address secret from Maurice. All this was relatively simple and I was pleased on the whole with the efficient way in which my creature coped. This was almost the most trying time for me. There was so little I personally could do to control events. Once the body had been brought to Monksmere I should be here to organise and direct. Now I had to rely on Digby to carry out instructions. It was Digby alone who must manage the business at the Cortez Club, and I had never been particularly happy about his plan to lure Maurice to the Mews Cottages. It seemed to me unnecessarily complicated and dangerous. I could think of safer and easier ways. But Digby insisted on bringing the Cortez Club into the plot. He had this need to involve and impress Luker. So I let him have his way—after all the plot couldn't incriminate me—and I admit that it worked admirably. Digby confided to Lily Coombs the fiction about the experiment to kidnap his half-brother and told her that Maurice had wagered a couple of thousand that it couldn't be done. Lily was paid a hundred in cash for her help. All she had to do was to watch out for Maurice, spin him a yarn about the dope traffic and direct him to Carrington Mews for any further information he wanted. If he didn't take the bait nothing would be lost. I had other plans for luring him to Carrington Mews and one of those could be used. But, of course, he took the bait. It was in the service of his art and he had to go. Digby had been carefully hinting about Lily Coombs and the Cortez Club on each of his visits and Maurice had typed out the inevitable little white reference card for future use. Once Maurice had arrived in London for his regular autumn visit it was as certain that he would show himself one night at the Cortez as it was that he would stay in his usual room at the Cadaver Club, the room which he could reach without having to use that small claustrophobic lift. Digby would even predict to Lily Coombs the night on which he would appear. Oh yes, Maurice took the bait all right! He would have walked into hell in the service of his writing. And that, of course, was what he did.

"Once Maurice appeared at the door of the Carrington Mews cottage Digby's part was relatively simple. The swift knock out blow, too slight to leave a mark but heavy enough to be effective, wasn't difficult for a man who had once been a boxing champion. The adaptations to the side car to convert it into a travelling coffin had been an easy matter for one who had built Sheldrake singlehanded. The side car was ready and waiting and there was access to the garage from the house. The slight body, unconscious and breathing stertorously—for Lily had done her part well and Maurice had drunk far more wine than was good for him—was slid into the side car and the top nailed in place. There were, of course, air holes in the sides. It was no part of my plan that he should suffocate. Then Digby drank his half bottle of whisky and set out to provide himself with his alibi. We couldn't know precisely when it would be required, of course, and this was a slight worry. It would be a pity if Maurice died too soon. That he would die, and die in torment, was certain. It was merely a question of how long that torment would last and when it would begin. But I instructed Digby to get himself arrested as soon as he was a safe distance from home.

"Later next morning, as soon as he was released, Digby set out with the motor cycle and side car for Monksmere. He didn't look at the body. I had instructed him not to open the side car but I doubt whether he was tempted. He was still living in the comfortable, imaginary world of the plot which I had created for him. I couldn't forsee how remarkably he would react when he could no longer pretend to believe in it. But when he set out secretly from Carrington Mews that morning I have no doubt that he felt as innocently excited as a schoolboy whose practical joke is going well. There was no trouble on the journey. The black plastic driving suit, the helmet and goggles were a perfect disguise as I had known they would be. He had a single ticket to Saxmundham from Liverpool Street in his pocket and before leaving the West End he posted to Seton House my description of the Cortez Club. It seems almost unnecessary to say that a typing style can easily be disguised but not the typewriter used. I had typed the passage some weeks earlier on Maurice's machine wearing a glove on my right hand and with bandaged left fingers. The passage about the mutilated body floating out to sea had been typed by Maurice and was taken by me from his papers. Using it was one of the small but agreeable refinements which I had incorporated into my plan when I learned about Miss Calthrop's idea for an effective opening for one of Maurice's books. It was in every sense a gift to me as well as to Maurice. To a large extent it determined the whole shape of the murder plot, and I made use of it brilliantly.

"But there was one vital part of my plot which I haven't yet mentioned. Strangely enough, although I expected it to be the most difficult, it was the easiest of all. I had to make Digby Seton marry me. I thought that bringing him to this might take weeks of skilful persuasion. And I didn't have those weeks. All the planning had to be done in those rare weekends when he was at Monksmere. I let him write to me because I could be sure that the letters would be burnt, but I never wrote to him and we never telephoned each other. But persuading him to this disagreeable and yet essential part of the plan wasn't the kind of thing I could do by post. I even wondered whether this would be the rock on which the whole scheme would be wrecked. But I misjudged him. He wasn't entirely stupid. If he had been I would never have risked making him a partner in his own destruction. He could recognise the inevitable. And after all, it was in his own interest. He had to marry to get his hands on the money. There was no one else he wanted. He certainly wasn't keen on a wife who would make demands on him or interfere in his life, a wife who might even want to sleep with him. And he knew that he had to marry me for one overriding reason. No one would be able to prove that we killed Maurice unless one of us talked. And a wife can't be made to give evidence against her own husband. It was arranged, of course, that we would divorce after a reasonable time and I was very generous about the marriage settlement. Not suspiciously generous. Just very very reasonable. I could afford to be. He had to marry me to keep me quiet and collect the cash. I had to marry him because I wanted the whole of his fortune. As his widow.

"We married by licence on 15th March at a London Registry Office. He hired a car and called for me early. No one saw us leaving the cottage. How could they? Celia Calthrop was away so there was no chance of her calling for me. Oliver Latham and Justin Bryce were in London. I neither knew nor cared whether Jane Dalgliesh was at home. I telephoned Maurice to say that I wasn't well enough to report for work. He was irritated but he wasn't concerned, and I had no fear that he might call at the cottage to see how I was. Maurice hated illness. He would care if his dog were sick. But then, he was fond of his dog. I find it very satisfying that he might be alive now if only he had cared enough to call at Tanner's Cottage that day, to wonder where I had gone—why I had lied.

"But time and this tape are runing out. I have settled my account with Maurice Seton. This is my triumph not my justification and there is still much to be told.

"Digby, driving the motor cycle and side car, arrived at Tanner's Cottage just before six o'clock on Wednesday. It was dark by then and there was no one about. There never is once dusk has fallen on this coast. Maurice was dead, of course, Digby's face was very white under the helmet as he prised off the lid of the side car. I think he had expected to see his victim's face contorted into a grimace of horror, the dead eyes glaring accusingly. Unlike me he hadn't read Maurice's text-books on forensic medicine. He didn't know about the relaxing of muscles after death. The calm face, so ordinary, so vacuous, so completely without the power to be either frightening or pathetic seemed to reassure him. But I had forgotten to explain about rigor mortis. He hadn't expected that we should need to break the rigor in the knees so that the body could be fitted into my wheel chair and taken down to the shore. He didn't enjoy that necessary bit of business. I can still hear his high nervous giggle at the sight of Maurice's thin legs, clad in those ridiculous trousers and sticking straight out like the broom-stick legs of a guy. Then Digby hit them and the rigor broke and they dangled and swung above the foot rest like the legs of a child. That small act of personal violence to the body did something to Digby. I was perfectly ready to take off the hands myself. I wanted to bring that chopper down. But Digby took it from me and waited without speaking while I laid out the hands ready for him on the thwart. I might have made a neater job of it. I doubt whether I would have enjoyed it any more than he. Afterwards I took the hands from him and put them in my mackintosh toilet bag. Digby had a use for them; he was determined to send them to Luker. But there were things I had to do to them first in the privacy of my dark room. In the meantime I slung the bag around my neck and enjoyed the feel of those dead hands, seeming to creep against my flesh.

"Last of all Digby pushed the dinghy out on the ebb tide, wading deep into the sea. I wasn't worried about bloodstains. The dead bleed slowly if they bleed at all. If there was spotting on the cycling suit the sea would wash it away. Digby waded back to me, glistening out of the darkness, hands clasped above his head, like someone who has been ritually cleansed. He did not speak as he wheeled me back to the cottage. As I have said, in some ways I underestimated him, and it was only on that silent journey back through the narrow lane that it struck me he could be dangerous.

"The rest of the night's work should have been the simplest. The plan was for Digby to drive as fast as he could to Ipswich. On the way he would stop at a lonely place on the bank of the Sizewell Sluice, detach the side car and sink it into the deep water. Once in Ipswich he would take the number plates off the motor cycle and abandon it in a side street. It was an old machine and it was unlikely that anyone would bother to trace the owner. And, even if it were traced to Digby and the side car found, we still had our second line of defence: the story of the experiment to kidnap Maurice, the innocent wager that went so tragically wrong. And we should have Lily Coombs to corroborate our story.

"My instructions to Digby were very clear. After abandoning the cycle he would first post Maurice's manuscript describing the handless body drifting out at sea. Then he would go to the station, still wearing his overalls, and would take a platform ticket. I didn't want the ticket collector to note the passenger who was joining his train at Ipswich with a ticket issued in London. Digby would push through the barrier when there was a convenient crowd, join the Saxmundham train, change his overalls in the lavatory, put them in a small hold-all, and arrive at Saxmundham at eight-thirty. He would then take a cab to Seton House where I would be waiting for him in the darkness to check that all had gone according to plan and to give him any instructions for the future. As I have said, it was the easiest part of the night's work and I expected no trouble. But Digby was beginning to sense his power. He did two very stupid things. He couldn't resist the temptation to detach the side car and drive at top speed around the village, even showing himself to Bryce. And he invited Liz Marley to meet him at Saxmundham. The first was no more than childish exhibitionism; the second could have been fatal. I was physically very tired by now and emotionally unprepared to deal with this insubordination. As I heard Miss Marley's car drive up and was watching them both from the shadow of the curtains, the telephone rang. I know now that it was only Plant making a routine enquiry for Mr. Seton. At the time it shook me. Two unforeseen things were happening together and I was prepared for neither. If I had been given time to take myself in hand I should have coped with the situation better. As it was, I quarrelled violently with Digby. There is no point in wasting time with what either of us said, but it ended with Digby driving off furiously into the night with the intention, he said, of going back to London. I didn't believe him. He had too much at stake to throw in his hand now. This was no more than another childish gesture of independence provoked by the quarrel and intended simply to frighten me. But I waited until the early hours for the return of the Vauxhall, sitting there in the darkness since I dare not put on a light, wondering whether one moment of temper was to undo all my careful planning, and scheming how the situation might yet be retrieved. It was two in the morning before I made my way home. Next morning I was back at Seton House early. Still no sign of the car. It was not until Thursday night when the telephone call came through to Pentlands that I knew what had happened. By then I had no need to simulate shock. It is good to know that Digby Seton will soon be paying for what he did to me during those twenty-four hours. He was surprisingly resourceful about it all. His story about the false telephone call was very clever. It would explain any hints about Maurice's death which he may have let out during the periods of babbling semi-consciousness. It strengthened his alibi. It made things even more uncomfortable for the Monksmere community. I had to admire his ingenuity, his inventiveness. And I wondered how long it would be before he began thinking about ridding himself of me.

"There is little more to say. The return of the chopper to Jane Dalgliesh was no more difficult than stealing it had been. The plastic cycling suit was cut into shreds and floated out on the ebb tide. I took the flesh off the knuckles of Maurice's hands with acid from the dark room and Digby posted his parcel. It was all quite simple. All according to plan. And now there is only the last chapter. In a few days' time I shall be able to dictate this again. I feel no particular hatred for Digby. I shall be glad when he is dead but I am quite happy to picture his agony without wanting to see it. But I wish I could have been there when Maurice Seton died.

"And that reminds me of the last explanation of all. Why wasn't I content for his dead body to be left in London, a bundle of flesh and clothes in a Paddington gutter? The reason is simple. We had to take off his hands. Those telltale hands with the knuckles torn to the bone where he had battered them against his coffin lid."

The voice had finished. For a few seconds the tape ran on. Then Reckless leant across and it clicked to a stop. Without speaking he bent to pull out the cord. Jane Dalgliesh got up from her chair and with a murmured word to Latham went out to the kitchen. Almost at once Dalgliesh heard the splash of running water and the chink of a kettle lid. What was she doing, he wondered. Getting on with preparing the lunch? Making fresh coffee for her visitors? What was she thinking? Now that it was all over was she even interested in that tumult of hate which had destroyed and disrupted so many lives including her own? One thing was certain. If she did later talk about Sylvia Kedge she wouldn't indulge in sentimental regrets of "If only we had known! If only we could have helped her!" To Jane Dalgliesh people were as they were. It was as pointlessly presumptuous to try to change them as it was impertinent to pity them. Never before had his aunt's uninvolvement struck him so forcibly; never before had it seemed so frightening.

Latham slowly released himself from his self-conscious pose in front of the fire and sank down into the empty chair. He laughed uncertainly. "Poor devil! Killed because of his choice of a nightdress. Or was it because of his choice of bedroom?"

Reckless didn't answer. Carefully he curled the flex of the tape recorder then tucked the machine under his arm. Turning at the door he spoke to Dalgliesh.

"We've dredged up the side car. It was within twenty yards of the spot you marked. Another lucky guess, Mr. Dalgliesh."

Dalgliesh could picture the scene. It would be pleasant on the bank of the lonely sluice in the early morning sun, a green peace broken only by the distant rumble of traffic, the singing water, the deep voices of the men as they bent to the tackle, the squelch of mud as the waders sucked at the river bed. And then the thing they sought would break surface at last, shaped like a gigantic striped marrow, the black hull festooned with weeds and glistening as the gouts of mud slipped away. He had no doubt that it looked very small to the band of toiling policemen as they urged and steadied it towards the bank. But then, Maurice Seton had been a small man.

When Reckless had left, Latham said belligerently:

"I must thank you for saving my life."

"Must you? I should have thought it was the other way round. It was you who kicked her off the roof."

The reply was quick, defensive.

"That was an accident. I never meant her to fall."

Of course not, thought Dalgliesh. It had to be an accident. Latham was the last man to live with the thought that he had killed a woman, even in self defence. Well, if that was the way he had decided to remember it, he might as well begin now as later. And what the hell did it matter anyway? He wished that Latham would go. The thought of gratitude between them was ridiculous and embarrassing, and he was too sore in mind and body to relish a morning of small talk. But there was something he needed to know. He said:

"I've been wondering why you went to Tanner's Cottage last night. You saw them I suppose—Digby and Kedge?"

The two square envelopes propped side by side were starkly white against the grey stones of the chimney piece, He would have to open Deborah's letter soon. It was ridiculous and humiliating this urge to throw it into the fire unread, as if one could with a single assertive gesture burn away all the past. He heard Latham's voice:

"Of course. The first evening I arrived. I lied about the time, incidentally. I was here soon after six. Soon afterwards, I walked along the cliff and saw the two figures with the boat. I recognised Sylvia and I thought that the man was Seton although I couldn't be sure. It was too dark to see what they were up to but it was obvious that they were shoving the dinghy out to sea. I couldn't see what the bundle was in the bottom of it, but afterwards I could guess. It didn't worry me. Maurice had it coming to him as far as I was concerned. As you seem to have guessed, Dorothy Seton sent me that last letter he wrote to her. I suppose she expected me to avenge her. I'm afraid she mistook her man. I've seen too many second-rate actors make fools of themselves in that role to fancy playing it myself. I hadn't any objection to letting someone else do the job, but when Digby was murdered I thought it was time I found out what Kedge was playing at. Celia told us that Sylvia was planning to see Reckless this morning; it seemed prudent to get in first."

It would be futile, of course, to point out that Latham could have saved Digby's life by speaking sooner. And was it even true? The murderers had their story ready: the bet with Seton; the experiment that went horribly wrong; the panic when they discovered that Maurice was dead; the decision to take off the battered hands in an attempt to cover up. Would it really have been possible without a confession to prove that Maurice Seton hadn't died a natural death?

He gripped Deborah's letter between his left thumb and rigidly bandaged palm and tried to insinuate the tips of his right hand fingers under the flap; but the tough paper resisted him. Latham said impatiently:

"Here, let me do it!"

Under his long nicotine-stained fingers the envelope ripped open. He handed it to Dalgleish:

"Don't mind me."

"It's all right," said Dalgliesh. "I know what's in it. It can wait." But he was unfolding the sheet as he spoke. There were only eight lines. Deborah had never been verbose even in her love letters but there was a brutal economy about these final staccato sentences. And why not? Theirs was a basic human dilemma. You could either spend a lifetime together laboriously exploring it, or you could dispose of it in eight lines. He found himself counting and recounting them, calculating the number of words, noticing with unnatural interest the spread of the lines, the details of the handwriting. She had decided to accept the job offered to her at the firm's American house. By the time he received this she would be in New York. She could no longer bear to loiter about on the periphery of his life waiting for him to make up his mind. She thought it unlikely that they would ever see each other again. It was better for them both that way. The sentences were conventional, almost trite. It was a goodbye without panache or originality, even without dignity. And if it had been written in pain there was no sign of it in that confident hand.

He could hear Latham's high arrogant voice running on

in the background, saying something about an appointment at an Ipswich Hospital to have his head X-rayed, suggesting that Dalgliesh might go with him and have his hand examined, speculating spitefully on what Celia would have to pay in lawyer's fees before she could get her hands on the Seton fortune, attempting once more with the clumsiness of a schoolboy to justify himself for the death of Sylvia Kedge. Dalgliesh turned his back on him and taking his own letter from the mantlepiece, laid the twin envelopes together and tore at them impatiently. But they were too strong for him and, in the end, he had to throw them whole into the fire. They took a long time to burn, each separate sheet charring and curling as the ink faded so that, at last, his own verses shone up at him, silver on black, obstinately refusing to die, and he could not even grasp the poker to beat them into dust.

Also available in Sphere Books by P. D. James

Death of an Expert Witness

When a young girl is found strangled in a field in the Fens, it looks like a routine job for the staff of the East Anglian Forensic Laboratory. But then the senior biologist is found dead in his lab and the murder comes closer to home. And Commander Adam Dalgliesh faces the most baffling inquiry of his career.

'Stunningly good' – *Evening Standard*

'A splendid success . . . A story that will delight all those who yearn for the golden age of Allingham, Christie and Sayers' – *Julian Symons*

'Forensic lab mystery marvellously illuminates murder's devastation' – H. R. F. Keating, *The Times*

'Improves with her every book' – Andrew Hope, *Evening Standard*

'The best recent crime novel I've read' – *Time Out*

'One of the best James mysteries yet' – *Publishers Weekly*

0 7221 4967 0 CRIME FICTION 95p

The Black Tower

P. D. JAMES

Hoping for a little investigation to enliven his convalescence, Commander Adam Dalgliesh accepts an invitation from an old friend to visit Dorset and solve a problem. But when he arrives at Toynton Grange, a private home for the disabled, he discovers that his host has died suddenly. Other more mysterious deaths follow and Dalgliesh finds that the 'problem' is an enclosed world seething with malice, intrigue, hatred and murder.

'Splendid, macabre piece' – *Sunday Telegraph*

'More expertise from Mrs James. The writing is excellent, the pitch of final terror beautifully sustained' – *Evening Standard*

'*The Black Tower* is a real novel, one which can be enjoyed without any reservation... You must read this book. And you must read all her other books' – *John Braine*

0 7221 5042 3 CRIME FICTION 95p

An Unsuitable Job for a Woman

P. D. JAMES

Cordelia Gray saw no reason why her job as a private detective was an unsuitable job for a woman. Until she was employed to discover why a renowned scientist's son had commited suicide. And she discovered his family's insidious secrets.

'A very ingenious, absorbing detective story of star quality' – *Evening Standard*

'One of the most compulsive and acutely observed thrillers of the year... A why-dunnit, rather than a who-dunnit; a study of the complex motives that make up the cold mind of a killer' – Peter Grosvenor, *Daily Express*

'Solid, well-written, ingenious, enjoyable' – Matthew Coady, *Guardian*

0 7221 5045 8 CRIME FICTION 95p

Cover Her Face

P. D. JAMES

Sally Jupp seemed the ideal girl to help Mrs. Maxie run a large house and look after her invalid husband. She was pretty, docile and grateful, or so it seemed, until murder shattered the tranquility of her new home. A puzzling, disturbing killing that brought Chief Detective Inspector Adam Dalgliesh to the quiet village in search of the murderer.

'P. D. James is in the front rank of thriller writers' – *Literary Scene*

0 7221 5046 6 CRIME FICTION 95p

'Outstanding story . . . a totally unexpected ending' is how the *Sunday Telegraph*, Books of the Year described

Shroud for a Nightingale

P. D. JAMES

A double killing within the gloomy precincts of the Nightingale Training College for nurses led Inspector Adam Dalgliesh into a web of intrigue and murder – revealing the carefully hidden trail of a Nazi war criminal.

'The characterization, from consulting surgeon to student nurse, is superior all the way through. . . This must rank as one of the best detections' – *The Guardian*

'Excellent' – *The Times*

'It's a long time since I've been gripped by a book as much as I was by P. D. James' *Shroud for a Nightingale*' – *Daily Telegraph*

0 7221 5039 3 CRIME FICTION 95p